Lex's Melody

Belfast Bound Book #1

By Leigh Stone

To Erin

So glad you finally
Won!

Love

Leigh Stone

XOXO

ISBN-13: 978-1503039520

ISBN-10: 1503039528

Copyright © 2014 Leigh Stone
All rights reserved.

No part of this book may be reproduced or transmitted in any form or by any means, electronic or mechanical, including photocopying, recording, or by any other information storage and retrieval system without the written permission of the author, except in the case of brief quotations embodied in critical articles and reviews.

This book is a work of fiction, all names, characters, places, and events are the products of the author's imagination, or are used fictitiously. Any resemblance to actual persons, living or dead, events, or locations is entirely coincidental.

All rights reserved. Except as permitted under the UK Copyright, Designs and Patents Act 1988.

Cover Art: © Kostudio, © yuran78
Fonts used include Georgia, Verdana, Tenderness and Comforta, these are open source fonts that are legal for commercial use.

DISCLAIMER:

This book contains explicit sexual content, graphic, adult languages and situations that some readers may find objectionable, including strong BDSM themes and elements, erotic elements, and fetish play. This book is for sale for ADULTS ONLY, as defined by the laws of your country of purchase. Please do not attempt to try out, or re-create any of the scenes from this book without the assistance and/or guidance of an experienced practitioner. The author will not be held responsible for any loss, harm, injury or death resulting from the use of any information contained within this work.

Dedication

To Joe Ferguson – You always told me that I should do something with my writing. I wish I had listened to you all those years ago!

You were right xoxo

CHAPTER 1

She stood in the hotel room completely naked, her arms by her sides, her eyes cast to the floor. Her heart pounded in her chest, her mouth was dry, but her pussy was wet and pulsing. This had been her first venture into Internet dating. She would never have believed that she would end up like this on a Friday night after work.

Alex circled her, letting his fingertips graze across the curve of her stomach. He watched as she swallowed hard and her breathing stuttered, and yet she still never lifted her eyes from the floor. He couldn't believe his luck. When he had found Melody's profile on the dating site he had been instantly attracted to her cheeky sense of humour. There had been something about her sparkling eyes and that smile of hers. She smiled like she had a dozen secrets that she would never tell. It made him wonder just what things she wasn't saying. He could never have imagined that she would be so into the darker sexual needs he possessed; there were so many possibilities. They started by exchanging a few emails and texts, and after a week or so, they seemed to like each other. They decided to take the plunge and arranged to meet for a drink.

~ ~ ~

Alex Matthews was six foot two, with dark messy short hair and rich sienna brown eyes enshrouded with long, thick eyelashes. He was 31 and had worked hard to set up his own firm, working as an architect in the Northern Irish city of Belfast. He was lean and muscular, and Mel's eyes widened when she saw him in the flesh. He had suggested that they meet in the oldest pub in the city, famous for its secretive little booths with doors. It gave him the chance to get her alone, and still be safe in a public place.

Mel was even more gorgeous in real life. Her long brown hair sat in waves around her shoulders. Her blue/grey eyes could penetrate the soul of any man who looked beyond her thick eyelashes for long enough. She was five foot six and her body was toned yet curvy. She had fantastic breasts, she had been naturally gifted with the kind of tits that some women would pay a lot of money for. Mel's smile was intense; it could vary from a sly curving at the corners to a full-blown gleam, showing off her unusually sharp canines. She sipped her drink and smiled at him. Her smile washed a wave of warmth over his body, hairs stood up on the back of his neck, and the blood pulsed into his cock making it stiffen against his jeans. She was intoxicating; he had never met a woman who made him feel so out of control and in a man who thrived on control that produced an exhilarating feeling. He was possessed with a need to know if she could ever accept his deeper desires and wants, but he had to find out.

"Would you mind if I kissed you?" He asked, holding her gaze, hoping to draw her in. She grinned at him, and her cheeks flushed with colour just a little. *You asked her?!* He thought, the notion that he would normally just take what he wanted taunting him.

"I think that might just be okay!" she laughed. He leaned in just a little closer, the smell of her perfume and shampoo mixed together in a heady scent that made his heart speedup, his mouth dry and his hard cock lurch against the denim that was keeping it prisoner. *Christ Alex, get a grip; you haven't even touched her yet!* He chastised himself. When she licked her lips, he was lost. He hastily closed his mouth over hers; Mel willingly opened her mouth to accept the thrusts of his tongue. She tasted divine and it added fuel to the fires of his lust and he instinctively ran his hands into her long silky hair. Her tongue lapped over his, caressing his as he probed her mouth. He pressed his lips harder against hers, he couldn't get enough of her, he wanted to take her, to have every last inch of her that very moment.

His hand tightened in her hair as he pulled it hard. *Too much!* His inner critic told him. To his surprise she moaned against his mouth and her hand moved to his hair as she ran her fingers through the dark brown locks at the nape of his neck. It sent a shiver down his spine and he tugged on her hair again.

He forced himself to pull away from her kiss and back into reality. "I'm sorry I pulled on your hair Melody," he winced, "I just got a bit carried away..."

She met his gaze and smiled, a short laugh escaped from her throat. "Ha, oh, don't worry about it," she blushed, "I actually like that kind of thing." She confessed. *That kind of thing.* The words echoed in his head. *Dear God,* he thought, *what other kind of things would this amazing creature consider doing?* She looked at him, and he could see the secrets that he wanted just sitting there on the surface. It was written in her eyes and all he had to do was ask.

"*That* kind of thing?" He pushed. She blushed more and licked her lips again biting her bottom lip nervously as she did. He could see from the vein in her neck that her heart was pounding. Was she just as turned on about the possibilities as he was?

"Well.... It's not something that I usually talk about with a guy I've just met in the middle of a pub..." She held his gaze, "but... I guess there's no harm in telling you a little," she swallowed hard again, trying to get the words out of her mouth, "I like an element of pain, I like being the one who is *not* in control."

She paused, trying to read his expression. What was she thinking? She had never freely told anyone that she was at least a little submissive; that receiving pain turned her on. He grinned back at her, and she was struck by just how ruggedly handsome he looked. His dark hair, his deep brown eyes that right now were shining with lust and possibilities, there was a hint of arrogance about him though not enough to make him seem unapproachable.

He breathed deeply and moved towards her lips again, locking his over hers forcefully. Something told him that he was going to thoroughly enjoy the secrets that she had to tell. Alex ran one hand along her denim covered inner thigh, and knotted his other in Mel's hair and pulled again. She moaned against his mouth. He broke free of her lips, and pulled her hair a little harder making her head fall back, exposing her throat to him. He nuzzled against the silky curve of her jaw and down her neck. She caught her breath, closed her eyes and licked her lips. She instantly felt that tell-tale heat growing low in her stomach. No one she had ever met had been able to turn her on so quickly as Alex had.

Alex's hand stopped high on her thigh and started to trace backwards and forwards over the denim as he opened and closed his hand, letting his fingertips tease. His nostrils flared taking in her sweet scent, fruity shampoo, lust and expensive perfume. He sucked gently on her skin when he got to her collarbone, and she let out another moan. His cock pulsed with need. He wanted to be inside her.

He pulled his face back from her neck and gazed at her. The desire on her face was clear, her mouth was parted, her cheeks and lips coloured, and her eyes closed. When she realised that he had stopped, she lifted her heavy lids and looked at him. Something close to insanity swept over him as he looked at her, and he leaned in, his warm breath brushing against her ear and asked.

"Do you like anal sex Melody?"

She went crimson, her lips moved a few times as if she were trying to decide on the right way to answer such a question. Without a shadow of a doubt she should be offended at such an indecent query. The thought occurred to her that she should be getting up and slapping his face, before walking straight out of there, but the heat that the question had caused to pool between her legs couldn't easily be ignored. Instead of feeling insulted, she felt on fire and driven to honesty.

"I enjoy it..." she said softly. Alex couldn't believe his ears. A million images of Mel on her hands and knees, her bare ass exposed and beckoning him forward appeared in vivid clarity in his imagination. His mouth uttered his proposal before his brain had even registered that it was going to.

"I think that you should be my little ass slut Mel."

Her eyes went wide and she shifted in her seat, out of the reach of his hands. *Shit! Jesus Alex, nice way to have her running for the hills!* His critic chided. He forced himself to look away from her, and took a long, slow sip of his drink.

Mel swallowed hard. This was not how she had expected the evening to go at all. *Get up! Get up, and get out of here now!* Her brain told her. But Mel couldn't move. She wanted to know more; she wanted to find out just what it was that Alex thought she could do for him as his "ass slut."

This is pure insanity! She thought to herself as she cleared her throat, and asked, "Just what does being your ass slut involve, Alex?" He forced himself to look back at her, and saw a hint of fascination flash across her features. *In for a penny...* he thought.

"Essentially, you would submit to me." He paused, letting that notion hang in the air for a moment before he continued, "I would spank you when I saw fit, and you would find my cock in your ass on a regular basis."

"Oh..." she murmured.

"We would both enjoy the experience that I can promise you." Alex pushed. Mel stared at him, her courage growing and her embarrassment subsiding.

"Oh, I know that I would enjoy the sex part!" she teased him, "But what makes you so sure that I would submit to you?" she queried, raising an eyebrow, challenging him.

He grinned. "Oh, I don't think that you will have any problems with that!" He said, moving slightly towards her again. "I think it's just what you need, Mel, a firm hand," he whispered, grabbing her hair, pulling so her head fell back exposing her long silky neck to him again, "right.... across.... your...backside." he breathed, punctuating his words with a kiss on her pulse point.

She closed her eyes and a sensual sigh slipped through her lips. Alex lifted his head and fixed his mouth against hers, he needed to possess her, to will her to submit. She pressed her lips hard against his; the tip of her tongue finding its way to his. She put her hand on his thigh, mirroring the movement that he'd made on hers just moments before. This time it was he who moaned against her mouth, pushing his fingers back into her hair and pulling, while his other hand cupped the side of her face along her jaw. His attraction for her had started the second he saw her. Now he knew he *had* to dominate her, to take her to the edge of everything she thought possible and beyond. He longed to have her over his lap and to bring his hand down firmly on her buttocks. He wanted to feel the heat he would be able to raise from her skin, and the need it would raise in her sex.

She pushed back from their kiss, breathless, and needing badly to answer his proposal properly. "I think you're right Alex, I think I should be your little sub."

He stared blankly at her, had he really heard her agree to give herself to him? He couldn't believe that he could be so lucky, to have such a beautiful creature agree to submit to his wanton dark desires.

He lifted her hand in his, "Are you sure about this Melody?" *Oh yeah genius, give her the chance to back out, it's not like you want her!* At some point, he would have to have a little chat with his inner critic for being so obnoxious, but he would think about that later, for now, he was just trying to be a gentleman; he needed her to be sure.

She blushed and nodded, "Oh I'm sure about it all right." She laughed nervously. "What happens now then?" She asked him, wondering how exactly you start out being someone's ass slut.

He grinned at her broadly and kissed the knuckles of the hand he was holding. "Now, we enjoy our drink, and we can make arrangements after!" He beamed.

~ ~ ~

For the rest of the evening, he had been a perfect gentleman in almost every respect, but there was always that hidden streak of desire and lust lurking just beneath the surface. He was more tactile with her than she would ever have accepted a man to be on a first date. Mel liked to live her life with the notion that she was in control. She was a strong, dominant woman, every day she was the one to support those closest to her, and she never let her guard down enough to let them return the favour for her. *Maybe that's why you need this so much?* She mused.

She had to admit that the thought of handing over the reins to someone else, even for just a little while was something that made her tingle with anticipation.

All too soon the evening was over, and Alex and Melody said their goodbyes.

"Text me when you get home safe!" Alex ordered her.

"Yes Sir!" She grinned. He glared at her cheekiness, swatted her ass playfully, and kissed her one last time as her taxi arrived.

"I'll text!" She shouted over as she jogged over to her ride home. Alex grinned watching her go.

~ ~ ~

Melody walked through the front door of her small house in the suburbs, dropped her coat on a hook and her keys into a dish on the hall table and went into the kitchen to turn on the kettle. She lifted her phone from her pocket and sent Alex a quick text as he had instructed.

Home safe – Mel x

Her phone chirped a few seconds later.

Took you long enough! A x

She laughed when she read his reply and messaged him back.

So demanding – how will I cope! X

She set her phone on the kitchen counter and made herself a cup of tea. Her phone chirped again as she put the milk back in the fridge. Lifting it, she read Alex's reply.

Because it makes you wet and we both know it ;-) x

She blushed. He was right of course, but to see that he was bold enough to call her on it made her cheeks heat. It also made her the exact thing that he accused of her of; she could feel the moisture clinging to her panties. Her moment of hesitation in replying seemed to be all the proof Alex needed as another message from him arrived.

I'll take your silence as proof! Go to bed, and think of all the possibilities! Sweet dreams Jellybean xo

~ ~ ~

He smiled knowing full well that her silence was an admission of the effect that he had on her. His phone chirped as her reply finally arrived.

Mmmm… wet dreams ;) Night! xox

He laughed and shifted on his bed. He stared at the ceiling going over the events of their evening. His cock was hard and his balls ached. Melody had turned out to be something he hadn't been expecting. Yes, she was beautiful, curvy in all the right places, but all of that paled into insignificance against her single admission to him, she wanted to submit to him.

Alex pulled back the covers exposing his body to the cool air of his bedroom. His hand went for his heavy erection; absently he started to stroke the length of his shaft until a vapid orgasm erupted and sleep claimed him.

~ ~ ~

It was late morning when Alex awoke. He was restless, he didn't usually sleep this long and needed to burn off some energy and clear his head, so he pulled on his sweatpants, a grey t-shirt, his well broken in running shoes and went out to pound the pavement.

The possibilities for a relationship with Mel swam through his head. *Relationship?* He scoffed at himself. *We don't do those bro! Remember Natalie!* Just the thought of her name was enough to have him trip over his feet and almost plant himself face first into the pavement. He cursed under his breath and fought to regain his stride. *It's simple!* He thought and continued to plot his simple plan for the next 10 miles.

~ ~ ~

Melody awoke refreshed. The events of the night before had driven her to give herself two of the best orgasms she had had in a long time before a deep and revitalizing sleep took over. She woke just in time for lunch. She jumped into the shower, dried off, and dressed in yoga pants and a tank top before heading to the kitchen for tea. As she waited for the kettle to boil she checked her emails on her iPad. Alex's name in the sender's list attracted her attention, so did the subject line.

From: Alex Matthews

To: Melody Anderson

Subject: A guide to your submission

Melody,

I hope you don't mind, but I took the liberty of drawing up some guidelines for you. I know you've not done this kind of thing before, but I think you'll find it helpful.

Questions:

What are your hard limits? (Things you will never do?)

What 3 things are you willing to try?

Describe 3 fantasy scenarios you'd like to try out.

Do you understand the traffic light system of safe words?

When was your last sexual health screen, and what were the results? Are you on birth control?

If there is any other information you think is relevant here, just let me know.

I will expect you to act a certain way when you submit to me:

Your usual stance will always be legs apart, (feet shoulder width apart) eyes to the floor. If you are on your knees, legs apart, hands on thighs, eyes down.

You will be naked in my company when we are alone unless instructed otherwise.

You will answer all questions put to you promptly.

You will address me as Master Lex whenever you are in a submission scenario with me.

You will not come without permission unless previously instructed.

Your submission to me is an incredible gift. I will not do anything to taint that trust. I will not misuse you, I will not permanently mark you, and I will not hurt you, you have my promise on that. I will also never break any limits with you.

I will push you, I will be strict, but I promise you will love every last minute of it!

Master Lex x

P.S. Attached is a copy of my recent sexual health check.

Well, you weren't expecting that! Mel thought, as she poured hot water over the teabag in her favourite mug. She lifted her phone from where she had left it charging in the kitchen the night before and sent Alex a quick text.

Thanks for your email (I think!) Will think it over and get back to you!

She opened her back door and stood on her back step sipping her mug of tea. *So formal!* She thought to herself as she went over Alex's email in her head.

~ ~ ~

Alex absently reached for his phone when he heard it chirp beside him as he watched the rugby match on television. He smiled when he saw it was from Mel and quickly read her message, but his smile faded when he read its contents. *Think it over?* He questioned. *She's having second thoughts!* The critic teased. He tapped a reply.

Sorry, I know it seems so formal! But I believe if something if worth doing, it's worth doing right, and I just don't want to ever betray any trust you place in me – A x

He hit send, locked his phone and dreaded her reply.

~ ~ ~

When Mel returned from her mum's house later that evening her head was clear and she knew exactly what she wanted to say to Alex. While she would never tell her mum what was going on, her mum's particular sense of humour had helped her without even needing to talk about Alex or her offer of submission to him.

Mel sat on her sofa with her laptop on her knee and opened her email. She re-read the email from Alex, and hit "Reply":

Master Lex,

Thank you for setting out your expectations of me so clearly. I appreciate the need for crystal clarity on such occasions.

First to address your questions:

What are your hard limits? (Things you will never do?)

Blood or other gross bodily emissions

What 3 things are you willing to try?

Various implements of spanking including a cane

Nipple clamps

Being officially collared

Describe 3 fantasy scenarios you'd like to try out.

New sex slave being inspected by a master who had just bought her

Schoolgirl and headmaster

A hotel maid who needs to "apologise" for poor service.

Do you understand the traffic light system of safe words?

Yes, Green = more please

Yellow = slow down, getting too much

Red = Stop!

When was your last sexual health screen, and what were the results?

Find enclosed attachment, checked 4 months ago and I've been celibate since. I'm on the pill, and because I'm in college I'm religious about taking it.

As for your point 5 (*You will not come without permission unless previously instructed.*) I'm going to have to really practice for that one!

Mel x

She smiled to herself, hit send, and closed her laptop before heading upstairs for a long soak in the bath.

~ ~ ~

He stared at the screen, taking in her reply line by line, over and over. She hadn't bolted. She hadn't told him what she thought of him. *You don't deserve her!* The critic whined, and whether Alex agreed or not, he was very grateful that Melody was going to be his for now.

~ ~ ~

When she got into bed there was already an email from Alex waiting for her.

Gorgeous Melody,

Thank you for your reply. I know I must have come across as a bit of a jackass, I'm sorry, I've just been a bit burned in these situations before, and I just had to be sure that you weren't the kind of girl who couldn't handle it.

Can't wait to have you as my little slut.

Alex x

She stared at the screen and reread his words several times. "Little slut." She whispered, trying out the words, knowing exactly the reaction it was having on her, she felt the liquid heat spreading out from within her, every inch of her skin became suddenly alive, like she had grown a million new nerve endings everywhere. She hastened to reply.

Alex, or should that be Master Lex,

When would you like to get your hands on your new "little slut"? I think even your new submissive would like it to be sooner rather than later!

Mel x

Mel hit send and waited excitedly for Alex's reply. It only took a few minutes for his response to arrive in her inbox.

Mel,

What are you up to on Friday evening? Your master needs you.

Master Lex x

She let out a little moan when she read his reply. *Needs me, huh?* She thought to herself. She felt a tightening in her stomach and replied again.

Master Lex,

I'm working on Friday night, but I am free from 9pm, does that still suit you Sir?

Your Mel x

She had barely had time to do anything else on the Internet before her email popped up with a reply from Alex.

Slut,

I will arrange something for after work on Friday night for us then! Something has already come up that you will need to take care of ;-)

Master Lex x

~ ~ ~

The rest of the week passed with a painful slowness for both of them. They had talked about what both wanted from Friday night, and Alex had explained the scenario that he wanted to start the evening with when they got together. He suggested that they meet on neutral ground for their first time, and said that he would book a room in the Europa Hotel, a five-star establishment just round the corner from where Melody worked. He had taken his cues from her email; playing out one of the fantasies she had told him about.

Mel was to take the role of a new little slut arriving in front of her new master for the first time. He expected her to come in, strip, and stand completely naked, hands by her sides, and eyes down, ready for him to inspect her, to see if she was truly up for the job of being his new sub. The terms he had set out for her had painted a vivid picture in her head and seemed to be permanently hardwired to make her pussy moist and in need. She wanted him to view her as worthy; she wanted to give her submission to him, to obey, and most of all to please him. He promised to never push her more than she would be able to take, to never make her regret her decision to give him this wonderful gift she was giving him, her trust.

As she walked out of her office building on Friday evening, he was standing there waiting for her. She pulled her coat around her; trying to get rid of the chill her nerves were causing her to feel. She walked up to him and smiled. He grinned back at her and held out his hand to take hers. He pulled her to him, and pressed his lips on hers, feeling her nervous shiver, he pressed himself against her, hoping to spark the fires of lust, and quell her tremble. When he felt her calm, he broke his lips away from hers and squeezed her hand.

"Are you ready, Mel?" He asked her, smiling. She couldn't help but smile back at him, but nerves had stopped the words from leaving her mouth and instead she nodded.

They walked together hand in hand through the streets of Belfast on the short walk to the hotel. Alex asked her about her day at work, until they stopped just across the street from the Europa hotel. Alex pointed up to about half way up the twelve-floor building.

"See that light shining out from that window?" he asked her.

She followed his gaze up the front of the building until she spotted the window he was talking about.

"That's our room, and at some point this evening I'm going to take you against that window." He grinned at her and her mouth fell open, her pussy already hot and ready for anything that he had in mind for her, but her mind was still struggling with the fact that she was doing this with someone she'd only just met.

Silently he led her by the hand into the elevator, and up to the sixth floor where their room was. He paused before he opened the door, "Do you remember what I said you should do?" he asked. She swallowed hard and nodded her head. Alex placed the card into the lock and opened the door stepping inside.

Mel stopped just inside the doorway. Her heart was racing, and she started to feel apprehensive. She knew what she was meant to do, she knew what she had longed to do all week, but now that she was there in the hotel room she was frozen, completely unsure of herself. She looked at him, pleading with him in her mind to help her. He took his coat off and looked back at her. He knew her fear, it was plainly written on her face. He walked back over to her, placed his fingers under her chin forcing her head up so she had to look into his eyes, and he kissed her softly, starting at her lips, and proceeding to her neck, nuzzling gently at her silken skin. "It's okay," he whispered in her ear, "You know how to stop at any time, you have the power my love; the sub always has the power." He kissed her neck again and walked away from her.

He had given her exactly what she needed. The second he turned his back on her she started to remove her clothing piece by piece, her coat, and her scarf, all the way down to her underwear. She paused for a moment, lingering with her hands on the clasp at the back of her bra. She let out a long slow controlled breath, steadying her nerves, driving herself on. She unhooked the clasp and the bra slid down her arms, freeing her ample breasts from their lacy restraints. She tucked her thumbs into the waistband of the matching lacy panties, slid them down over her hips, and shimmied them to the floor. She had never felt so exposed, and yet so liberated all at the same time. She lowered her arms to sides and bowed her head, her eyes staring at the floor before her.

Alex grinned when he turned around to see her. His cock sprang to life seemingly admiring the sight as much as he was. He glided silently over to where she was standing. She truly was a sight to behold; it was enough to make him want to run his hands over his cock right then and there. She was setting him on fire, and he was starting to think that she was going to burn him alive. He moved around her, letting his fingertips graze over her flesh, and when he got behind her, he pressed himself against her, making sure that she could feel his cock against her ass. His arms reached around her, and his hands kneaded into her ample breasts.

"Hmmmm." He muttered sounding very much like someone who was trying to decide which of the fruits he was squeezing was the ripest. His fingers went to her nipples, which were peaking invitingly. He pinched, and he heard her breath quicken, he twisted them, rolling them between his fingers and thumbs. He watched her bite her bottom lip, and yet she never moved, and never lifted her eyes from the floor. He let go of her nipples and ran his hands over her arms, feeling the goose bumps that were prickling her flesh, gliding his way round to her ass. He grabbed at her ass cheeks and squeezed them roughly.

"Mmmm..." He sounded behind her, "not bad." He stated. He pushed his knee between her legs and pushed them apart, he let his hand slide from her ass to her now soaked sex. He gasped when he discovered how wet she was.

"Tsk tsk tsk, my, you really are wet aren't you? Truly a little slut!" he teased her. "I think I will keep you, I think I might have a use for you after all!" He gloated. "Get on your knees slut and follow me on all fours."

Mel blushed, sinking to her knees, and crawling after Alex as he strode across the room and sat himself on the sofa by the window. When she arrived in front of him, she did exactly as he had instructed her to in their emails; she rested back on her heels, legs parted, head bowed, and hands on her thighs. She realised quickly the reason for such a position, her pussy and tits were exposed for Alex to view as he pleased, with very easy access to her should he want to do anything else. He leaned back on the chair and drank in the glorious sight of her, this beautiful, strong woman kneeling at his feet ready to submit to his will. His cock was thick and straining against his trousers and his balls were painfully full. *There's only one thing for it!* He thought. He stood before her, unzipped his trousers, and removed his cock from its fabric confinement, pulling it out of his grey cotton boxers, and letting it bob freely straight out before him. He thought he caught Mel looking at his straining cock, but her head was still dipped and he wasn't sure.

"Slut." He said demanding her attention. "You can thank me now for allowing you to be in my service. Show me how grateful you are!" He admonished.

He took a step towards her, his cock hanging just in front of her mouth; he grabbed it with his hand, and presented it at her lips, waiting for her to make her move. Without looking up at him her lips parted, and she moved forward over the head of his now heavy penis. Her tongue ran along the underside of his glans, and circled over the top, he moaned and grabbed a handful of her hair. She sucked, rolling her tongue around his cock, slipping further down it with each suck. Alex's eyes rolled back in his head, and he moaned again. *Jesus Christ!* He thought. *She's going to drive me insane!* He pushed his cock deeper into her mouth, holding her head still with the hand he had in her hair. He didn't mean to get to this point so early in the evening, but with Mel he just couldn't help himself, she quickly drove him into a frenzy of lust. She had skills with her mouth and tongue on his cock that he would never have thought possible and no matter how hard he tried to keep his control he couldn't, he found himself thrusting deeper into her mouth, into her throat. Any regret he may have had in handling her so roughly so soon was quickly washed away when she controlled her gag reflex with seemingly effortless ability breathing through her nose. His breathing became ragged, he could feel that tell-tale tightening in his groin, his hand tightened in her hair, and he thrust into her mouth with quicker thrusts, racing to get the release he craved with her so readily. She lifted her hand to his balls, and his orgasm ripped through him, he let out a stifled moan, spurting hot come down the back of her throat. Her hand disappeared from his balls, and she kept his cock in her mouth, teasing out every last drop, cleaning him, letting him soften in the warm, wet enclosure of her mouth.

CHAPTER 2

A simple self-satisfaction filled Melody as she licked the taste of Alex from her lips. He put his finger under her chin and forced her head back so she had to look up at him. He looked pleased with her performance, he looked sated, and that simple fact made the heat in her groin encompass her whole body.

He smiled warmly down at her, letting go of her chin so her eyes could return to the floor. He tucked himself back into his boxers and refastened the button at the waist of his trousers.

"Your gratitude was very well expressed slut." He purred at her. "Now stand up." His voice containing the illicit element of a man not to be disobeyed.

"Yes Master Lex." Mel breathed, rising to her feet. Alex grinned at the sound of those words falling from her lips; his cock lurched, suddenly deciding that it was ready for another round. He stepped up against her, putting his hand around her waist and pulling her against him. He leaned over and his lips made contact with hers. Her arms twitched instinctively wanting to wrap them around his neck, but Alex ran his hands down her arms to her wrists and held them tight to her sides. His kiss was slow and sensuous, his tongue toyed with hers and she felt herself melt in against him, becoming pliable to his will.

He broke their kiss and turned her so her back was against his chest. He lazily swept her hair away from her neck and kissed her before whispering in her ear.

"I'm going to see just what I can do with you now Melody, I'm going to break you in as my little ass slut, push your limits and see just how much you will submit to me." With his final words his hand found her breasts and he kneaded them roughly in his hands, his lips back onto her neck.

Her nipples pinched painfully into tight little peaks begging for attention from Alex. He bit into her shoulder, his index fingers and thumbs found her hard nipples and he teased them, rolling them at first before pulling them out from her body roughly. A panting moan escaped from her lips, and she started to feel the moisture between her legs slick on the tops of her thighs. Alex directed her to the bottom of the bed, took a single step back.

"On the bed on your hands and knees" he demanded.

Mel slid her hands forward on the bed, until her knees came up on it with her, and she stopped, her head dipped, her thighs parted, her ass and pussy completely exposed to Alex. He stood there for a moment completely drinking in the sight before him. She was so wet for him, he could see where her inner thighs had become slippery, he could practically smell the arousal coming off her presented derriere. His cock throbbed and he absently rubbed himself through his trousers. *She's going to fucking kill me!* He thought to himself. *But holy hell! What a way to go!*

He stepped towards Mel, and his hands spread across her ass, groping her pert cheeks firmly, squeezing them, rubbing a thumb up and down the crack of her ass. Without warning his thumb dipped lower and slipped into the hot wetness that was spread all over her labia. She hissed out at the sudden attention her pussy was getting. His touch scorched her; she was hungry for more, and on the verge of begging him for it when his hand disappeared. She groaned at the loss and no sooner had the sound escaped from her than his hand smacked down on her right buttock. She jumped in surprise and let out a squeal, her ass cheek burning under the sting of Alex's hand, the sizzle went straight through to her clit, making her pussy clench wanting to be filled. Alex's ran his hand over the cheek that it had just struck to soothe and tease her, again he allowed his thumb to dip down into her wetness. Mel's hips came back, trying to get more from him than just a fleeting torment, and her left buttock received the same attention as the right. Again she jumped, but this time it was a little groan that escaped from her lips instead of a yelp.

Alex's fingers smoothed over her heating ass, giving her the same relentless treatment over and over. Hands stroking her backside to soothe her heated flesh, thumbs slipping in and out teasingly of her hot, sopping sex, followed by a hard smack on alternating cheeks. He had thought she couldn't get any wetter for him; he was wrong. Mel moaned, pushed back against him, and she was more and more drenched every time his thumbs tempted her. By the time he had made her ass bright red and he could feel the heat coming off her tortured skin through his trousers, he could barely contain himself.

"Don't move!" he told her, and gave her an extra hard slap on her left buttock, she hissed at the contact. He pulled his t-shirt over his head and grabbed his little wash bag out of his holdall. His shoes were kicked off, quickly followed by his trousers, socks and cotton boxers.

Mel heard the tell tale ripping of foil, and held her breath, waiting to see what was going to happen next.

"I'm pleased with how you are responding to me, my glorious little sub!" he said, his voice feeling like velvet over every inch of Mel's sensitive skin. "But I can't wait any longer to find out how it's going to feel to slide my cock into your lush little ass!"

The breath that Mel had been holding rushed from her lips when she felt Alex rub a cool, wet fluid over her tight little asshole, and he began to push his slippery finger into her most intimate place. As his finger penetrated her, she pushed back on his hand, and he groaned, playfully spanking her ass as a warning.

"Stay still!" He hissed.

He pulled his finger out of her, and she felt him instantly replace it with the tip of his hard thick cock. He held onto her hips and pushed against the muscles of her ass, she gasped at the feeling of pressure as he teased himself into her. He groaned feeling Mel's body opening to him, allowing admission to the head of his erection.

He paused, she was hot, and she was tight. He was savouring this moment completely, this was too good a feeling to rush. He heard her panting, heard a groan escape when he stopped moving. Suddenly she was pushing back on him, her need to feel him deep inside her so great that she couldn't stop herself, she moved pushing back against him, her hips moving back. His fingers dug into her hips and he groaned, he couldn't take it; she was pushing his limits of control, beckoning him forward with her silent demands. He thrust forward, his length fully inside her, his balls against her soaked pussy.

"Jesus Christ Mel!" He groaned as he felt just how delicious it was to be lost inside her. Every inch of his skin tingled, this woman was intoxicating, and he couldn't stop himself from wanting more and more. He pulled back a little before thrusting against her again, a moan rumbled deep in her throat, that sound alone was enough to break him. The raw pleasure and lust in that sound had his cock twitching inside her as he started his hard pounding into her sweet ass, harder and harder, faster and faster. Her breathing quickened her entire body humming with her building orgasm. Every time his balls slapped against her pussy she moaned. He grabbed her hair, pulling her head back as he showed her delicious backside no mercy. Her hips fell into rhythm with his own, rising to meet him as if Mel needed to have him deeper and deeper with every stroke. He felt her tighten around him, knowing that her orgasm was about to seize her. He felt a tingling at the bottom of his spine, the pulse starting to throb in his cock, the tightening in his balls. He pounded into her like a madman in a frenzied need to mate with her, to claim her, to have her fall apart beneath him.

Melody felt like she was losing her mind, the fullness of Alex deep inside her ass, his unyielding fucking of her to a fever pitch. The fact that he was clearly coming undone under her influence, all fed into the passion that was almost crashing over her.

"Come Melody.... Oh God, come now!" he breathed on the verge of his own orgasm. Those words pushed her over the edge and the world around her fell apart to the sound of her own voice crying out.

"Yes... oh Master Lex, YES!"

She was still mid-climax when Alex shouted out behind her, "Oh fuck! Fuck! FUCK!" He slammed his hips against hers one more time, grabbing both her hips again as he pumped deep into her in a blistering finish.

His legs wouldn't support him any more, he held her tight against him, and came down on the bed with her. They both landed on their sides, spooning against each other, Alex still semi-erect and inside her. His arms went round her and he cradled her against his bare chest, keeping her like that as their breathing calmed, and their heart rates slowed down again. He nibbled on her shoulder; little kisses and nips with his teeth grazing the skin. His fingers lazily traced over her pebbled nipples, and she shivered against him.

"Are you okay?" he whispered against her neck. She smiled trying to make her brain focus long enough for her to reply.

"Yes Master Lex, very okay!" she grinned back at him.

For a moment, he allowed himself to get lost in her smile and the satisfied look on her face. But quickly a knot started to tighten in the pit of Alex's stomach and he needed to escape. He took his arm from around her, grabbed hold of the condom, and allowed himself to slowly slide out of her. Melody sighed at the loss of him, and he instantly regretted breaking their connection. He slid off the bed and tied a knot in the condom before throwing it into the waste bin. He looked at her backside as he returned, still burning red and his control returned. He went into the bathroom and started to run the water in the shower. He came back into the room and sat on the bed beside her.

"Don't fall asleep yet!" he whispered in her ear. "Come on, get up, and come with me." She groaned as he pulled her arm, she was comfortable and sated, but she was still compliant. She lazily rose from the bed and followed Alex.

She stopped at the door of the bathroom, looking at him.

"Get in." He beckoned holding out his hand to her, she bit her bottom lip and slipped her hand in his as he led her into the shower.

The warm water was so soothing over her skin as she let the shower flow over her. Alex got in behind her and reached around her for the shower gel. He lathered it up in his hands and started to tenderly wash all over her body starting at her shoulders. He massaged as he washed, letting his hands caress every inch of her. A satisfied moan from Melody broke the silence, and she turned to Alex, reaching for the shower gel when he stopped her.

"Not tonight my little slut." He smiled. "I rode you too hard, you'll be sore tomorrow, but this should help. Next time you can wash me." He told her, placing a small kiss on the tip of her nose. He turned her back under the spray so that he could rinse her. When Mel was free from soap suds, Alex led her out of the shower, and wrapped a towel around his hips before turning back to Mel to dry her off. He was gentle over her buttocks, taking care not to cause any more irritation to her skin.

"That's going to still be red tomorrow, and I would say that you'll have a reminder every time you sit." He told her almost regretfully.

She grinned back at him, a glint in her eyes. "God I hope so!"

Alex laughed shaking his head. "You're dangerous, woman!" he smirked.

She presented him with a full on wicked grin, "Oh I know, Master Lex!" she said raising an eyebrow.

That look was undoing him again. He had planned to rub lotion into her scalded rear end, and lead her into bed to sleep. Instead, he found himself pulling her towards him, he pressed his lips to hers, probed her mouth with his tongue, fisted his hands in her hair. She challenged him; there was no other way to describe it. She looked at him with that eyebrow, and it was as though she was provoking him with her defiance. She wrapped herself around him in response to his kiss, her nails running down his back teasing him. He grabbed her hands and firmly held them behind her back as he kept claiming her mouth as his. Mel's breasts pushed forward when he held her hands tight behind her, her towel slipped, and she found herself skin to skin against him. His chest hair tickled her nipples and she moaned into his mouth, pushing herself forward, needing more friction from his chest on hers.

It was too much. She was too much. Alex grabbed her and pulled her to her feet. He whipped the towel away from around her, discarding his own towel as well. He grabbed a condom and led her to the window.

"Put your hands on either side of the window frame!" Alex commanded as he rolled the condom down over his length. Melody obeyed, standing naked and visible in the window, high above the city with people still moving around in the street below in their Friday night of revelry, if they looked up she would surely be spotted if she hadn't been already. Alex moved in behind her, he pushed his knee between her legs, forced them apart, allowing him more access to the delights that lay between her thighs. She felt his cock sliding through her drenched sex as Alex gripped her hips harshly and thrust upwards. She gasped as her sensitive flesh was taken, her muscles flexing and adjusting to accommodate Alex's girth and length. He settled quickly into a fast pace, ceaselessly riding her hard.

She had to grip the window frame tightly to stop from falling, but Alex's harsh thrusts had her pinned against the window anyway. Her breasts collided with the cool glass of the window every time Alex pushed into her. The cold glass against her nipples only seemed to exaggerate the heat everywhere else, and a long moan escaped from her lips.

Alex took that as a sign that he needed to speed up, and he started to grind into her pussy, harder and faster. Mel began to pant; that exquisite feeling had started to build inside her.

"Don't you dare come yet!" Alex growled into her back, pounding into her like his life depended on it. Mel clenched around him at his growl, trying to focus on the people on the street below instead of the delicious sensation of Alex relentlessly hitting that one perfect spot deep inside her over and over again. She whimpered, fighting the orgasm that was trying to hit her like a tsunami. She heard the change in Alex's voice behind her and she knew that he was close.

His hands moved from her hips to her breasts, he grabbed them roughly pulling on her peaked nipples.

"Come!" he barked and pushed so hard and deep inside her, his own release ripping through him as he continued to pull on her nipples as she had her own climax. As she stilled his hands became gentler on her breasts, and his lips nuzzled against her neck to place tender little kisses along it and her shoulder.

Alex continued to nuzzle her as he pulled back, holding the condom as he slid out of her. She shivered at the loss of his body from hers, but she didn't move, she knew not to. He tied off the condom, and threw it into the waste bin before returning to Mel. He ran his hands along her arms, still fixed to the window frame. He eased them down, rubbing her shoulders a little and turning her to face him. He cradled her head in his hands and kissed her, his mouth gently caressing hers as he coiled his tongue with hers.

"Mmmm," he whispered against her lips, "You have pleased me tonight slut!" He smiled at her kissing her sweetly again.

She looked up into his almost black eyes. "Thank you Master Lex!" She smiled back at him. He took her by the hands, led her over to the big bed and pulled back the covers.

"Time for some rest wouldn't you say?" He grinned.

"Definitely Master Lex!" She said as she stretched and then placed herself into the bed. He pulled the covers round her and kissed her on the forehead, before going to the other side of the bed and getting in. He settled down, reaching for the switch on the bedside lamp.

"Sweet dreams Jellybean." He whispered into the darkness once the light was off.

Alex woke in the middle of the night to find his limbs tangled with Melody's. He allowed himself to look at her as she slept, drinking in the peaceful expression on her face in the pale light coming from the bathroom. She was stunning, and yet she was so much more. He'd never had someone submit to him in such a passionate and complete way. He kissed her forehead, and she stirred, moving her head from his shoulder to his chest. He flinched, holding his breath as she settled back into a deep slumber. He fell asleep again with the sweet scent of flowers and Mel in his nostrils.

CHAPTER 3

As they left the hotel the next morning, Mel felt like she was floating on air. Alex had been right, every time she sat down, or moved in a particular way she received a reminder of the night before. Her thighs were stiff in muscles she hadn't even realised she had, and her buttocks ached. He had smirked when he noticed her sitting down gingerly, trying not to encourage the twinge of pain when she sat.

She drove the ten miles home and felt already like she was missing something. *How is it possible to miss him already?* She laughed to herself. She was just pulling into her driveway when her phone chirped from an incoming text message.

Thank you for an amazing evening! A x

She read it as soon as she turned off the car, not even waiting to go into the house. She replied instantly.

I had an amazing time myself! Thank you too x

~ ~ ~

Sitting on his sofa, Alex grinned at his phone, glad to hear that Mel had experienced the same amazing evening as he had. *Early days yet!* His inner critic started. Just this once he wanted to ignore his inner critic, just this once, he wanted to let go. He texted her back:

What are you doing tomorrow night? A x

He knew that he should be playing it cool, but after last night he couldn't resist, her submission was truly something else, and he couldn't wait to get his hands on her again, the firm yet ample curve of her backside, how greedy she clearly was for him, letting him ride her hard. His phone sounded out that he had a text message and distracted him from his thoughts.

I'm working on a college assignment with some of the guys tomorrow night, but I am free the night after :)

His grip tightened on his phone. The guys. He knew her background; he knew that she was a student working on her Masters degree in Computer Science. He knew that she was one of the few women on the course at all, and that in a particular class that she was talking about, she was the only woman in the class. But that didn't stop that feeling rising up in him. *You're jealous!* Came that voice. *Getting attached already!* It chided. Alex sighed and pushed his jealousy down and replied again.

How would Ms Melody like an evening of lust and debauchery? A x

He was already breaking his rules by asking to see Mel again so soon, but he couldn't help himself. Normally when he had a submissive, he would never play during the week. Normally. But with her, the wait for the weekend to come around again was just too long. The screen of his phone lit up with an incoming message from Mel.

Why thank you kind Sir! That sounds divine! :D Just heading to the college library to get some work done. Text later xx

He gripped his phone again. *What is with this alpha male shit?!* He thought. Alex took a deep breath, and went and got himself ready to go out for a run. Time to rid himself of these frustrations by pounding on the tarmac for a few stress relieving miles.

Mel looked around the third floor of the library for the other guys from her class. Jonathan, a cute looking 24 year old with broad shoulders, dirty fair hair, and soulful blue eyes which always had a cheeky twinkle in them, waved over to her smiling his usual big and bright grin. She found a smile spreading across her own face. She couldn't help herself; there was just something about Jonny that always made her feel better. He had been her closest friend since almost the first day of college, and over the last 3 years they had been through a lot together. Within months of knowing each other, she and Jonny had been such close friends that lecturers had asked if they had known each other before college, sure that they seemed to have known each other for years.

She slumped down in the chair beside him and flinched. Jacob, the lean tall dark haired, youngest in the group at just 22 years old, looked across the table at her with a puzzled expression on his face.

"What's up with you?" He asked her pushing the glasses he always wore up his nose, his blue eyes laced with genuine concern.

Jonny glanced over and grinned more. Of course, her best friend had known where she was going and why the night before. Jonny had her back, he was her safety net, she would never have been to a hotel with someone who was practically a stranger and not have Jonny know.

"I slipped on the bottom step this morning and bumped my butt a little hard, I'm okay Jake!" She lied to Jacob.

Jacobs's usually cute baby face screwed up and he hissed. "Ouch! You okay sweetie?"

Mel nodded, and Jonny smirked. She glared at him and pulled out her laptop. She knew that on the first smoke break that Jonny needed she would be grilled about what happened.

"So, how is fixing that replication error going, Dylan?" She asked, looking at the tall, dark, handsome 26 year old part-time personal trainer, hoping to change the subject.

"Nate and I have been working on it." Dylan said turning the laptop round for Mel to see what they had done. She glanced at Nathaniel, who was sitting tapping his pen on the pad in front of him. Nate at 23-year-old was the lead singer in a rock band called "Remembering Tomorrow" and Mel had never seen him without a pen in his hand, always writing lyrics or drumming out a beat, no matter what they were doing. Nate sighed and ran his fingers through his long red hair.

"We think we have the damn thing fixed, but, you'll know it better than me!" Nate smiled.

She and the guys spent the next two hours slaving away on their Master's project. Jonny sighed and sat back with his hands laced behind his head.

"I think it's time for a smoke break!" He grinned at Mel, "You coming?" He asked.

She rolled her eyes, Dylan and Nate looked up at her, both smirking.

"We'll keep working here, but get me a Coke will you?" Nate asked.

She sighed, "Sure," and turned towards Jonny. "Let's go then!" She said, getting up from her chair and starting to walk away to the elevators. Jonny got up and started after her. He waited with her in silence at the elevator doors, they got in together, and Jonny pressed the button for the ground floor. They remained in silence until they were standing in the smoking area outside the library. Jonny pulled out a packet of cigarettes, lit one, and took a long draw.

"So are you going to tell me how it went last night or not?" He smiled.

Mel laughed, "You want all the gory details Jonny, or just the highlights?" Jonny exhaled a cloud of smoke. "Well, I know that your ass is sore you dirty bitch, so why don't you start there!" Mel blushed. "Jesus Jonny!" She bit her lip, thinking over what happened last night, and thinking about what to tell her best friend. "It was amazing... He was amazing.... And yes, he gave me a damn good spanking, and my ass is still tender today!" Jonny smiled at her, he liked to see his best friend happy, he'd seen her go through the pain her ex had put her through, and he'd been there through it to help her, to put her back together.

"Amazing huh?" He smirked. "Like toe curling amazing, or just sporting a big cock like me?" Mel laughed again and slapped him on the arm.

"I told you before, stop mentioning how big your cock is unless you're willing to prove it!" She covered her face and laughed. "Jonny, he was both, and I know that you're worried about me, but I promise you, it's just some fun. You know I'm not looking for anything serious after Kyle."

Jonny stubbed out his cigarette on the top of the bin before throwing it in. "I know Mel, but I do worry about you, it's my job!" The smile that grew across Mel's face was genuine and heart-warming for Jonny, and he returned it with everything that he had.

She wrapped her arms around him. "Thank you sweetie!" Mel squeezed him tight, and he returned her hug and kissed her forehead.

"Let's go get Nate his Coke." He smiled, turning back towards the library.

It was after nine by the time that Mel made it home from the library. She dropped herself onto the sofa exhausted from a long day of studying. They had worked hard and were getting on well with their project. She smiled to herself thinking about Alex and pulled her phone out of her pocket.

Just got home! Have a good day? X

Mel set her phone down and went to get herself a cup of tea. When she got back to the sofa, she found a message waiting for her.

Had a run and an afternoon at rugby. Tough day at the office? A x

She smiled and sipped her tea while replying.

Big time! But at least we're finally getting somewhere with our project. We'll be hard at it again tomorrow. Just about to get into the bath and relax.

She hit send and lazed back against the cushions. What she needed right now was a warm bubble bath and a good book. Her phone chirped again.

Tease! Making me think of you naked and wet! I should spank you for that! A x

She grinned when she read his reply. She couldn't help herself; she had to tease him again.

Oh, it's worse! I'll be naked, wet, and in the company of a hot alpha male!

She hit send on her phone and got up to put her cup in the kitchen sink.

~ ~ ~

Alex looked at his phone in disbelief. *An alpha male?* He repeated in his head. Was she teasing him? Was she seeing someone else? He took a deep breath and texted back.

Alpha male? Do I have a rival for your affections?

Minutes passed before her reply came in.

Do you want my affections? X

Alex felt exposed. He wanted to say yes, but he couldn't, not so soon, maybe not ever. He paused thinking of the right words to reply with.

I do NOT share Melody. Ever.

He hit send and tried to ignore his inner critic. *Possessive asshole!*

Melody read the text and her whole body heated. The demand and the dominance were dripping off every word. It shouldn't leave her feeling turned on, but it did. His possessive need for her made every nerve in her body awaken. She gathered her hair on top of her head, turned off the taps and stepped into the bubbles.

I know Master. I am getting into the bath with a book containing a hot alpha male xx

Mel sighed and relaxed back into the bubbles, lying in soothing heat. She pulled the bath rack over and opened Cooper by Harper Sloan, letting the warm water, and the hot actions of Asher Cooper unwind the tension of working on her degree project all day. Her phone chirped again.

Read about a lot of hot alpha men?

Mel smiled. She owned more books that anyone she knew. Especially ones with hot alpha males; aside from computers it was her number one addiction. She hit reply.

I read a lot, period. I'm a bit of a book junkie, especially if they contain hot alpha men ;)

She set her phone down and sank back into the bubbles with her book.

A book junkie? Alex laughed, suddenly his head was swimming with a fantasy about a sexy librarian, being able to take her over a big leather-covered desk, or pushing her up against a row of shelves. His cock throbbed and he adjusted himself in his jeans. It was starting to feel like he had been hard non-stop since he met Melody. His lust for her was stronger than anyone else he'd ever met, and his possessive need to keep her all to himself was something else he'd never experienced before. She was drawing him in, he felt like he was fast becoming a fly caught in a spider's web, unable to escape. He wasn't even sure he wanted to escape.

Don't fall asleep in the bath Jellybean! Enjoy your book x

CHAPTER 4

Mel sat in her car and sounded the horn to let Jonny know that she was outside and waiting for him. A few minutes later his front door slammed and he bounced into the passenger seat beside her.

"Morning sweetie!" She smiled.

Jonny groaned and rubbed his face. "It's too early on a Sunday for this shit!" He grumbled.

Mel laughed and pulled away from the front of Jonny's house. "It's for your own good and you know it buster! Get your Masters and you'll be unstoppable!" She smiled.

Jonny put the car window down and lit a cigarette. "I know! I know! And you know that I appreciate you dragging my ass out of bed, but it's 10 on a Sunday morning!" Mel rolled her eyes at him and laughed.

Ten minutes later they arrived at the college library, Jonny glanced over at Mel. "How's your backside today?" He grinned.

"Painless." She smirked, only to watch Jonny's grin grow.

"Have you told him that?" Mel raised an eyebrow at him. "No? Why?"

Jonny's grin had grown to shit eating proportions. "Tell him…. Then tell me what he says!" He laughed and walked towards the main library doors.

Mel took her phone from her pocket to put it on silent before going into the library, but she couldn't resist texting Alex first to see if they were still going to see each other later that day.

Hey, x do you still want to see me tonight?

The reply came back almost instantly

Of course, I do Jellybean! Does 8pm suit? BTW, how's your backside today?

Mel grinned at her phone and Jonny glanced over at her as they waited for the elevator to take them to the third floor where all the Computer Science material was held. She texted him back.

8 is perfect! And my ass is lovely and white, with no pain. I think you need to try harder next time Master. Just heading into the library, might be a bit slow to reply x

She hit send and dumped her phone into her bag.

"What?!" She asked Jonny when she caught him staring at her again.

"Oh, nothing at all, just remember to tell me what he says." He winked. She stuck her tongue out at him and giggled, walking to where Dylan and Nathaniel were waiting for them.

Alex stretched out on his bed and thought about what he was going to do with Melody when he was back in her company. Just thinking about her was enough to make his heart quicken and his cock throb. He put his arm behind his head and closed his eyes, daydreaming of what would happen between them in just a few short hours.

At lunchtime, Mel finally got time to look at her phone. There were 2 messages from Alex waiting for her.

> Your ass looks untouched? Damn Mel, I'm going to have to try harder next time. I can't spank you tonight though; it could cause deep tissue damage. At the weekend, I promise a more lasting experience! A x

She grinned and blushed deeply before skipping to the next text.

> I'd like to take you out for dinner. But I would like to play a little game at the same time if that's okay with you ;-) A x

Mel texted back asking the nature of his game and went back to her lunch with the guys from her course.

Later in the afternoon, Jonny dragged Mel outside with him for his smoke break.

"Well?" He asked after taking his first drag.

"Well what?" She asked, prolonging the moment for just a little longer.

Jonny grinned at her and raised an eyebrow. "You know perfectly well what I'm talking about!"

Mel sighed, she knew that Jonny wouldn't quit asking her until she gave in and told him.

"Fine, he said that he would have to try harder to make my ass stay red and sore next time... Happy now?" She glared watching Jonny laugh as he exhaled smoke.

She rolled her eyes, "You are an ass Jonathan Tyler, a complete fucking ass!"

He stubbed out his cigarette still laughing and as they walked towards the library doors he slapped her on the ass and walked back towards the elevators.

Alex left his house at 7.30pm ready to take Melody out for dinner. He'd left her specific instructions on what to wear, and where to meet him. She was to take a taxi because he would be driving her home afterwards and he told her to meet him outside.

At 7: 58pm he looked up from his watch to see Mel smiling at him from a few feet away. His stomach flipped when he looked at her and he couldn't help but grin back at her.

"I'm not late am I?" She asked nervously. He reached out, took her hand and pulled her closer to him so that he could kiss her briefly, allowing his lips only a moment's brush against hers.

"No Jellybean, right on time." She smiled up at him; even in heels Alex was at least 4 inches taller than her. He looked into her eyes and felt his cock stiffen. He raised an eyebrow, hoping she would understand. She blushed, and her hand went into his, feeling the small key ring that she was placing against his palm he grinned again and leaned down to place another kiss against her lips. When his lips left hers he tilted his mouth to her ear.

"I do hope the vibrator I have the control for is in the place I asked it to be." He warned her.

Her face turned crimson and she nodded. He kissed her cheek and smiled, staring into her eyes. "Then let's go eat!" Alex kept her hand in his and led her into the restaurant.

The waitress came over and took their drinks order, and Alex asked for a few more minutes before they ordered.

"Do you trust me to order for you Mel?" He smiled at her.

Mel's eyebrows went up in surprise. "That's very gentlemanly of you Alex, and a little old fashioned!"

Alex leaned over the table, his hand going to his pocket and the remote control hidden within. "That's Master Lex, Melody, you wouldn't have me take you over my knee in front of all these people now would you?" He grinned at her, her eyes going wide and staring at him.

He pressed the 'on' button on the remote and pressed the other button to select a vibration setting. Mel felt the vibe suddenly start to buzz on her clit, and a small squeak of shock escaped her lips.

"Now, now Mel, keep control of yourself, you don't want the entire restaurant knowing what a dirty girl they have in their presence!" She stared at him as he watched her struggling to keep her composure. She swallowed and licked her lips and his eyes were instantly on her mouth. His thoughts immediately wandered to taking that mouth, to the sight of his cock slipping between her greedy lips and hitting her throat. His cock sprang to life in his pants as if it agreed with him on where it needed to be at that moment.

"I'm waiting for a reply Melody." He prompted.

Mel looked down and cleared her throat. "Sorry, Master Lex." She said, just as the waitress reappeared at the table with their drinks.

Alex flicked the off switch on the remote and smiled politely at the waitress, who was looking at Mel with a smirk on her face. Mel glanced up at her saying thank you for her drink, and at that moment knew that the waitress had heard her calling Alex 'Master Lex.' Her face grew crimson, and Alex laughed.

"We're ready to order now I think." He smiled.

Mel glared at him again across the table, and again he turned on the vibrator. She instantly shifted in her seat and let out a long breath.

"For a starter, I think that we'll both have the chicken liver pate, followed with medium rare steak for me, and the linguine pomadoro with chicken for the lady. I'd also like a mineral water with ice and a slice of lime, and a glass of Sauvignon Blanc for my guest." Alex handed the waitress the menus and looked across the table at Mel, turning the vibrator off again as the waitress walked away. "Do you approve of my choices?" He smiled at her, taking a mouthful of the scotch on the rocks.

"I do, thank you... Master Lex" she hesitated before taking a sip of her orange juice.

They chatted as they waited for their starters to arrive. Alex asked about her course, how her project was progressing, and whom it was that she was working with. *You're fishing!* That inner voice started to nag.

"They are great guys. It's Jonny, Jacob, Dylan, Nate and me. We make a great team, we work well together, we get on well, and we help kick each other in the backside when it's needed!" Mel smiled, she loved working with her group, and they were all good friends to her. Alex felt his jealousy starting, to see her smiling and practically glowing about the group that she worked with had him feeling at odds. He knew that he shouldn't be jealous. Hell, he didn't want to *be* jealous, even if it was something that was allowed. His mouth tightened into a hard line, and Mel's smile started to fade.

"Are you okay?" She asked, reaching across the table and touching his hand. Her contact jerked him back into reality, his eyes falling to where her hand was on his. He took her hand in his and traced over her wrist with his thumb.

"Yes, sorry, talking to you about working had me thinking about a big project that I'm working on myself. Not very polite of me, Jellybean, I'm sorry." He lifted her hand to his lips, kissing her knuckles. Over her shoulder, he noticed that there was a waiter coming their way with their starters and he reached into his pocket again, flicking the vibrator back on. He kept a hold of Melody's hand, feeling the goose bumps rising on her skin as he turned the vibrator to a stronger setting.

"Looks like our food is here." He smiled, letting go of her hand so he could lean back and make space for the plates being set in front of them.

The general chitchat continued as they ate. Alex tried to keep away from the topic of Melody's college friends, and they got to know each other more generally, learning each other's likes and dislikes. Throughout the meal, Alex varied the vibrations of the bullet on Mel's clit, keeping her burning and needy all evening long, without ever letting her get to orgasm, holding her on that knife edge of coming and not quite being ready to. Alex paid the bill, took Melody's coat and held it out for her. They left the restaurant, Mel placed her hand in his, and they walked to where his car was parked in a side street. Cutting down an alleyway Mel pulled Alex against her and crushed her lips against his. Her hands gripped his hair holding him close, her body pushed him back until they made contact with the wall, her leg slid up the side of his hip, grinding her pelvis against his. His tongue duelled with hers, his hands went to her hips and grabbed her, pulling her tight against him, his hard cock pressing against her pussy and stomach.

She broke their kiss, panting, "You're a cruel man Alex Matthews!" She teased breathlessly. Alex's hands went to her hair and he pulled, her head dropped back and her neck was exposed to him. He traced tiny kisses from her collarbone up to her earlobe.

"That's Master Lex to you, slut." He breathed in her ear before nibbling on her neck just below her ear. Mel let out a groan into the darkness. Alex spun her, her back now against the wall, he pulled her earlobe between his teeth, and her hands found their way under his jacket and she started to pull his shirt out of his waistband, needing to get her hands on his bare skin, wanting him to feel her nails in his back. His lips met hers again, his hands slipping from her hair to her hips again, one hand dipping to her thigh, lifting her leg around his hip, running his fingers down to her knee and then back to her ass, kneading them into her backside. She moaned against his lips, and he pried his mouth from hers.

"Jesus Mel..." he hissed, dropping his hands away from her and backing off. "Come on!" He hissed, grabbing her hand and practically dragging her to his car.

They pulled into Melody's driveway 20 minutes later. Alex jumped out and around the car to open the door for Mel. She took him by the hand and led him to her front door, lifted her keys from her bag, opened the door, and led him inside. The second, the door closed behind them his mouth was back on hers. He backed her up against the wall in her hallway, his lips crushing against hers, his hands finding the hem of her dress, and pulling it up, his lips parted from hers just long enough to allow her dress to be pulled off over her head before coming back harshly on hers. She pushed his jacket off his shoulders and started on the buttons of his shirt. One of Alex's hands skimmed her breasts through her lacy bra, kneading into her flesh causing her nipple to pebble beneath his touch; the other fondled her ass roughly, pulling her hard against him. Her hands fumbled with the buttons and she grabbed it, pulling it apart in haste, sending buttons flying in all directions. She needed her hands on him, she had to feel his skin against hers, and she couldn't wait a minute longer. Her fingertips grazed his chest hair, skimmed over his nipples, and she raked her nails down his sides as she headed for his fly. Alex growled against her mouth, pulling himself back away from her as he pulled off the rest of his shirt, she lifted herself off the wall as he did, reaching behind her back to undo her bra, letting her breasts fall free. This was Alex's undoing, the sight of her there in stockings, heels, and lacy panties was more than his cock could take, and he pounced on her again. He hitched her up against the wall, pulling her legs around his waist, her arms around his neck clinging to him. He stooped just enough to pull one of her nipples into his mouth, drawing it against his tongue, elongating it with each suckle. A long moan erupted from Mel's throat and her back arched. Alex straightened, lifted Mel higher against his body, reaching beneath her, he undid his fly and shimmed his boxers and pants down his thighs. His eyes met hers.

"Please, Alex!" she begged breathlessly, and pulls his head towards her again, their lips bruising against each other's, lust and need driving them forward. Alex pulled Mel's panties to the side, yanked the vibrator away from her clit, pushed her back against the wall, and in the same movement sank inside her completely in one thrust.

Mel cried out at the fullness she felt, the delicious pressure already building, breathless as Alex started to thrust into her roughly, fuelled by his own desire.

"God Mel... Your pussy... You're fucking perfect." He groaned as he pushed deeper and deeper inside her with every thrust. Her nails digging into his shoulder blades as she hung on to him. As he pounded her against the wall her mouth nibbled his shoulder and neck. Alex could feel her orgasm coming, her pussy tightening around him, pulsing as he grabbed her ass hard, and pulled her tight against him. His mouth on her neck was all the trigger that she needed, and the world around her shattered into a million pieces and fell away leaving her floating, only anchored to reality by Alex's thick shaft grinding into her. She could feel him throbbing inside her as her climax started to dissipate. He nibbled on her shoulder, relentlessly thrusting into her. His hand slipped round to her asshole, she felt him spread her wetness against it, and his finger pushed inside her, all at once a second orgasm she hadn't been expecting crashed into her.

"Alex! Fuck yes! Alex!" She screamed out, and as she did Alex's teeth sank into her shoulder, and a long growl erupted from his own lips as he came hard, still thrusting deep inside her.

"Oh Melody." He moaned before catching her mouth with his own, his tongue teasing her in a long, slow and languishing kiss. He eased his finger from her ass, and her body shivered. He slowly savoured the taste of her mouth on his, giving her time to recover enough for her legs to not buckle under her.

When they had both calmed enough, he broke their kiss and slid his cock out of her, and let her feet drop to the floor, ready for her to stand unsupported. She gazed up at him.

"You okay?" he whispered to her. She nodded her head and licked her swollen, well-kissed lips.

"Uh huh." She smiled at him. She looked at his button-less shirt lying beside them. "Sorry about the shirt." She grimaced.

Alex let out a small laugh, "Jesus Mel, don't even apologise for that! I think it's very hot that you couldn't wait to get a hold of me." He reassured her, leaning towards her and kissing the tip of her nose. He lifted his hand to her face and caressed her cheek. "Tonight has been amazing Jellybean." He said almost regretfully. Mel looked deep into his eyes and understood what he was trying to say.

"You have to go." It wasn't a question—she already knew his answer.

"I have to. I have work in the morning, and at the very least I need a new shirt now." He smiled at her, leaning in, his lips gently caressing hers. "I've had an incredible evening Mel. Thank you." He said, kissing the tip of her nose again. He pulled up his boxers and pants, and put on his button-less shirt. Mel grabbed her dress and pulled it over her head so she could see him to the door. He reached to open the door and paused, turning to crush his lips against hers for one last time, he wrapped his arms around her drawing her into him.

"Goodnight Jellybean." He smiled at her when he broke their kiss. He turned the door handle and opened the door.

"Goodnight Alex!" She called as he got into his car. She watched as he started the car and drove out of her drive and round the corner disappearing out of sight before she closed the door. She floated upstairs, fell into bed, and slept deeply.

CHAPTER 5

Juliet Malone had worked at Matthews Architecture for two and a half years. The 25-year-old was a petite yet curvy woman with bright blue eyes and wavy blonde hair, which today she had up in a tight bun. She turned the corner of the office coffee room to find an unexpected sight.

"Alex?" She asked.

Alex spun around with an empty coffee cup in his hand. "Hi Juliet." He smiled. Juliet studied him for a second and then looked at her watch.

"You know that it's only quarter to 8, right?"

Alex frowned at her. "Juliet I do know how to get into work before 10 you know.... But I'm not great at setting up this coffee machine... Can you..?" His voice trailed off looking at the coffee machine on the counter top. Juliet laughed. "Sure thing boss. And I know that you can make it to the office before 10 it's just that I've never seen you here before 8!" She teased, taking the coffee cup from his hand and started to prep the machine. "Why don't you head back to your office and I'll bring it in for you." She said rolling her eyes.

"Thanks, Jules, I knew you were my assistant for a reason!"

Alex sat behind his desk looking out the window over the city when Juliet walked in behind him setting his coffee on the desk.

"So Mr Matthews, what gives?" She asked as she took a sip of her own coffee. Alex looked over to Juliet and lifted his mug.

"I don't know what you're talking about Ms Malone." He said raising an eyebrow. Juliet smirked and shook her head, she had quickly become firm friends with Alex, and she was one of the few that he let see past his tough exterior.

"Fine! Fine! There's no reason that you're in work 2 hours early completely out of the blue. Do you want to go over the meetings you have scheduled today?" Alex nodded absently, and Juliet started to take him through the appointments scheduled for the day and the projects that they were related to. As she was about to head out of the office, Juliet turned and called over her shoulder.

"Oh, Alex, don't forget that tender you have with the college for their new computer building. Professor O'Neill is coming in tomorrow about it."

Alex smiled, the thought of the tender bringing Melody back to the front of his thoughts instantly. He lifted his phone to text her.

Hey, Jellybean x Hope you slept well after last night
A x

He didn't get a chance to set his phone down before Mel had replied.

Go away :P some of us are still sleeping! ;)

He laughed as he read her reply.

Sleeping all-day and healing quickly, are you sure you're not a vampire? Lol x

He hit send and again, within moments Mel had replied again.

Oh, I'm a vampire alright, only I don't drink blood, and it's not your neck I'll be sucking on ;)

He groaned as he read her reply and his cock began to spring to attention in his pants. Just at that moment Juliet knocked on his office door and announced the arrival of his colleagues ready to start his first meeting of the day.

Mel had been blissfully dozing when her phone sang with an incoming message from Alex. She had been lost in a dream about him, but contact with the real thing was a million times better. It was only Monday morning, and she was already wondering when she would be seeing him again. Seeing him twice since Friday, and being very well fucked on both occasions was proving to be a slightly addictive situation to find herself in. *Get a grip Mel, it's just sex... Good sex, but still just sex!* She scolded herself. Even if that was the case, was there really anything wrong with getting a lot of good sex? She decided that there wasn't, and deciding that her sleep was over, she got up and put herself into the shower.

She drifted into the library rather absentmindedly. Dylan looked up from his computer and his gaze turned questioning.

"You okay?" He whispered when she approached.

"Yeah sweetie, I'm fine, just a little fuzzy-headed today."

Nate smirked, "Sex hangover?" he asked her.

Melody blushed. "I'm going to kill Jonny..." She let her voice trail off as Nate and Dylan started to laugh. She'd guessed correctly the origin of their knowledge was indeed Jonny. "He'll be in late by the way... Maybe he'll be nursing his own hangover and you can pick on him instead." She grumbled, sticking her tongue out at her group.

After a few hours, Melody's phone buzzed across the table with an incoming message. She glanced at the screen only to find herself disappointed. It was Jonny and not Alex who was texting her.

Just arriving, having a smoke first, want to join me? :-)

She lifted her phone and put it in her pocket.

"Back shortly guys." She told the group and went downstairs to meet Jonny.

When she pushed open the big main doors at the front of the library, Jonny was already standing there, cigarette in hand. She walked over to him and he smiled at her. Once by his side she slapped him round the back of the head. He laughed and rubbed the spot where her hand had connected.

"What the fuck was that for?" he asked.

She glared at him.

"You know very well what that was for!" She scolded. "Nate asked me if I had a sex hangover!"

Jonny roared with laughter, and other people stared as they walked to and fro from the library. Mel glared more fiercely. What she had with Alex was new and uncertain. She had no idea what it was, or if it would even go any further. She hadn't wanted anyone else to know, least of all the lads in her group.

"Are you really that pissed off?" Jonny asked her, the cigarette hanging from his mouth jumped up and down as he spoke.

"YES! You fucking know I am." She hissed through gritted teeth.

Jonny took the cigarette from his mouth and exhaled. "Why? For fuck's sake Mel, you've seen the guy twice in one weekend. That doesn't sound like a bad thing to me.

You've been single for a while now, is it a bad thing that your friends know?" He reasoned.

"Jonny, I don't even know what it is! Yes, I've seen him twice, but it might just be nothing but sex. I don't need the lads to know about the sex I'm having." She said, sounding offended.

"I'm sorry, Mel. But relax, these guys are your closest friends! They just want to see you enjoying yourself.... Well, not literally.... You know, they just want the vague hint that you're getting yours." Jonny smirked.

Mel sighed. "Cock."

Jonny laughed again. "Does this mean I'm forgiven?" He asked her grinning, the cigarette back to bobbing about in the corner of his mouth.

"I'll think about it." She huffed. "Now suck up your cancer stick, you need to get some work done since you missed half the morning on your walk of shame!" She smirked at him, and now it was Jonny's turn to huff and glare.

"Who was it?" She asked.

"No one you know." He said curtly, and stubbed out his cigarette, stomping off towards the doors. He paused to see if she was following him, she smirked and jogged to where he was holding the door open for her, and they went back to work.

~ ~ ~

It was the weekend before she saw Alex again. He had been busy with work, and she had been busy with her project for college, work, and a night out with the guys. They had planned out a scenario in advance. Melody was a naughty little schoolgirl. She was to arrive in uniform at Alex's house, and she would find out the rest of the details when she got there and they played out in front of her. Alex had emailed her a few days before.

From: Alex Matthews

To: Melody Anderson

Subject: The School Rules

Melody,

Thank you for your application to our School. I have enclosed the uniform list and some rules and regulations. I look forward to seeing you on your first day, Friday 22nd.

Yours Sincerely,

Headmaster Lex.

UNIFORM GUIDELINES:

Grey skirt (MUST be knee length)

White cotton shirt (tucked in)

White knee socks

Black leather shoes (no heels!)

Black blazer

School tie

Underwear should be white cotton, no lace

Hair will be tied up

No make-up

SCHOOL RULES:

The school principal will be addressed as Headmaster Lex at all times.

The uniform guidelines must be obeyed at all times; failure to do so will result in punishment.

You will be silent at all times, unless directly asked a question, you may notify the Headmaster that you wish to speak by raising your hand.

You will move quickly and quietly to and from each class.

When you arrive at your classroom, you will knock on the door, enter in silence, and sit on the chair provided.

The school is a boarding school, and as such you will be provided with all meals and sleeping arrangements will have been taken care of.

Tardiness of any kind will not be tolerated.

Please note: Headmaster Lex will hand out whatever form of punishment he sees fit. These can be in a manner of different forms, from writing lines, detention, and more corporal forms of punishment.

Start time: Friday 22nd at 7:30pm

Mel had re-read the email a few times, a plan formulating in her head. She had some of what she needed, and had been happy to buy more props for the rest. She put on her outfit, went out to the car, and drove to Alex's house.

The door knocked, and Alex's heart started to race. He couldn't wait to see Mel again, but the added excitement came from the little role-play that they had figured out together. He couldn't wait to see how she looked and how she would act.

He opened the door and looked at the sight in front of him. She had listened to his rules, but he could already see that she hadn't obeyed them perfectly. A grin skimmed his lips as she looked at him.

"Headmaster Lex?" She asked him.

He moved aside to let her in. "I am, and you must be Melody. I've been expecting you my dear." He told her, his voice velvet smooth yet firm.

As she moved across the hardwood floor, he could hear the clip-clop of heels as they made contact.

"Stop!" He commanded as he closed the front door. He stared at her, his eyes burrowing into her. "In my school, young lady, we have an uniform inspection. You will stand here, hands by your sides, back straight, eyes on the floor. Do you understand?" He cautioned.

"Yes, Headmaster Lex." She exhaled softly. Mel did as she had been told. Her eyes at the floor in front of her, her hands by her sides, and she waited.

Alex began to circle her. Her black leather shoes had a kitten heel, her knee socks were perfect, her skirt was grey, but it was no where near knee length, her blazer was black as he had asked, her shirt white and figure hugging, He could see the bra underneath was plain white, her tie he recognised as being from a local secondary school, her hair was neatly tied into pigtails hanging at the sides of her head, and her face had the tiniest trace of lip gloss and mascara. Alex let out a series of tut-tut sounds and finished with a long sigh.

"It would appear Miss Anderson, that you are not capable of obeying the school rules." He informed her. "I know you understood that if you didn't obey the school rules that you would be punished young lady, so I can only guess that punishment is exactly what you were seeking." He chided, he had hoped that she would do this. It proved two things to him. Firstly, that she was perfect for him, she knew what he wanted without having to be told, and secondly, that she was more and more willing to submit to him. "I count three indiscretions Miss Anderson. You are not allowed heels in this school, your skirt is not knee length and therefore not appropriate, sluts wear short skirts Miss Anderson, and I see make-up on your face. You will receive ten swats for every rule broken. Do you understand girl?"

Mel nodded. "Yes Headmaster Lex." She answered.

"Follow me." He barked. Mel followed Alex down the hall a short distance, before he turned into a room. "This is my study." He explained. "All of your punishments will be completed here. I do hope you don't make it a habit of being in this room Melody." He scolded.

Mel scanned the room. It was a classically decorated study. Dark wood panelling covered the walls, a wrought iron chandelier hung from the cream coloured ceiling. Everything was made from mahogany, the large desk with a red leather inlay on the top, the large bookcases that filled two of the walls. There was a large draughtsman's table by the window, and two large chesterfield sofas in front of an ornate Edwardian fireplace. Melody was in awe. The room was just amazing, truly a classic piece of design, in keeping with the age of the house. Alex watched her taking in the room, allowing her a moment to take it all in before issuing a command to her.

"You will bend over the table girl." He instructed, leading her by the arm, and pushing her over the leather table top. "Your hands will be placed palms down like this," he instructed placing her the way he wanted her, with her arms bent at the elbows, and her forearms flush with the table, "and your nose will touch the table, you will NOT let it move from here." He directed. He moved to behind her, stooping to his knees, his hand on her inner thigh, caressing her as he moved her legs apart. "Your legs will be held apart, like this." He smirked, feeling her shiver under his touch, but giving her nothing. "When you come into my room, and you are to receive swats, this is the way that you will present yourself across my table." He commanded. He heard her suck in a breath and knew that if he touched her now she would be soaking wet for him. "Do not move!" he told her, his tone unyielding.

Mel froze to the spot, waiting for what he would do to her next, she wanted to please him with this more than anything, she had been disobedient on purpose; she couldn't help herself. She wanted his control and his discipline more than anything at this moment.

She breathed out a hiss when she felt his hands on her thighs, but she didn't move. He slowly slid her skirt up her thighs and over her buttocks, her white cotton underwear on full display. She swallowed when she felt Alex's fingers skim over her hips to the waistband of her panties and he pulled them down her legs to rest at her knees. He walked around the desk to a drawer; he slid it open and lifted out a thick wooden ruler. Mel's heart began to accelerate, and her breathing became fast and shallow. Alex caressed her bare backside with the wooden ruler, rubbing it softly over her cheeks.

"You will count each stroke. If you pause, I will add on two more per pause. If you lose count, we will start over. Is that understood?" He asked.

"Yes Headmaster Lex." She said, her voice shaking with need.

Alex pulled the ruler back and cracked it against Melody's exposed rump. She jumped at the contact. "One!" She called out against the table top.

Strike. "Two!"

Strike. "Three!"

Strike. "Four!"

By the time, they had got to 29 Mel was crying. Every strike of the ruler sent a blaze of fire through her groin. The burning in her buttocks was matched by the burning desire she felt in her sex. She was drenched, and she was so frustrated that she couldn't hold back the tears. She was scorched with lust and need; she needed Alex to make her come. She wanted to beg and plead. It felt like if he just connected the ruler with her clit a certain way that she would explode into a climax. She didn't know if it was possible to come from a spank on the clit, but she was sure she would like to find out. Alex paused; she waited for the last swat to hit her backside. His hand caressed her heated skin, every nerve within enflamed by her punishment.

"One more Melody." He told her, and she held her breath waiting. Suddenly something cold and slippery was pressing against her asshole, demanding entry. She felt it penetrate her with ease until the base of it sat against her skin. He was torturing her—she was convinced of it. "You seem to be enjoying your punishment young lady, perhaps this will remind you that you were disobedient. I will remove this when I think that you have behaved sufficiently!" He informed her. She understood what he had done. He had slid a butt plug inside her. She groaned, the feeling of frustration had intensified, between the heat in her buttocks, the want in her sex, and the fullness of having her anus plugged, she just couldn't take it. Alex interrupted those thoughts with the last crack of the ruler across her backside. She had been lost in her own lust, and he managed to catch the butt plug in his swat causing it to give a little thrust into her. It was all she needed.

"30!" She cried out as her body started to convulse and the orgasm that had been threatening erupted around her.

"When you have composed yourself Miss Anderson, you will meet me in the kitchen!" He called to her through her keening and closed the door behind him. Mel instantly sagged against the table, her knees buckling beneath her. *Sweet holy fuck!* She thought to herself. *That man has just made me come by spanking and plugging my ass! This has to be a fantasy!* She exclaimed inwardly. She concentrated on calming her breathing into slow deep breaths, knowing that would have the same calming effect on her heart rate. She didn't want to leave him waiting too long. Once she was sure that her legs could support her, she lifted herself off the table, pulled up her panties and rearranged her skirt. She checked that she was presentable enough, and walked out of the study in search of the kitchen.

CHAPTER 6

After opening a few other doors, Melody pushed the kitchen door open and walked in. She looked around, taking in the cream walls, modern oak cabinets, and granite counter tops.

"Welcome to your first lesson girl. You will prepare me something to eat from the ingredients that I set on the kitchen counter." Alex announced from where he was standing looking in the fridge. She stared at him. *What?* She thought. *He wants me to cook for him? Oh shit!* She panicked, the only time that she had eaten with Alex, they'd been at a fancy restaurant in town. Alex pulled the butter, sliced ham and cheddar cheese from the fridge, setting them on the counter. He moved to a cupboard and pulled out two slices of bread, from a drawer next to that came a knife. Soon Melody had all the ingredients in front of her for a grilled ham and cheese sandwich. He looked at her with a smirk. "You didn't think I would be *that* cruel do you Miss Anderson?"

"I did wonder, Headmaster Lex." She admitted honestly. He grinned and walked towards the breakfast bar taking a seat and looking back at Mel.

"I expect the perfect cheese and ham toasty Melody. I expect a dark golden brown colour, I wish it cut on the

diagonal, and I expected it served as soon as possible."
He instructed.

Melody started moving about the kitchen for her task.
She started to prepare a sandwich, thinly slicing the
cheese, melting the butter in a pan. She could feel Alex's
eyes on her as she moved around, watching her, as he
scrutinised and no doubt planned how to punish her
next. Soon Mel had the sandwich finished, cut on the
diagonal, and placed on a plate that she presented to
Alex. She nervously moved on the spot, waiting for his
reaction.

"Got ants in your pants?" He asked her. Mel stilled.

"No Headmaster Lex." She answered. He took a bite
from the sandwich and munched quietly. She watched in
silence as he took bite after bite, and all the while he said
nothing. *Jeez, he wouldn't be eating it all if he didn't like
it, right?* She thought to herself, but she longed for him to
tell her himself what he thought of it.

Once he had finished he lifted his plate, and put it in
the dishwasher, knowing Mel was watching him, waiting
for his approval. He turned to look at her. "I think you've
learned something here Melody." He told her. "What do
you think that you've learned?" He asked.

"Patience, Headmaster Lex?" she queried.

"No." He stated. "You've learned that no matter what
the task is, you long to please me." He informed her. Her
cheeks blushed, he was right. It had been a simple task, a

mere grilled sandwich, but she longed for it to please him, she wanted to get it right so that she would satisfy him. She couldn't believe it had become as basic as that. An instinctive need to please him while she was in his company as they played out each scene together. She dipped her eyes to the floor, suddenly very conscious of herself and the revelation of just how submissive she was around 'Lex.'

Alex's fingers stroked under her chin and lifted her head up, forcing her to make eye contact again. "Never be ashamed of your submission Melody. It's an incredible gift, and I am so very honoured that you would present it to me." His lips melted against hers for a moment, causing goose bumps to ripple over her skin. "I think it's time for a physical education lesson." He told her. "Come with me." He beckoned.

Mel followed Alex upstairs and into the master bedroom. Once again she was in awe of the room. An opulent king-sized, four poster bed sat against one wall, two doors on the wall opposite either side of a large Edwardian fireplace. A large bay alcove with three large windows filled the far side of the room, a large leather armchair with footstool sitting to one side of the alcove. Light came from ornate wrought iron wall sconces on either side of the bed. Alex opened the door closest to the entrance to the magnificent bedroom.

"You will hang your blazer in here, and put your shoes on the rack." He instructed, gesturing to the appropriate places within the large walk in closet. Mel swallowed and licked her lips, the room itself was amazing, but when she thought about the fact that she was now in his bedroom with him for a lesson in "physical education" her sex began to heat and she started to clench around the plug in her ass.

She quickly did as she was instructed, taking off her shoes and blazer, re-emerging moments later. Alex took her by the hand, leading her over to the armchair by the window.

"Sit." He commanded. Mel sat on the chair, and Alex sat on the footstool in front of her. "Now we're going to see how you cope with prolonged physical activity Miss Anderson." He told her, staring intently into her eyes.

She shifted in her seat, wriggling against the pressure the chair was causing against the plug in her behind. She was becoming needy again, longing for him kiss her, to have his hands on her skin, to have his cock deep inside her.

"Give me your foot." Alex demanded. Mel lifted her foot and set it on his lap. He slid his hands from her foot up her calf to the back of her knee, slipping his fingers under the top of her sock, and pulling it down her leg and off her foot. He pulled her foot to his chest where he let it rest against him. He reached under the footstool and produced a leather cuff. He wrapped it carefully around her ankle and buckled it securely. She looked at the thick leather strap with its soft lining surrounding her ankle, a thick dog leash style clip hanging from it. He lifted her foot from his chest, kissed it, and set it back on the floor.

"Now the other one." He insisted. Mel looked at him as she lifted her leg to his lap. Alex's eyes roamed down her body, falling at last on the flash of panties that she was giving him in this position. He stared, and she felt her skin flush and her pussy clench. She was soaked, and he could see it. He lifted his eyes from her panties and met her eyes with a look of pure carnal desire shining in his chocolate brown eyes. Again he slid his hands up her calf until he reached her knee. Slipping the sock down her leg and off, he placed her foot on his chest, and wrapped her other ankle in a leather cuff. He lifted her foot to his lips, and his hand slid up her thigh as he kissed her foot. He pushed her panties to the side and dipped a finger into her wet folds. She shuddered under his contact, a short moan escaping from her lips. Alex pulled his hand away and set her foot on the floor, staring at her mouth. He lifted the hand still glistening with her own slickness and pressed them against her lips.

"Suck." He commanded his eyes sparkled. She parted her lips and Alex's fingers pushed between them. She ran her tongue over his fingertips savouring her taste, before sucking on them greedily, teasing him, and making his mind wander to other activities. He glared at her and a growl reverberated in his throat.

"Stop that."

Melody stared back at him, and sucked his fingers deep into her mouth until she reached the knuckles on his hand, her tongue tracing over the underside of them. Alex snatched his hand back—his face growing menacing. Mel held his stare, challenging him, defying him, willing him to take her.

"Give me your wrists." He snarled at her, holding her stare with his own. Melody straightened her back and put her hands out in front of her. Alex lifted two more leather cuffs from under the footstool and fastened one around each wrist, each one a perfect match to those around her ankles, complete with clips.

"Stand." He ordered as he stood himself, standing so close to her that their chests were almost touching. He took her by the wrist and led her over to the foot of the bed. He slid the knot of her tie down and loosened it, removed it, and draped it around his own neck. His fingers then moved to the buttons of her shirt.

"I see you're still not understanding the importance of doing what you are told and following the rules Miss Anderson." He said softly, slipping her unbuttoned shirt off her shoulders and throwing it to the armchair. He lowered his head slowly and moved his lips towards hers. She closed her eyes, and tilted her head to grant him better access to her mouth; she held her breath and waited. Alex pressed his finger against her lips, letting it slide from them over her chin and down between her breasts. He turned her towards the bed, her back to his chest. He reached for the zip at the back of her skirt, slowly undid it, and slid her skirt down over her hips letting it pool at her feet. He bent to remove it, tapping each ankle in turn to encourage her to lift each foot in turn. He threw it to the armchair to join her shirt.

"Now, Miss Anderson." He breathed in her ear. "It's time to correct that defiant nature of yours if you wish to continue in this school. You do want to stay here, don't you Melody?" He asked, one hand sliding over her ass, and pressing on the base of the butt plug and the other hand reaching around and pulling on her nipple through the cotton of her bra.

"Yes Headmaster Lex!" She moaned.

"Good girl." Alex smirked behind her. He unfastened her bra, his eyes gleaming when her breasts were exposed to him. He bent to take a nipple in his mouth; his hands skimmed her hips and found the waistband of her panties. He pulled them to the floor. Her underwear joined the rest of her clothing on the chair.

He ran his hands over her until his hand circled around her wrists. He lifted her arms over her head. "Stay." He ordered, and moved away from her disappearing into his walk-in closet. He reappeared moments later with several pieces of silk rope. He threw one piece over the top cross bar of the four poster, a small loop on each end of the length of rope allowed him to use the clips on each of Mel's wrist cuffs, keeping her secured with her arms above her head unable to lower them even if she wanted to. A second length of rope was passed behind the legs of the bed, and the clips on her ankle cuffs were attached to it. Mel was secured to the bottom of the bed, standing facing it in an inverted Y shape, stuck and completely at Alex's mercy.

Once he had Melody secured he stepped back to admire how she looked in front of him. His cock throbbed in his jeans, begging to be freed. It urged him to forgo what he had planned and just take Mel roughly over and over until neither of them could see straight anymore. He palmed his erection through the denim, trying to relieve some of the tension and calm his baser needs. *God this woman will be your undoing!* His inner critic told him. Alex shook his head, pulled the tie from around his neck and used it to cover Mel's eyes, tying it behind her head as a makeshift blindfold.

"Do you understand that you need to be disciplined Miss Anderson?" he asked at her back.

"Yes Headmaster Lex, I understand." She trembled.

Alex moved behind her, cupping both of her breasts in his hands. He kneaded them roughly, groped her and made her gasp. His fingers and thumbs found her already pebbled nipples and he pulled on them harshly. Melody let out a long moan. Alex smirked at her back. "You like this don't you Miss Anderson." He taunted her.

"Yes Headmaster Lex." She breathed.

"Let's see how *much,* shall we?" He taunted right beside her ear, one hand dropped from her breast and dipped into the moisture between her legs. "Just as I thought. You're not really a good girl at all Miss Anderson. You're a dirty little slut. You enjoy someone punishing you!" Melody's whole body flushed in response to Alex's words. He pushed two fingers deep inside her and bit down on her shoulder. Melody gasped and pulled on her restraints, her hips moving involuntarily against his fingers. Just as Mel was starting to feel an orgasm building within her groin, Alex removed his fingers from inside her. She felt him touch them against her lips, and she opened her mouth to receive them.

"Clean." He commanded, and she licked her wetness from his fingers, sucking on them, savouring the taste of her own essence.

His hands went back to kneading her breasts. They caught hold of her nipples and twisted them, causing Melody to cry out in a moan.

"I wonder just how much your nipples can take." He whispered. "I have some lovely clamps to attach to these beauties, but we'll start with some easier ones first." He said, and suddenly he disappeared from behind her. Mel heard him moving about the room, but was so distracted by the sound of her heart thumping in her ears that she couldn't make out what it was that he was doing.

Alex climbed onto the bed in front of her, allowing him better access to her supple tits. She jumped when she felt his mouth on her nipple; he sucked on it harshly, his mouth coming away from her breast with a pop. Suddenly there was something cold and metal biting into her nipple instead. "Oh, Miss Anderson, the sight of you with a clamp on your nipple is the most amazing thing." He told her and then she felt his mouth on her other nipple. The same cool metal bit into her flesh after his warm mouth. Once both were in place, Alex flicked both clamps with his fingers, which only increased the biting feeling that Melody was experiencing. Each little movement in the clamp was instantly hot-wired to her pussy, it made her clench with need, her sex sopping with evidence of her desire. Alex moved up against her and skimmed his hands across her ass. "Green, Yellow, or Red Miss Anderson?" He asked near her lips.

"Green Headmaster Lex!" She gasped. With that confirmation Alex crushed his chest against hers, crashing his lips into hers, and seized her in a searing hot kiss. His tongue fucked her mouth, mimicking what he wanted to do with her later. She wriggled against him. God, he just couldn't get enough of this woman. He raised his hand and slapped her backside as he kissed her. She jumped and groaned against his mouth. He knew she was turned on by it; some of his previous submissives would have yelped out in shock, but no, not Melody—she moaned out in lust, and craved more. He pried his mouth from hers, keeping his forehead against hers.

"You fucking love this, don't you Mel? Later, I'm going to show you just how hard you make me! But first, you needed to be punished Miss Anderson." He breathed against her mouth.

He pushed himself off the bed and reappeared behind her again, his hands skimmed across her backside. "I have a paddle here." He explained. "I'm going to use it on your ass. Use your safe word if you need to." He told her. He pressed himself against her back, his hand found her pussy, and she felt a bullet vibe buzzing at her clit. She gasped and felt her body tense, an orgasm building up within her. Her breathing increased, and she started to moan and writhe against Alex's hand. When she was close, Alex pulled back, away from her, and she felt the first contact from the paddle against her ass. It wasn't enough to hurt her, but it stung, and made her flesh start to burn, and her whole body hum each strike increasing the deep need she felt in her pussy. After ten strikes on her backside, Alex pressed himself back up behind her again, his fingers teasingly pushed the vibe back in against her clit. He kissed her shoulder, while his other hand cupped one of her breasts and flicked at the clamp on her nipple. Just like before, Alex coaxed her to the brink of orgasm and then stepped back and slapped the paddle against her ass.

Alex continued this treatment until Melody had been denied the opportunity to orgasm seven times. "Orgasm denial—it's such a dirty trick isn't it Miss Anderson?" He breathed near her ear.

"Definitely Headmaster Lex!" She answered her voice raspy.

"Do you want to come Melody?" He asked her.

"Yes Headmaster Lex, please, oh God please let me come." She begged him.

"Five more hard swats with the paddle. After that, I will allow you to come." He told her. Mel held her breath and waited for the first strike to arrive on her backside. When it did she leapt against her restraints and cried out. Alex rubbed his hand across her heated skin. He cracked the paddle on her backside again. Again Mel cried out, and Alex's hands roamed over her red flesh.

By the time the fifth swat arrived on Mel's rear, her previous tears had returned. This time it was the worse kind of frustration she had ever experienced. Every nerve ending in her body was on fire. She needed to come; she needed it like she needed air to breathe. She strained to listen for where Alex was in the room, but she couldn't quite make out where he was. She tried to pull her legs back together, in an attempt to get any kind of friction on her clitoris. She heard him moving behind her, and she stopped wriggling. He pressed himself in against her back, she felt his naked skin touch hers, and she felt his erect and heavy cock against her back. He kissed her shoulder and ran his hands from her hips to her breasts, kneading them, careful to avoid the clamps on her nipples. She moaned loudly and pushed her ass out against him, silently begging him to take her. His hands slipped back down to her backside, he gripped the base of the butt plug and slid it out of her. He wrapped it in a tissue and dropped it to the floor.

Alex palmed his throbbing cock; rubbing it in the lubricant he had squirted into his palm, and guided the head against Melody's asshole. The plug had been keeping her open for hours, and he slid his length deep inside in one stroke. Melody growled, a low, wild sound erupting from her as Alex started to pump his cock in and out of her ass. Almost instantly Melody started to feel her climax building within her. Alex felt it too as she began to clench around him. He grabbed a tight hold of her hips and drove himself roughly into her over and over, until suddenly Melody screamed at the top of her lungs as an earth shattering climax ripped through her body, shattering her into a million tiny fragments. Alex didn't stop, he kept up the pace that he had set, and continued to pump into her. No sooner had she come down from the first orgasm than she started to feel a second one building within her. Alex kissed her shoulder and neck, nibbling on her, encouraging her second climax. Melody's breathing became faster still, and again he felt the tell tale signs that she was close. He pulled her hips hard against him, slamming into her, and his hands reached for her breasts. Melody screamed out again, clenching hard on his cock as her body convulsed in orgasm, and Alex released the clamps on her breasts. The release and following burn that happened as the blood flowed back into her now super-sensitive nipples made her breath catch in her throat and she shouted his name all over again. "LEX!" She cried, her body twitching and jerking as she came apart for the third time. Alex's hands went back to her hips. "Fuck Mel!" He called out as he came hard and deep into her body.

He let his semi erect penis slide inside from her body; he reached up and took the tie away from her eyes. Bending, he released the clips that kept her legs apart. He stood, releasing the clips that held Mel's arms above her head. He scooped her into his arms and carried her into the bathroom. Alex set Mel on the toilet seat and turned on the bath taps, letting the huge tub in his ensuite fill. He kneeled in front of Melody, and undid the leather cuffs on her wrists, rubbing the red marks that circled her wrists. He released the cuffs on her ankles, rubbed them with the same care as he had shown her wrists, gathered up the cuffs, and removed them from the room. Mel sat there silently in a post orgasmic haze. Alex returned, poured some luxury bath oil into the water, and turned to Mel. Gently he removed the bands from Melody's hair, allowing it fall loosely over her shoulders.

"Baby." He whispered to get her attention as he turned off the taps. "Come and get into the bath with me." He said, guiding her up from where she sat and he stepped into the bath, encouraging her to do the same. He slid into the warm water, assisting Mel to do the same, and positioned her in front of him. He pulled her gently against him, took the sponge from the side of the bath, dipped it in the water, and started to tenderly wash the water and soothing oil over her skin. He lay in the bath holding her and squeezing the sponge over her body until her head fell back onto his shoulder and she sighed.

"That was incredible." She told him. He smiled and kissed her neck.

"No baby," he grinned, "*you* were incredible!" He told her and dropped the sponge into the water so he could just hold her tenderly against him. She sighed again, and he felt her body start to relax into him. He kissed her shoulder. "Come on sleepy head. Time to get out, and sleep."

Alex helped her out of the bath, dried her off, wrapped her in a towel, and scooped her up in his arms again. She grinned as she nuzzled into his chest.

"I can walk you know." She said.

"I know." Alex laughed and kissed her forehead. He set her on the floor by the bed took the damn towel from around her, and she sat on the edge of the bed.

"Lie down." He whispered as he scooped her feet from the floor and tucked her into the bed. He crossed the room to the other side of the bed, turned the lights down to a dim glow and crawled into bed behind Melody. He pulled her in against him, holding her close.

"Night Jellybean." He whispered and kissed her shoulder.

"Night sweetness." She whispered back and drifted off to sleep. He held her, feeling her breathing change to a slow, steady pattern, which told him that she was asleep. *Sweetness?!* He thought to himself and drifted off to sleep along with her.

CHAPTER 7

Alex sat alone in his study, the only light in the room came from the flickering flames of the dying fire in the hearth. He rolled the scotch around in the bottom of the crystal tumbler, staring at it, mesmerised at how the light from the fire caught the amber liquid and the decorative cuts in the glass. Restlessness had driven him to get out of the bed where Melody lay beside him, beautifully peaceful in her sleep. His mind kept fluttering back to seven years ago. To Natalie Carter and all of the broken shards of the man that he used to be. His mind focused on that night, the night he had left an empty shell. He thought back to the apartment that they had shared together and watched as his mind replayed the events of that evening in crystal clarity.

Natalie reached for him. "Alex baby, we can fix this!" She pleaded. He looked at her in disgust.

"Don't fucking touch me!" He hissed at her and pulled his arm from her grasp. "FIX THIS!?" He boomed at her. "You think that we can ever fucking fix this?" He looked at her, her face stoic and without a shred of comprehension. "You fucked my best friend Natalie!!

Jesus Christ!" He cried out in exasperation and started to pace the room, running his hands through his hair.

A look of panic settled across her features.

"I'm sorry!" She told him, her eyes starting to fill with tears. "I can't ever tell you enough times how sorry I am!"

Alex stopped and stared at her in disbelief. *Does she really think that sorry will be enough?* He asked himself.

"Not half as fucking sorry as I am, Nat." He shook his head in anger and started to pace again. "You let my best friend fuck you, Natalie! And as if that wasn't a big enough fucking insult, you let him get you pregnant! I'm just the dumb son of a bitch who sat holding your hand in the hospital while you lost what I thought was OUR son... You have no fucking idea how 'sorry' will never ever cut it do you!?" He spat out with venom, glaring at her.

Natalie's head slumped forward, and the tears that had been welling up in her eyes finally spilled down her cheeks. She looked up into Alex's injured brown eyes, as she spoke softly.

"You think I didn't feel his loss too Alex?" She asked.

Alex sighed, and for a brief moment his anger washed away, "I know you did Nat. I do." He sighed, his shoulders sagging in a moment of defeat. Natalie saw it as her moment to strike.

"We can help each other, we can make each other better." She told him, as she moved towards him and grabbed his hands in hers. Alex looked at her, then looked at where she held his hands in hers. He pulled them from her grasp like just touching her was enough to taint him forever.

"You broke my fucking heart in two, Nat. You can't make this better, you're the last person I want to try and make this better! I can't even stand to look at you!" He snarled, shaking his head in disbelief, and moved towards the front door.

"Please Lexy, don't go!" She pleaded, calling him the pet name that he hated, but she insisted was cute.

He turned and glared at her. "I hate that name!" He shouted at her, pointed a finger at her and moved a step closer. "I will never trust you or anyone else as long as I live." He moved back towards the door. "I'll send someone over for my stuff." He told her before opening the door and walking out of their apartment and Natalie's life.

"You okay?" Melody asked from where she leaned against the doorframe of the study wrapped in just a sheet. Alex was jolted from his memories and his eyes flew to where Mel was standing.

"Shit, I'm sorry! Did I wake you?" He asked her, setting his scotch on the end table beside him, and stretching his hand out to her, to beckon her into the room.

She walked over to him and took his outstretched hand in hers. "No, you didn't." She smiled sweetly. "I just woke up and wondered where you were." Regret flashed over Alex's face and Mel frowned, sitting in his lap.

"Hey you." She said, cupping his face in her hands. "What's that look for?" She asked. Alex closed his eyes and let his head fall into Mel's hand, nuzzling his cheek against her. "Alex?" She questioned again.

"I'm sorry." He sighed. "I just... had a bad dream." He told her.

Mel stroked Alex's hair off his forehead. "Oh sweetie." She sighed. "You should have woken me." She said, placing a kiss on his forehead as she wrapped her arms around him, and held him tight against her. Alex's arms went around her and held her tight. Letting her comfort wash over him. She kissed his cheek, letting go of her hold around him. She pulled herself from his lap and took his hand in hers.

"Let's go back to bed." She smiled at him. Alex glanced up at her and knew that there was nowhere else he wanted to be than back in bed curled up beside her, wrapped up in her arms.

~ ~ ~

Alex woke to find the bed beside him empty. He got up, pulled on his favourite lounge pants and went downstairs. He walked through the kitchen door to find

Melody dressed in one of his shirts, making breakfast. She smiled broadly when she saw him.

"I have scrambled eggs, bacon, toast, orange juice and coffee. Sound okay to you?" She asked.

He looked at her in surprise and then gave a small laugh, "That would be great!" He answered, and took his place at the breakfast bar and waited to be served.

"Mel, can I talk to you about something?"

She turned and looked at him, a wooden spoon in her hand. "That sounds serious?" She said, wondering what was coming next.

"It is, and it isn't." He replied. She smirked and turned back to cooking the eggs.

"Go on." She told him.

Alex sighed, he needed to say this, but he wasn't sure how. "I just wanted to talk about what's happening here."

"Breakfast?" Mel replied cheekily, trying to lighten the mood.

"No, cheeky! I don't mean the breakfast." He smiled. "I mean the 'you and me' thing."

"Uh huh... what about it Alex?" Melody asked, feeling unsure.

"Mel I love spending time with you, and I don't want that to stop, but I can't offer you anything other than dominance, I don't do relationships."

Melody was silent. She planned out her reply in her head.

"Will you be dominating anyone else?" She asked.

"Hell no." he replied.

Melody went silent again. Alex sat watching her, waiting for some kind of response. Finally, she turned to put the eggs she had been cooking on the plate and brought two plates to the breakfast bar with her.

"I..." She started, and then let out a large puff of air with a hum. "Look Alex, I like you. I want to keep seeing you." She told him. "I think it's pretty obvious that I like you dominating me." She blushed. "I appreciate that you're being honest with me, and to be honest, as long as you're not talking about screwing other women, or dominating other women, I think I can handle what you're saying." She paused, registering the confused look on his face. "Why are you looking at me like I'm some kind of alien?" She smiled.

"Because you aren't going ballistic at me." Alex admitted, staring at her.

"What's the point in that?" She asked him. "You can't give what you don't have in you to give; me wanting anything else, or disagreeing with that isn't going to change it."

"Do you want something else?" He asked her.

"Some day, maybe. But I have to be honest with college, and the work I need to put in there, I'm kind of happy enough to go with the flow right now." She looked at him and lifted her hand to his cheek. "I'm going to assume you have a reason for the 'me no relationship'." She said putting on her best Tarzan impression. "When you're ready to share it, I hope you know that I'm here to listen. Until then, I don't think I could go back to not having you as my master even if I wanted to. I'm really enjoying this time with you Alex, I'm happy to keep doing that if you are."

Alex sighed. His heart should have felt lighter. He had been honest with her, he couldn't give her romance, or hearts and flowers. But he could give her dominance. *But you already want to give her the heart and flowers, don't you?* His inner voice taunted.

"I have to be honest Jellybean, I've never wanted to explain to a submissive that I can't give them a relationship, I would have ditched them the second that seemed to be an issue with them. I don't want that to be an issue with us. Can we be friends? Does this qualify as a friendship?" He asked, feeling like he was digging himself a hole.

"If I say that friends with benefits is fine with me, will you stop fretting over it, and worrying about it?" She said softly with a smile.

Alex sighed and smirked at her. "It would seem my friend knows me well already."

Mel rolled her eyes. "Daft sod. Eat your breakfast."

"Yes Ma'am." He grinned back at her and tucked into his plate of scrambled eggs and bacon.

~ ~ ~

Melody sat staring out of the library window, adrift in her own little world. Jonny nudged her elbow. "You okay?" he whispered.

Mel glanced in his direction. "Hmm?" She asked.

"Are you okay?" He repeated.

"Shit! Yes... Sorry, I wasn't paying attention." She said shaking her head and dragging herself back to reality.

Jonny eyed her suspiciously. "Uh huh..."

Mel stuck her tongue out at him. "I'm fine! I just didn't sleep much." She grinned.

Jonny groaned. "Eww, too much info baby, too much info!"

Mid afternoon arrived, and Mel and Jonny met up with the others of their little group in the café that was attached to the college library. Jonny sat in their corner booth beside Mel, Dylan on her other side at the head of the table, and Nate and Jacob sat opposite.

"So what about this new man you've got?" Dylan asked as Jonny smirked beside her.

"Yeah Mel, what about Alex?" He grinned.

"Oh Alex, is that his name?" Dylan smirked.

Mel sighed. "I hate you nosy bastards, I really do." The waitress approached their table to take their orders. Once the food and drinks were ordered, the guys went back to teasing Mel. "So what does Alex do?" Nate asked.

"I think that question would be better phrased with, what doesn't he do?" Jonny corrected. Mel punched him on the arm, and he laughed.

"We always knew you were a dirty bitch Mel, so come on, spill it." Dylan laughed beside her.

Jacob blushed. "Maybe it's private!" He scolded the others, causing even Mel to laugh at that.

"Oh, Jake sweetie, it's okay I can talk about sex." She said sticking her tongue out at him. "So Dylan, what was it that you wanted to know?" She smirked. "Is it the multiple orgasms you want to hear about? Or the bondage? Or maybe you're looking for tips on anal?" Mel grinned, and every set of eyes at the table fell on Jacob. He had turned a beetroot red and was looking incredibly uncomfortable. Everyone burst out laughing, and Jacob stared at the floor.

"I hate you guys, you know that!" He huffed. Just like that, the fascination with Mel and Alex ended, and talk moved to a night out that they were all planning for the Wednesday night.

"Pizza first, and then pool in the SU?" Dylan asked.

"But of course bro!" Jonny confirmed. "You driving Mel?" He asked.

"As always sweetie." She replied as the waitress reappeared with a tray of drinks for the table. Chatter continued, food arrived, and the group relaxed, discussing who was going to win the most games of pool, who would drink too much with the most money on Jacob. Eventually, their food was finished, their conversations had faded, and they decided that it was time to head back into the library to get some more work done.

Mel stopped outside Jonny's house and turned off the engine. He flicked the ash off the end of his cigarette and looked at her. "So are you going to tell me what was eating at you earlier?"

Mel sighed. "Alex told me that he couldn't offer me a relationship, and we settled on a 'friends with benefits' kind of setup."

"And you're not sure if you like that offer?" He asked, exhaling a puff of smoke.

"I don't know. I like him, I like the buzz I get from what he can do, but what if I want more, further on down the line?"

Jonny touched Mel's hand. "You can't keep denying yourself happiness no matter what form it's in, just in case something bad happens, baby. If he makes you feel good what's the problem?" Mel looked like she was trying to think of a response when Jonny interrupted her. "Anderson, stop fucking overthinking it!" She sighed and took the cigarette from his mouth, took a long drag on it and handed it back to him.

"Yes boss." She said exhaling smoke.

"Feel better now?" He asked.

"No, my throat's on fire." She croaked. Jonny laughed, leaned over to the driver's side of the car, and gave her a kiss on the cheek. "Tomorrow?" he asked.

"You bet buster! Bright and early." She coughed.

Jonny groaned. "Not too early Mel, please!" He pleaded, lifting his behind out of the passenger seat.

"I'll call you later sweetie." She smiled and Jonny waved as she drove away.

~ ~ ~

Mel lay in the bath and did what she did best, over-thought. She thought about what Alex had said about them being friends with benefits. She thought about the fact that he said that he didn't do relationships like that, but she also thought about the fact that he had said that he was already treating her differently to the way that he had treated other submissives. *Other submissives.* Just the thought of those words made her stomach feel like lead. She couldn't bear the thought of anyone else being with him, getting pleasure from his body like she had. *Get over it Mel! So he wasn't a virgin neither were you!* She told herself. But, telling herself that didn't seem to calm the sickening feeling that arose any time she thought of being "just another submissive." She thought about what she wanted from Alex. *Are you really happy just being just friends with benefits with him?* She asked herself. She thought about her degree, and thought about all the work that was coming up. She decided that the friendship wouldn't hurt, nor would the ability to have a little 'stress release.' Mel sighed. For now, being Alex's friend and submissive was enough for her. She couldn't escape the thought that she would eventually want more, but she put it to the back off her mind, and refused to let herself think about it. She sank lower into the bath, until her thoughts drifted away in the soothing warmth of the water.

CHAPTER 8

"Jules, can you come in here a minute, please?" Alex asked into the intercom of his office. A moment later Juliet knocked on his door and walked in. "I have a problem."

"You can get a cream for that." She smirked.

Alex glared. "Ha, bloody ha!"

"Sorry oh, great one. How may this humble assistant, help you?" She grinned.

Alex sighed.

"Oh dear, I smell woman troubles." Juliet teased.

"I wouldn't say troubles..." Alex's voice trailed off. Juliet walked to the chair on the opposite side of Alex's desk, she sat back and watched her employer and dear friend closely. She waited for him continue. "I've been seeing someone over the last couple of weekends." He looked at her waiting for a reaction. Juliet said nothing, just looking back at him, letting him know that she was waiting for more information from him before she would say anything. "Her name is Melody. She's 26, brunette, a Computer Science student in the final year of her masters. She's submissive, and she's... well, to be honest, she's fucking amazing." Alex smiled, the thought of Mel filling him with warmth. Jules smirked at her friend.

"I'm failing to see a problem here, Boss." She said. Alex squirmed trying to explain himself properly.

"Mel was asleep beside me, and I had a nightmare about Natalie." Juliet became straight-faced. She watched Alex's expression intently, trying to see if she could read the worry on his face.

"What bothers you more Alex? Dreaming about Natalie? Or that it was your closeness to Melody that probably triggered it?" Something quickly flickered across Alex's face. If Juliet had blinked, she would have missed it. "Oh... You *like* this girl." She accused, and another expression flicked across his face. "Oh Alex, you have it bad!"

"Stop it!" Alex exhaled through gritted teeth. "You know what Natalie did. I can't, Jules, I don't even know how anymore." He sighed.

Juliet looked at her friend and smiled. "I think you do. I think it just scares the shit out of you that for the first time in ages, you actually want to."

Alex took a deep breath, puffing out his chest, holding it in, and then let it out slowly as if it would stop the panic from rising in his guts. His hands went through his hair, and then he pulled them down over his face.

"You know what happened with Natalie, Jules, how do I allow myself to get into that again? How do I know if I even want to?"

"You're overthinking it, lovely. Sometimes, good things happen. I know I wasn't around for Natalie, but I know what happened, and I know that I would be pretty fucked over by it too. But Alex, if you sit here, and you never let anyone else in, hasn't she won?"

Alex slumped forward in his chair, his elbows resting on his knees, and his head in his hands. Juliet walked over to him and placed a hand on his shoulder. "When was the last time you were home with Emily?" She asked him.

"Not since the start of the month."

Juliet sighed. "There's nothing happening this afternoon, go and see your damn sister. And TALK to her about this! Tell her about Mel." She scolded him.

Alex put his hand on Juliet's, rubbing it. "Remind me to give you a raise." He smiled meekly.

"Oh, fuck off, you know that you could never earn enough to pay me what I'm really worth!" She said as she squeezed his shoulder and walked out of the office. "I'll call Emily and tell her you're on your way." She called as she closed the door behind her.

~ ~ ~

Alex walked up the drive to the front door of his sister's house. Before he had a chance to ring the doorbell, Hannah had swung the door open and bounced out and into Alex's arms. "Uncle Alex!" She squealed. Alex grinned and held the five year old tight. "Hey,

Hannah Banana!" Emily appeared at the door behind her daughter.

"Hey kiddo." She smiled when she saw Alex with her oldest daughter swinging from his neck.

"Hey Em." He smiled back. "Does this belong to you?" he said, pointing at his niece and grinning.

Emily laughed. "Nope, nothing to do with me. I think I have a crowbar under the stairs if you want to try and pry it off?" She offered, smirking and standing back from the door so Alex could walk in. He stepped through the entrance, kissed his sister, and prepared himself for the rest of his Godchildren.

"Uncle Alex!" Came the shriek from the hallway, and the thundering of children's feet sounded out as Emily's son and other daughter ran towards their uncle. Alex leaned over as two-year-old Jessica and seven-year-old Ethan attached themselves around his neck with Hannah.

He kissed and squeezed them all before their mother shouted.

"Oi! Monkeys! Can we show some manners and not swing from Uncle Alex like he's a tree?" She scolded. Three little faces grinned at Alex and looked at their mum guiltily, their feet touching back on the ground with a little assistance from their uncle.

"Scram!" She ordered. "Mum and Alex are going to have coffee!" Three pairs of little feet stomped their way back to the living room. "BEN?" She hollered upstairs.

"YEAH?" A distant voice replied.

"Alex is here, kids need you in the living room." Within seconds, Emily's husband Ben appeared at the top of the stairs.

"Yes boss." He grinned. "Afternoon Alex, don't let her shout at you." He said as he walked down the stairs. "She's been on everyone's case today." He grinned as he walked past his wife, who smacked him on the backside as he passed. "See!" He smirked, and Emily shoved him towards the living room, rolling her eyes. When she turned back to Alex he was laughing.

"Shut it you." She warned with a laugh of her own.

Forty minutes later, Emily was staring at her brother with a cup of coffee in her hands as they sat on the sofa in her conservatory. "So let me see if I have this right... You like this girl."

"Melody." He corrected.

Emily held a hand up in surrender. "You like this Mel... But you are fretting over her being another bunny boiler Natalie incarnation, so you don't want to get involved with her?" She asked and took a sip from her cup.

"Well, I don't think it's as simple as that..."

"Isn't it?" She smirked. "Seems like it to me." She leaned forward and set her cup on the coffee table in front of her and took Alex's free hand in both of hers. "My darling, baby brother. There will never be another Natalie, thank Christ!"

"Jules said pretty much the same thing."

"I've always loved that assistant of yours, such an incredibly smart woman!" She grinned. "Natalie was a... well to be honest sweetie, she was a fucking asshole. But she was only one person Alex, and not every woman is like her. Now I'm not saying that you won't get your heart broken again. That, kiddo, is always a risk, but it's worth it dear brother, very, very worth it!"

Alex sighed. He knew that he liked Mel, he knew that his sister was right, but he still just wasn't sure if he could take that plunge.

"Are you dominating her?" She asked quietly.

Alex almost spat out his mouthful of coffee. "What?!" he coughed out, setting his cup on the table, and cleared his throat.

Emily sighed. "Alex, Naomi was never a discrete woman, do you really think that it wouldn't get back to me through her sister?"

"Naomi?" Alex asked, feigning ignorance of the name of one of his previous submissives.

"Kiddo..." Emily said in warning. "Let's not pretend that you don't know who and what I'm talking about. It's your life, I won't interfere, but I can see how you might use that to keep yourself at a distance and guarded."

Alex shook his head. Emily had always been able to jump right to the exact issue at hand. "Yes." He sighed.

Her mouth formed a grim smile. "Don't you want more?"

"Yes." He whispered. "I never did before. But I do now." Emily threw her arms around her brother and squeezed him tight.

"Then you need to decide what you want to do with that. But she's not Natalie, and you have to stop treating them all like they might be."

Some of his troubles melted away through his sister's hug. Some of them came to the forefront. He had a decision to make, was Melody worth taking a chance on. *You already know the answer to that butthead, you've known it for over a week now!* His critic scoffed at him. Emily let go and looked at her brother. "I'm making pasta for dinner. You staying?" Alex loved his sister's cooking.

"God yes!" He grinned at her.

~ ~ ~

After an amazing pasta dinner with his family, and three bedtime stories each for his nieces and nephew, Alex finally thought about heading home. He stood at the door, hugged Ben and said goodbye before his brother-in-law was called upstairs by Ethan. Emily hugged her brother tightly. "You need to come here more often Alex.

We miss seeing you." She scolded. "Don't forget Ethan is eight in a fortnight! There's a party here at the house. I'll call you about it at the weekend."

Alex smiled, feeling contented from an afternoon in his sister's company. "I'll be there." He promised, pulling her into another hug. "I love you Em."

"I love you too kiddo." She smiled warmly. "Just think about what I said."

"I will! I will!" He agreed and turned to head back down the drive to his car.

As he waved and pulled away from the house containing a happy little family, he started to think about the options that lay before him. To trust Mel, or not. To trust himself and his decisions, or not. To let his emotions rule, or not. He thought about what he said to Emily. Melody made sex more than that; she made submission more than something that he could control. Something that he wanted more of, simply because it was with her. Only time would tell how he would react, and if he could handle letting go of his fears from the past and be able to have something more with Melody, something that he was already starting to want.

When he arrived home he sent two text messages. One to Juliet, thanking her for pushing him to go and see his sister, telling her that it was just what he needed and that he would fill her in tomorrow. The second he sent to Mel.

Hey Jellybean. Just in from my sister's and I thought I'd say hello. Have you any free time over the next couple of days? A x

He put his phone on silent and climbed into bed, falling into a deep and dreamless sleep for once.

CHAPTER 9

Juliet looked positively green by mid-morning, when she opened the door of Alex's office. Alex glanced up at her and was instantly concerned. "Jesus Juliet, are you okay?" He asked, walking over and putting a protective arm around her.

Juliet leaned against him. "Actually I was going to ask if you minded if I headed home." Juliet suddenly covered her mouth and bolted for Alex's private bathroom. When she emerged all the colour had drained from her face and she looked at Alex feeling guilty for being sick in his bathroom. Alex handed her a glass of water.

"Kennedy has a car ready to take you home."

Juliet smiled weakly. "Thank you. Kate should be able to cover for me until tomorrow."

Alex studied her. "Jules, don't you dare come back until you're feeling better."

"I don't want the boss to think that I'm skiving off on the sick." She said, attempting to smirk at him.

"He's a bastard anyway." Alex winked at her. Kennedy knocked on the door of Alex's office and entered.

"Alright Boss, God Juliet you look like death." He greeted them. Alex smirked, and Juliet extended her middle finger in greeting.

"Thanks, Ken, I feel like it." She said rolling her eyes. Kennedy put an arm around her and walked her out of the office and headed for the elevators.

Alex lifted his desk phone. "Kate?... Yeah, Juliet has had to go home sick..... Would you? Thanks, I'd really appreciate that.... Okay, see you shortly." Hanging up, he sat back down on his leather high-backed chair and went back to prepping his tender for the university.

~ ~ ~

It was around 12:30 when Melody arrived at Alex's building and smiled to the pretty redhead sitting outside his office. "I'm here to see Mr Matthews." She smiled at the assistant.

"Do you have an appointment?" The assistant asked.

"I don't as it happens, I just took a chance on calling in to take him to lunch." She explained.

"There isn't anyone in with him at the minute. May I take your name?"

"Mel Anderson."

Kate pressed the button on the intercom. "Mr Matthews? There's a Miss Anderson here to see you."

The intercom crackled and Alex's voice sounded through the speaker. "Send her in."

Kate gestured towards the open doorway, and Mel walked through the door of his office. She was wearing a red and blue paisley patterned sundress. She smiled at him as he sat staring at her.

"Hello, Sir." She grinned. Alex slid from behind his desk and stalked over to the entrance behind Melody.

"Kate, hold my calls will you." He told Juliet's stand-in before he closed the door and bolted the lock. He stepped directly behind her and pulled her against him, holding her to his chest. His hand swept from her hips to her breasts, and he palmed them through her sundress, his lips finding her neck.

Mel moaned, "After your text last night, I was going to offer you lunch."

Alex pulled on her nipples through her bra and dress, "You already are, I know exactly what's on the menu." He breathed against her ear and ground his hips towards her rear, letting her feel the hardness of his cock through his trousers. Mel moved forward, releasing herself from Alex's grasp. She moved quickly across his office, rounded his desk and dropped herself into his chair, swinging her sandaled feet up to rest them on top of his desk.

"So this is where you slave away all day huh?" She asked with a smirk.

Alex scowled at her from across the room. "Sometimes... Sometimes I'm out on site, sometimes I work from home... Get your feet off my desk!" He said as he closed the distance between them, stopping at the end of the desk which was serving as Mel's foot stool. She grinned at him, feeling playful and turned on by his handling just moments before.

"Make me." She laughed raising an eyebrow and running her tongue over her right canine. Alex pounced. He grabbed her ankles, swinging her feet to the floor, he grabbed her by the upper arms and yanked her from his chair. In a split second, his lips were crushed against hers. He held her tight against him, hungry for her, as if he needed to fuse their bodies together. His tongue fucked her mouth and she moaned against him. He slid a hand to his tie, loosened it without undoing it, and broke their kiss just long enough to take his tie off over his head.

His lips were instantly on hers again his tongue probing her mouth, licking her tongue. He ran his hands down her arms starting at her shoulders, keeping her tight against him. When he reached her wrists, he forced her hands behind her back, holding her wrists together as he slipped his tie around them and pulled it tight. Mel moaned against his lips, and he broke their kiss again, keeping his forehead against hers, both panting against each other's skin. He spun her around, her back how against his chest again. He cupped her tits roughly before yanking down the top of her dress and her bra, allowing her breasts to spill out. His finger and thumb went straight to her nipples and he pinched them, pulling them out from her body. She hissed at his contact, her head falling back against his shoulder.

"Such a naughty girl coming in here to tease me while I'm working." He snarled breathlessly against her neck. Mel hummed out a moan. Alex's hands slipped from her nipples and went for the hem of her sundress. He flicked it out away from her to gain access underneath it. His hands found the waist of her panties and he yanked them down. He stepped back to allow himself the space he needed to remove her panties from her completely. He couldn't resist lifting the hem of her dress and biting her butt cheek while he was there. Melody gasped. Alex stood, panties in hand, and pulled her back against him. He balled her panties up in his fist and moved Mel to face his desk.

Alex moved Mel's hair off her shoulder and brushed his lips against it before he nipped at it with his teeth. Mel breathed out a sigh, and his lips travelled towards her neck. The feeling of her hands tied, Alex, hard and behind her, and being pantie-free in his office made a long, loud moan fall out of her mouth. Alex's hand quickly covered her mouth, and her panties were shoved between her lips, gagging her. Her breathing sped up. His hands found her nipples again, pulling on them, and kneading her flesh roughly.

"You can tease me all you want Miss Anderson, but the entire office doesn't need to know you're here.

Hopefully, your little pantie gag will remind you to keep quiet." He breathed in her ear, then he returned his lips to her neck and shoulder.

Her back pressed against Alex's chest, Mel moved her hands in an attempt to brush against his cock and encourage him to take her. He growled when her fingers grazed against his length. He pushed her forward so she was bending over the desk, and pushed his knees between her legs forcing them apart.

"I'm going to discipline you for this later Melody. But for now..." His voice trailed off as his hands skimmed across her thighs and lifted her dress up to her waist exposing her bare ass to him. Mel groaned against her pantie gag. Alex lifted his hand and struck a swift spank on her bare backside, before rubbing it softly, his hand circling her backside, a finger sliding between her legs and penetrating her. Mel let out a muffled moan and clenched around the finger pressing into her. Alex pulled his finger from her sex and lifted it to his mouth, sucking it in and tasting her.

"Mmmm.... Fuck, you taste incredible." He smirked and dropped his hands to his fly. His cock bobbed in front of him, thick and heavy when he freed it from his slacks and boxers. He took Mel's hips between his hands and stepped against her, his cock finding itself at the entrance of her wet pussy. He dipped his pelvis against hers, and his erect penis slid home. Alex groaned.

"Jesus Mel! You're always so wet for me!" He slowly pulled back and out of her, before slamming himself back into her roughly. A series of appreciative whimpers sounded around the panties in Mel's mouth, and Alex continued to pound into her. He scooped around her to pull her back against his chest again. He nuzzled into her neck and seized her tits coarsely in his palms. He thrust hard into her over and over as she stood in front of him, the position only serving to strike her deep inside on that super sensitive bundle of nerves. He could feel her tightening around him; he knew that she was going to come. His lips were on her earlobe and his finger found her clit.

"Come for me Jellybean." He whispered.

Melody's entire body tensed as her orgasm rushed through her. She bit down on the panties in her mouth, a long stifled groan vibrating across her lips. As the ripples of pleasure pulsed through her, she fell limply against Alex's chest. He felt her juices flood around his cock and kept up his relentless thrusting deep inside her. No sooner was her first orgasm ebbing when a second one rushed to take its place. Alex pulled the panties from her mouth as she cried out again, swallowing her sounds with his mouth on hers. He felt her vaginal walls clenching on him, coaxing him to his own orgasm. "FUCK!" Alex hissed through gritted teeth as he came, collapsing back onto his office chair, pulling Melody with him so she landed on his lap, his cock still buried inside her. Her panty gag falling from her mouth as she moved.

Mel's head fell back against his shoulder, and she looked up at him. He held her tight against him with an arm around her waist, a hand cupped her jaw and kissed her deeply holding her close to him. Mel pulled against the tie, freeing her hands and held on to Alex's arm, not ready for their post-orgasmic bubble to burst just yet. She broke their kiss and gazed at him. "Does this mean you don't want any food?" She smiled.

"Don't tempt me to eat you, Jellybean." He grinned and kissed the end of her nose. He glanced at his watch. "I have time for a quick bite." He said and raised an eyebrow.

"Let me put my panties on and we can go for something." Mel said, about to reach for her discarded underwear. Alex grabbed her hand and laughed.

"Oh no. You were a teasing little slut Miss Anderson. You can go without your panties while we have lunch. I want them as a little reminder." Mel tried to reach the lacy knickers perched on Alex's desk again, wriggling in his lap as she did, his cock lurched inside her, and she exhaled softly. Alex grabbed her hips and ground his against her. "If you keep doing that, we'll both go hungry!" he warned her. She looked at him intently, trying to decide which idea she liked better.

"Jellybean." He growled in warning.

She leaned in and kissed his cheek gently. "Okay."

He lifted her up off his lap, biting his lip to stifle the groan that threatened to escape his throat as his cock slid from inside her. Melody shivered at the loss.

"Can I freshen up before we go out?" She asked. "You know if you're keeping my knickers." She smirked.

"There's a bathroom through that door." Alex said, pointing in the direction of his personal bathroom, and swatting her on the backside as she walked away. She jumped and gave a little yelp, grinning at him over her shoulder as she walked away.

Once Mel had closed the door of the bathroom, Alex lifted the lacy underwear from his desk, opened a drawer and dropped them inside. When she re-emerged he grinned, and offered her his arm, leading her to the office and heading out in to grab some lunch. He couldn't help but smirk when he watched Mel constantly pulling at the hem of her dress, trying to make sure she didn't accidentally expose herself.

~ ~ ~

It was almost 2:30 by the time Alex got back to the office after having lunch with Mel. He had found it difficult to prize himself away from her. He buried himself in work for the rest of the day. Once Kate had left for the day, he went to get a document from his drawer, finding Mel's panties instead. He grinned, running his fingers over the delicate garment, before scooping them into his pocket and heading for the door, and home.

CHAPTER 10

Mel pulled into an empty space outside the Student's Union, Dylan jumped out of the front seat followed by Jonny, Jacob and Nate out of the back seat. She joined them at the back of the car, locked it, and they all headed across the street to the old-fashioned Victorian bar for drinks and cheap pizza.

Jacob arrived back from the bar, and passed each of them their drinks, pear cider for Mel, bottles of beer for Jonny, Dylan and Nate, followed by a chilled bottle of rose in an ice bucket and a glass for himself.

They chatted about their classes, about their lecturers, and they talked about their lives away from college. Dylan was excited about a Bachelor Party that he was going to, heading off to Majorca for some sun and beer craziness; Nate was heading off to see his favourite metal-core band, and Jacob was talking about a holiday that he and his boyfriend were thinking of taking to Prague. Mel sat and listened to them all, smiling at the wonderful group of people that she had surrounded herself with. She looked at Jonny, who was sitting quietly listening. Nate and Jacob got up to get the pizzas and side orders from the bar, and Dylan spoke to Jonny before Mel had the chance to. "What's your problem dude? You're sitting there like a spare part!" Dylan smirked.

"Nothing mate, just not sleeping as usual." He held up his almost empty beer. "Give me another of these and I'll start to liven up." He laughed. Dylan whistled at Nate, shook his beer bottle and put up 3 fingers. Nate nodded, and he and Jacob returned with pizzas and more beers.

Well fed, and with a few drinks downed, Mel, Jonny, and the others headed over to the SU for a few games of pool. "I hope you've been practicing, Jakey." Dylan laughed.

"Oh hush." Jacob pouted.

Dylan roared with laughter and patted Jacob on the shoulder. Mel smiled at them. "Oh Dylan, don't be mean!" She scolded. "Besides, you saw him last time, even if he hasn't, sweet Jesus he can't get any worse!" The murderous look on Jacob's face made her burst out laughing.

"So mean!" Jacob sulked. "You're always picking on me!"

Jonny laughed and put his arm around Jacob. "Aww, but we only do it because we love you! If we can't take the piss out of you as your best mates, who can?"

The rest of the evening was filled with laughter, jokes and fooling around. Dylan and Jonny got very competitive; Nate started to try and throw them both off their game, resorting to pinching their backsides, and making faces over the pocket that they were aiming for. Anything he could to put them off. Jacob decided the touchy-feely approach was best, and kept lying over the back of each man as he leaned over to take his shot. Mel delighted in joking with Jonny about his new admirer since Jacob seemed to hug Jonny a lot more than Dylan.

Mel was just getting ready to take her shot when her phone vibrated on the table. "It's Alex." Jonny grinned. She stuck her tongue out at him and potted the yellow ball in the middle pocket. While Jonny took his shot, she read the text that had arrived.

Hope you're having fun tonight x Fancy calling into mine on the way home? A x

Mel smirked. Jonny stood beside her. "Getting your freak on tonight then?" He laughed. Mel stroked the side of her face with her middle finger, which only made Jonny laugh harder.

"Are we ever going to meet this bloke?" Dylan asked her.

"Ah, let me think about that... Umm... No." She laughed.

"Are you ashamed of us, sweetie?" Jacob asked.

Mel shook her head. "No Jay, nothing like that, it's just early days yet." She cast a glance in Jonny's direction who potted the black accidentally giving Mel the game. Mel cheered, and Jonny cursed, providing enough of a distraction that the others in the group let the topic go.

All too soon it was time for Nate to catch the last train home, and Mel had promised to take him to the station.

The group said their goodbyes and parted on a high. Everyone passing around hugs as they left. Nate thanked Mel for giving him a lift to the station. "Hey, it's all good sweetie, you know I don't mind." She reassured him. "I needed to head on anyway."

"Is this to see the new boy-toy?" He joked.

She laughed. "He's not a 'boy-toy'! But yeah I'm going to see him on the way home."

Nate smiled. "He seems to put a smile on your face, and that's good in my book. But you tell him, if he ever upsets you, he'll have a squad of us coming for him."

Mel laughed. "Thanks, sweetie, I appreciate that." She pulled up outside the station and Nate hugged her tight and disappeared through the side entrance. Mel pulled away from the kerb and headed to Alex's house.

Mel pulled into Alex's drive and turned off her car. He appeared in the doorway, light from behind him, pouring out into the night, and making him even more of a dominant presence in front of her. She got out, locked up, and walked slowly towards him. He took her by the arm and pulled her against him, his lips sinking down onto her, his mouth sucking and nibbling on hers, his tongue dancing with hers in her mouth. After a moment, Alex pulled back from her. "Hello." He smiled.

"Hi there." She whispered breathlessly.

"Coming in?" Alex smirked.

"Ohh yes!" Mel grinned.

Mel followed behind Alex as he headed for the living room. "Wine?" He offered, holding up a bottle. "Or would you prefer a pear cider? I have some in the fridge."

Mel grinned at him. "You got pear cider for me?" Alex nodded. "Ohh I would LOVE one!" She smiled, and Alex disappeared off, returning with an open bottle and a glass with ice. Mel took the bottle from him and took a drink. He smirked when she didn't take the glass from him. "Such a tomboy Miss Anderson!" Mel grinned and set herself on the sofa, Alex setting himself beside her.

"I was about to watch a film, have you any preferences?" He asked.

She took a mouthful from the bottle and settled back into the seat. "What's on?"

Alex brought up the onscreen guide, flicking to the movie channels. Mel grinned.

"That one!" She pointed at the comedy channel.

"The Full Monty?"

"Ohh yes!" She grinned. "It's a good laugh, and I've not seen it in ages!"

Alex laughed. "Your wish is my command, M'Lady."

Mel laughed and they snuggled back against each other, and watched Robert Carlyle strutting his stuff as an out of work Sheffield Steel worker. Alex watched as Mel laughed, and blushed her way through the film.

"What would you like to do now?" Alex asked, turning the volume down on the TV.

Mel grinned. "Is Hot Chocolate on Spotify?"

"Are you going to strip for me Miss Anderson?" He grinned.

"I'm not, no." Mel smirked. Alex laughed and ran his fingers through his hair.

"I see." He said, and got up and walked to his stereo system. He tapped on the screen of the docked iPod and Hot Chocolate "You Sexy Thing" started to play through the speakers. Mel grinned and raised an eyebrow suggestively. Alex started to gyrate his hips in time with the music. He circled them as he pulled his shirt from his jeans and started to unbutton it at the top. Mel giggled as he moved sexily around his living room. He turned his back to her, wiggled his bum from side to side, gave her a heated glance over his shoulder, and shrugged his shirt off his shoulders and down his back. He tossed it in her direction once it was off, turned to face her, and undid his jeans.

Before he moved his jeans, he stood in front of her, his flies open, and ran his hands slowly up over his abs, over his chest, and up behind his head. Mel stared at him and licked her lips, Alex grinned, loving how turned on she was getting. He turned back away from her and shimmied his jeans and boxers down over his hips, exposing his bare ass to her, which he smacked as soon as it was bare. Mel started biting her bottom lip and laughing. *Damn this man is sexy and a lot of fun.* She thought to herself. Alex dropped his boxers and jeans to his ankles and kicked them away, his used his hands to provide some modesty, and turned to face Mel again, dancing towards her, thrusting and swaying his hips. She reached up to touch him.

Alex smacked the back of her hand "Ah! Ah! Ah!" He scolded. "No hands on the dancers please Miss."

Mel threw her head back and laughed. "Don't you offer private dances?" She asked.

"I'm very expensive!" He smirked.

"That's a shame." Mel sniggered. "I'm a poor student. I guess I couldn't afford you." She challenged.

Alex took her by the hand and pulled her to her feet. "Maybe we can work out some other way for you to pay me?" He smirked.

Mel put her hands on Alex's chest, skimming her fingers over his skin. "Perhaps..." she said, looking deep into his eyes. Her arms went around the back of his neck and her lips brushed his. "Depends on what you have in mind." She smiled when she pulled her mouth away. Spotify changed the song to Paul Young's "Wherever I Lay My Hat" and Alex forgot his modesty, pulled Mel into him, and started to slow dance with her. They swayed against each other, and he started to sing in hushed tones, emphasizing certain words in the song. "If so I'd like for you to know that I'm not worth it, you see..." He sang softly and kissed the tip of her nose. She tightened her grip around him and nuzzled into his chest. She longed to tell him that she thought that he was worth it. She longed to ask him who had hurt him so much. She knew he had nightmares. He'd had a few while she had slept beside him, his body would tense and become covered in a cold sweat, he'd start to move around, mumbling about something she couldn't quite make out.

The song came to an end and they stood there entwined together for a moment, Whip It by Devo started, and Mel looked up at Alex before both of them started to laugh and all trace of the sadness that was starting to surround them disappeared. "Don't even think of it." Mel grinned.

Alex looked at her with a fake offended expression. "I'm sure I don't know what you mean!"

Mel gazed into his eyes again. "A whip Mr Matthews... No!" She smiled. His hand roamed down over her backside before giving it a little smack

"Are you sure you couldn't be tempted?" He grinned.

"Perfectly!" She smirked back. "Now, what happened to this private dance?" She said pushing him back and admiring the view. Alex took a step back from her, covered his now erect penis with his hands and turned allowing her to take all of him in.

"If you like what you see, I'm sure we can work out a way for you to pay lip service to my dancing skills." He said, swaying his hips.

Mel licked her lips and stared intently. "Lip service huh?" She said and raised an eyebrow. "Better be a damn good dance mister." She smirked.

Alex raised an eyebrow in disbelief. "Would there be any doubt, Miss?" He asked, and started to gyrate his hips in slow wide circles in time with the music.

"I guess not... I suppose I can agree to pay you *lip service*."

Alex looked like the cat that got the canary, and started to flex his body in Melody's direction and move towards her. She watched intently as he performed his best erotic dance in front of her. Her panties grew wet as she watched, her heart pounded in her ears, and she wanted nothing more than to run her hands over every last inch of him. He smirked and lifted one hand beckoning her with his index finger to come towards him. Mel moved slowly, stalking towards him. He pulled her against him, his erection thick and heavy against her. "I think you have too many clothes on." He whispered in her ear and started to pull at her t-shirt. She helped him slip it over her head and threw it to the sofa. Alex let his teeth graze over her neck as he nibbled his way down to her shoulder.

The music changed to Prince's 'Kiss' and Mel manoeuvred Alex so that his back was to the sofa, and she pushed him back until he fell back onto it. She took a step back from him and started to move in time to the music, turning the tables on Alex. "Consider this a part payment." She winked at him over her shoulder as she swayed her ass over his lap. His hands went to her hips, and she smacked his hands away. "I think you know the rules, mister!" She teased, and turned to face him. She put a finger on her lips and dipped it into her mouth in mock oral. Alex groaned, and Mel grinned, letting her hand drop from her mouth, and join her other hand in skimming over her neck to her chest. She grabbed her breasts in her hands and kneaded them before she slipped her hand over her stomach to the button of her jeans. She slipped the zipper down and skimmed the denim over her hips and to the floor. She stood in from of him, placed her hands on his thighs, and leaned over so her face was level with his. She slid her hands down to his knees, and reached behind her back, and opened her bra, letting the lacy cups fall from her soft tits. She tossed it onto the sofa with her t-shirt and put her hands back on Alex's thighs. The chorus of the song came round again, and Mel puckered her lips in a kiss.

Alex couldn't take it anymore, he grabbed Mel's wrists and pulled her into his lap, crushing his lips against hers. "Payment satisfied." He murmured against her mouth, before pressing his against hers, and demanding access with his tongue. She moaned, and pressed herself against him as much as she could from her position on his lap. As he kissed her, he pushed her back, sliding her off his lap so that her backside was on the sofa beside him. He moved from beneath her, manoeuvring himself to be between her thighs as she lay back on the sofa. He pried his lips from hers and leaned back to take in how she looked, spread out on his sofa and in need of him. His gaze fell on her panties, and a wicked smirk formed on his lips. Mel looked wide eyed as she took in his almost predatory expression. His hands skimmed over the flesh on her inner thighs, setting every nerve ending in her body alight. His hands skimmed across the tops of her legs and stopped on one hip. Her lacy panties were in pieces in mere seconds, and Alex pulled the scraps of material away from her body and tossed them to the floor. Mel's breathing was fast and shallow and she watched as Alex brushed his body against hers, until they were face to face, chest to breasts and hip to hip. He paused over her for a minute, looking into her eyes. His mouth opened as if there was something that he wanted to say, but the words caught in his throat, and never made it past his lips. *Coward!* His critic laughed. Mel's hand went to his cheek and caressed his face. The words clung to their hiding place within him, and he did the only other thing he could, he kissed her, hoping that she would understand from that what it was that he couldn't say. He kissed her deeply, yet tenderly and ground his hips against hers. She moaned into his mouth her hands stroking his back. He moved against her, shifting his position between her thighs yet keeping his mouth on hers. She felt the head of his cock pushing between her slick labia, and his tongue plunged deep into her mouth as he thrust his length into her. Mel cried out, the delicious pressure from being filled so completely growing in her groin. Alex stilled, allowing her body to become accustomed to his trespass. He broke their kiss and gazed again into her eyes, watching her panting beneath him. "Do you know what you do to me Mel?" he asked, licking his lips. Mel shook her head.

"I want you." He breathed and circled his hips, allowing his cock to withdraw slightly before grinding it deep inside Mel again. A sensual sigh erupted from within her as he did. "Can you feel what you do to me?" He asked, circling his hips to pull out half way, before thrusting in deeper. Mel moaned out in reply. Her hands roaming to Alex's backside, willing him to do more than the exquisite tease that he was doing at that moment. His ass clenched under her hands, and he started to pull back and push into her in a deliberately slow pace. Her back arched in perfect synchronisation with his movements. He groaned, torturing himself as much as Mel with his steady pace. His head slumped forward against her shoulder. Again things he wanted to tell her tried to bubble to the surface, bursting just before they formed into words in his mouth.

He buried his face against her neck, nibbling on her neck. Frustrated with himself for not being able to be as honest with Mel as he wanted to be. A long soft keening erupted from her and his instincts took over, he lifted his face to be able to look at her and started to drive into her over and over again in a frenzied pace. Mel started panting, heat pooling low in her stomach; that familiar tightening feeling rising as Alex continued to grind his length into her.

"Ohhh Alex!" She cried in pleasure as her orgasm began to take over her.

"You. Are. Mine." Alex growled, thrusting hard into her, pushing his cock deep inside her as she tumbled over the brink of her climax. Her back arched and her whole body tensed, the air rushed out of her body and she screamed out in euphoria as he fucked her deeply. Her nails dug into his backside, pulling him tight and hard against her. "Fuck me, Alex!" She encouraged. "Oh fuck, YES! YES!" She cried as a second wave of orgasm swept over her body. Alex kissed and bit at her shoulder, "You're mine Mel. All mine!" He hissed in her ear and gave one final thrust into her, his own waves of pleasure engulfing him as he erupted deep inside her.

Mel clung to him as the last shivers of pleasure rippled through them both. He lifted his head from her neck, and looked deep into her eyes, and in that second he knew that she understood. There was something happening between them that he couldn't explain and that if he thought too long about his fears would threaten to pull it to pieces. Instead, he just lay there with her, looking into the face of the woman that in the moments he held her made his fears dissolve into the ether.

~ ~ ~

Mel woke the next morning to find Alex's side of the bed empty. She looked at the clock on the bedside table to see just what time it was. 10:42 blinked back at her from the display, and she stretched, deciding to get up and see where Alex had gone. She wrapped herself in his bathrobe and ventured out into the rest of the house in search of Alex.

When she stood in the door frame of his study, she found him dressed in just a pair of soft jersey lounge pants and wearing his glasses while staring at the screen of his 27 inch iMac. She smiled when she saw him. "What are you up to?" She asked as she approached him. Alex jumped when he heard her voice, he had been so engrossed in his task that he had been unaware of her presence. He looked up at her and reached to pull her into his lap when she was close enough. He sighed "I'm trying to find a present for Ethan."

"Ethan?" Mel asked.

Alex snuggled her close against him, his arms wrapped around her. "My nephew. His birthday is next week, and I have to find him a gift." He explained.

Mel glanced at the screen. "What age is he?"

"Turning 8." Was his answer.

Mel grinned, "And you thought that was a good gift for an eight-year-old?" She said, biting back a laugh. Alex's fingers instantly found her waist and he began to tickle her. Mel squealed and started to squirm in his lap. "Are you saying that there is something wrong with buying him that?" He asked as Mel howled on his lap with laughter.

"Stop!!" She begged between giggles. "I give in!" She laughed.

The tickling abated, and Alex kissed Mel on her now bare shoulder, when it had been exposed as she writhed around on his knee. "What would you get him then Jellybean?" He asked as he nipped her shoulder. Mel closed her eyes and sighed. Alex's mouth moved towards her neck and he kissed her soft skin. Her head fell back onto his shoulder, and she moaned. Alex slapped her thigh playfully.

"Jellybean!" He growled. "Present picking first, pleasant fucking after."

Mel grinned and elbowed Alex in the ribs so she could get to the keyboard. She opened up Safari, went to the

Apple website, and opened the page about the iPad Mini. "Get him one of these, you can buy educational apps, as well as games, books and films." She said, and moved back against him. He wrapped his arms back around her.

"You really think that this will be okay?" He asked, nuzzling back into her neck.

"Mmmm. I'll even go with you to the Apple Store later." She said before getting off Alex's knee so that she could turn and straddle his lap instead. "But that's later." She grinned and moved against his hips. He reached between them and undid the tie on the robe she was wearing. "You look good in my robe." He told her as he pulled the front of it open. "But I like how you look naked even more." He cupped her breast in his palm and grabbed her ass with his other hand, crushing his lips against hers.

It was about three in the afternoon by the time they finally made it out of the house and headed for the Apple Store in the high-end shopping mall near House of Fraser. "iPad first. Then you need to feed me!" She teased him as they walked out of the car park to the back of elevators.

Alex bowed as he pushed the button to call the elevator. "Your wish is my command M'Lady." He grinned at her. Mel laughed and rolled her eyes. The lift arrived and they got in alone, pressing the button for the

"Upper Ground" floor. As the lift moved Alex grabbed her hand and pulled her against him. "Damn shame this thing doesn't have a stop button." He grinned and gave her a quick kiss on the cheek. She laughed at him, and he walked out of the elevator without letting go of her hand, pulling her along with him to the Apple Store.

Three hours later, and they had played with almost everything in the Apple Store, and had amazing Japanese food in one of the restaurants in the centre. Alex took Mel back to his house, and they collapsed side by side onto the sofa in the lounge. "Thank you." He smiled at her, pulling her in against him.

"For spending your money?" She laughed. "Anytime!"

"Funny woman!" he said and squeezed his arm around her tight in a play headlock. Mel laughed and jabbed her elbow in his side to get free.

"Seriously though," she grinned at him, "you're welcome."

Alex sighed and closed his eyes. "Are you staying this evening?" He asked her sleepily.

"Are you kicking me out?" She smirked.

"No."

"Then I'm staying. Poor you, you're stuck with me for another evening!" She said, and lifted the cushion from beside her slapping Alex across the stomach with it. He opened his eyes and grabbed for her waist again. Mel squealed.

"Yeah, poor me... Such a burden." He said, letting the comment drip with sarcasm. Mel laughed and struggled in his grasp, trying to escape his tickling fingers. Finally, she broke free and bolted for the door, fleeing into the rest of the house. Alex laughed and bound out of the room after her.

CHAPTER 11

Her phone bleated with an incoming text.

What are you up to tomorrow night? A x

She read the message and laughed as she replied.

I'm free, but you are a busy man with a birthday party to attend remember?

Her phone chimed again within moments

Yes, I am aware of that Miss Anderson! Such cheek! I mean after that, you're free? A x

She texted him back.

Yes, perfectly free, what does Sir have in mind? x

Again, Alex messaged her straight back.

Well... I have an idea ;-)

Mel replied that she was interested in hearing more about Alex's idea, and he sent her back a list of instructions for the next evening and his sister's address.

She pulled into the street where Alex's sister lived at midnight, just as he had asked. She was wearing her knee high boots, a short figure hugging baby doll negligee, and a tiny pair of matching panties, over the top of this she had her favourite red mac which was long enough to cover her outfit, but short enough that it only came down to her mid-thigh. Tucked into her panties, tight against her clit was a bullet vibrator operated wirelessly by remote control.

Alex appeared from the dark driveway and got into the passenger side of Mel's car. "Hello gorgeous!" he smiled as he put his seatbelt on. Mel smiled back, "Hello Master Lex. This is for you." She put the control into his hand and his smile turned into a full-scale grin. Mel started the car and drove down the street. "Good evening?" Mel asked nervously, waiting for Alex to start pressing buttons on the remote control. "Not bad." Alex smirked, rubbing his fingers over the remote. Mel glanced at him as she watched the traffic before merging out onto the main road. "I have a feeling it's about to get better though!" He grinned again. "How many settings are on this again?" He asked her. She bit her lip and tried to concentrate on her driving, "Seven." She glanced again in his direction and caught the sly smile on his lips as he turned the vibe on. Mel gasped, feeling the little bullet come to life against her clit. "You okay there?" Alex asked, grinning like a Cheshire cat. "Mmmm, yes, but this might be..." her reply faltered when Alex pressed the button again, she sighed and continued, "ahh, be, um, a little hard to explain to any police." Her sentence was interrupted again by Alex turning the vibrator to a pulsing rhythm instead of a steady buzz. Alex laughed,

"What would you need to explain to the police?" Mel glared at him and laughed, "Oh I don't know, sorry officer, we had a little accident because, mmmm, my master has a vibe on my clit and was playing with the remote control, ohhh, teasing me as I was driving along!" Alex changed the pattern of the vibrations again, and Mel let out another little moan. "You're doing very well at keeping focused Melody, I'm impressed!" Alex teased her. She glared at him again and groaned as he pressed the button on the controller again.

Melody clenched her thighs together, trying to get more friction on her clit as she drove back to her house. Alex kept changing the pattern of the pulsations coming from the vibrator. Her sex was so slick that she couldn't get as much contact as she needed to get any relief, instead it kept her on a slow burn. She tried to distract Alex from his quest to keep her needy by making small talk, she asked about his evening, his parents, how his week had been, unfortunately, nothing swayed him from his mission to keep her on the edge, right where he wanted her.

When she pulled into the driveway of her house and turned the car off, Alex turned off the vibrator, leaned over, finding her lips with his in a slow tender kiss. "Take me inside." He commanded. Mel led Alex through the front door and into the living room. He pounced, kissing her deeply, pulling her tight against him, ravenous for her touch. His fingers knotted in her hair, and he tugged, her head falling back exposing her neck to him, ready for him to kiss and nibble along its length. As he kissed down to her shoulder, both hands moved to the collar of her red coat, pushing it back off her shoulders, kissing the skin it left exposed. Her coat fell to the floor, and Alex stepped back to see the beautiful scene before him. He could see the peaks of Mel's nipples straining at the material of the baby doll nightie. "Turn." He growled, his voice letting her know just how the setting was arousing him too. Mel turned on the spot slowly, glancing over her shoulder through lidded eyes as she reached the back. Alex hissed at the sight of the split at the back of the outfit, revealing the lush globes of Mel's ass, barely covered by the matching panties she wore. "Stop!" he ordered as he reached for the belt on her coat, pulling it free. "Hands behind your back!" He instructed. Mel obeyed. Her hands coming behind her back, ready for Alex to do what he wanted. He wound the belt from her coat around both wrists, securing them behind her back, just above her buttocks. His hands skimmed over her ass cheeks, and quickly found themselves on her forearms as he again pulled her tight against him, her ass lined up perfectly with his swollen cock. From her arms, his hands roved across the front of her body towards her breasts, cradling them in his hands, squeezing them roughly, feeling them rise and fall as Mel panted against him.

With her hands behind her back, her breasts were shoved forward, the stiffness of her nipples looking more exaggerated in this position. He kissed along her shoulder as his fingers teases those stiff little peaks and a sigh escaped from Mel's lips. He slid his hands up over her shoulders, slipping the straps of her baby doll down so that the cups of the negligee became loose around her cleavage. Alex's lips and teeth found her shoulders again, and he pulled the front of her outfit down, freeing her breasts. Again, Melody moaned, the brief moment of friction from the fabric of her baby doll teasing her. She need not have worried about the loss of attention on her nipples, within seconds Alex's fingers were on them, rolling them between his finger and thumb, kneading her tits roughly, pulling on her nipples. One hand left her, and she groaned at its loss, only for it to turn the vibrator back on again and return to her nipples with haste.

Mel's head fell back onto Alex's shoulder, her body melted against his, open to all of the attention that he wanted to give her. Between his kneading hands, tugging fingers, his nipping and kissing mouth, and the pulsing vibrations on her clit Melody felt her body flush with heat. "Please!" She begged him. Alex turned her to face him and moved his mouth to her nipples and his fingers to her clit and the vibe. Melody's moans got louder; she wanted to run her hands through Alex's hair, to hold him against her. Instead, she tried to push her chest out more, attempting to encourage him take her to the edge. He looked up at her and grinned broadly. He started to kiss a trail down from her breasts to her belly button and down further still. She felt his lips graze the top of her mons and a loud groan escaped from her lips. "Master Lex!" she begged him again. "Please!" Hearing her delicious torture Alex just couldn't resist dipping his tongue against her clit while pushing the vibe back into her tight pussy. He felt her flood against his mouth at the extra sensations that he compelled her to experience. His lips slipped around her clit, and he sucked, Mel felt her knees shake as her orgasm threatened to overtake her. Alex's hands arrived at her hips to steady her as her body started to shudder and a climax ripped through her. Alex kissed a trail back up her skin, pulling her nipples into his mouth as he did. A shiver ran through Mel's body. She felt his hands on her shoulders pushing her back onto the sofa behind her. He put his arms around her and moved her so that her head hung back over the arm of the chair. He moved and stood above her head, looking down at her. She looked up at him and licked her lips, knowing what was coming next. Alex slowly undid the fly on his jeans, lowered them, and stepped out of them, throwing them to another chair in the room, he reached forward over Mel to pull her nipple into his mouth; his thick, hard, boxer covered cock straining to get free. She leaned up reaching out to it with her tongue. Alex hissed at her attempted contact, released her nipple and stood up. He tugged the front of his boxers down letting his rock hard dick dangle in front of her face, stroking its length as he glared down at her. "What is it that you want Melody?" He asked her, a wicked smirk growing across his lips. "Please, Master Lex!" She pleaded. "Tell me what you want, slut, I won't know until you tell me!" He teased her. He understood completely what her need was, but he needed her to verbalise her want, to express her need to him precisely. She licked her lips and looked up at him, "I need your cock in my mouth Master, please!" She breathed out, looking up at him, leaving her mouth open temptingly. Alex growled; his eyes fixed on her parted lips. "I could never deny you what you want, Melody." As he spoke he leaned over, dipping his hips towards her, and pushing the silky head of his shaft past her lips, and into her moist mouth.

She felt exquisite around him. The second his tip pressed against her tongue she began to lick and tease him, applying a gentle suck to encourage him deeper. He thrust gently into her mouth, pushing a little deeper with every stroke. She ran her tongue along the upper side of his cock with each thrust, circling the tip each time he pulled back. A moan escaped from his throat, and his thrusting sped up, pushing further into her throat on every stroke. She was so turned on by him. She pushed her head back to allow him easier access to her throat, clamping her legs together, trying to achieve the friction she needed to come along with him. Alex bit his bottom lip, sucked in a deep breath, and pulled back, out of the warmth of Mel's sweet mouth. His hand ran from his balls to the tip, catching the pre-cum between his thumb and forefinger, before putting them on Melody's lips for her to lick it off. She suckled on them greedily and he let out a sigh. "Get up!" He commanded, pulling her arm and moving her directly in front of him, her back against his chest. "Bend." He instructed, and with his assistance, Mel folded over the arm of the sofa, her face in the cushions, and her ass up in the air. Alex's fingers dipped into her moist folds, spreading her juices over her asshole and his hand. He ran his slick hand around the head of his cock and down the shaft before pushing the tip against Mel's tight hole. "Spread your legs." He growled and her legs slid wider. He pressed against her, applying constant pressure until he felt that familiar give as the muscle of her ass finally allowed him to enter. He heard her gasp as he was allowed access into her most intimate place. He couldn't hold back, he felt her pulse around him almost instantly, and he drove deep into her, his balls colliding with her wet pussy with the first stroke. Melody cried out beneath him, the sound that she produced was almost feral, like some sort of animalistic mating call, and on hearing it, Alex lost all control. He started to pound into her ass without mercy, needing to claim her, needing to make her his, needing to erase every other man from the world so that she existed only for him, so she always would be his and his alone. He was panting hard, pulling on her hips to keep her with him, knowing that with her hands still tied behind her she wouldn't be able to stop herself from slipping forwards. "Fuck...." He heard her hissing beneath him. "Harder Master!" She moaned. Alex pulled almost all the way out before slamming back into her, their bodies crashing together with an audible slap. Mel shuddered and called out to him. "Yes Master. Fuck, YES!" He felt her entire body contract around his cock as she exploded beneath him crying out with the hardest orgasm he had heard her have. Her body held and tugged on him like a hand stroking him tightly to a finish, and seconds after Mel, Alex's own climax ripped through him. "Oh Jesus.... MEL!!" he shouted out as his cock pumped his hot seed deep inside her. He collapsed over her, barely able to keep his weight off her as he waited for the stars in his vision to clear, and for his legs to be made from something other than jelly. He tugged on the belt around her wrists freeing them, and she placed one hand around him behind her, moving with him so that they ended up side by side on the sofa, spooning together with Alex's semi erect cock still buried deep inside her. Alex pulled her tightly against him and nuzzled her neck. Mel wrapped her arms around his as they crossed her body.

Soon they both drifted into a sleep, still tightly tangled together.

Mel awoke some time later to find Alex stroking her hair. "Are you okay, Jellybean?" He whispered before placing a soft and chaste kiss against her lips. She smiled up at him, shifting around slightly to caress his cheek. "Oh, I'm better than alright." She grinned up at him. "Good." He said kissing the tip of her nose. "Let's go to bed." He smiled down at her. She licked her lips while looking deep into his eyes, pausing before she answered him. Whatever answer it was she was looking for, she seemed to find in his face, and she smiled. "Okay." She replied. Alex pushed himself up off the sofa from behind her, stood, and outstretched his hand offering to help her up. Mel placed her hand in his and when she stood intertwined her fingers with his, turned off the light and led him upstairs.

CHAPTER 12

Alex woke with a start, sitting bolt upright in bed, covered in a cold sweat, his heart hammering in his chest. He tried to calm his breathing, taking in long deep breaths. He glanced over to Mel, worried that he had woken her with his reaction. He ran his hands through his damp hair. *Jesus Matthews, get your fucking shit together!* His critic scolded. His hand brushed over his face as he tried to wipe away the memory of his nightmare. *Every damn time.* He thought to himself. He needed a drink; he eased his legs round, put his feet to the floor, and gently got off the bed. Mel moved in her sleep with a sigh and he froze. When he was sure that she wasn't going to wake, he tip-toed out of the bedroom. He stood on the landing and sighed, the nightmares were still coming to him even after all these years, and every time he lay beside Mel and fell asleep they became their most vivid. He crossed the landing and walked into the bathroom, blinking as he turned on the light. He leaned over the sink, turning the cold water on and splashing it over his face. He sighed. *Never going to get over this shit are you buddy?* His inner voice asked. He was starting to think that it was right, worse still, he knew now that he wanted to get over it. He wanted to be with Mel in a way that was more than just sexual, but every time he was close to her that fear nagged constantly in the back of his mind. And every time he lay beside her and slept, the nightmares that Natalie burned into his skull surfaced.

Alex felt like a caged animal, he needed to pace and move around. He turned off the water and dried his face, turned off the light, and headed downstairs. He wandered around Mel's lounge, distracting himself by looking at her photos, knick-knacks, and her book collection. He stopped at the frame of Mel and an older woman who looked very similar. He smiled, it pleased him to think of Mel and her family. His eyes moved to the frame beside that, Mel standing with a pool cue in her hand, grinning, with two men young men standing beside her, a pang of jealousy ran through Alex. *Oh, they're just her college mates butthead!* His inner critic reminded him. He studied the two men in the photograph with her. A red head with piercings and tattoos stood with her grinning, and behind them a young looking dark haired guy with glasses was sticking his tongue out. He looked at how well she fitted in with the rest of the group. He looked at how her smile reached her eyes, as did the smiles of everyone around her and his heart leapt in his chest. *No good will come of this!* His critic warned.

Alex sighed, and he ran his fingers along the spines of the books on her bookshelf. She had been honest when she had text from the bath, her collection of books was extensive, and not restricted to any one genre. There were literary classics, Bronte, Dickens, Austen and Shakespeare. There were novels of sci-fi television shows like Star Trek, Quantum Leap and the X-Files. There were as he discovered by reading a few blurbs, a lot of erotic romances, from Fifty Shades of Grey to authors Alex wasn't familiar with, like Victoria Ashley, Laurelin Paige, and J S Scott. There were even a few on crafts and DIY. He smiled, he felt like he was slowly getting to know more and more about the girl who seemed to capture him so completely. Something else on the shelf caught his eye, and a plan formed in his head for something that he wanted to do with Mel.

He smirked and walked to the kitchen to get a glass of cold water. As he drank it, he glanced out the window, her back garden was illuminated by the moon, and the stars twinkled above. A plan was forming in his head. Something nice that he would be able to do for Mel. He finished the water, rinsed the glass, and went back to bed.

~ ~ ~

Mel woke the next morning and stretched out, finding herself in a tangle of limbs. She gazed at Alex's slumbering form beside her. She couldn't help but smile when she looked at his handsome face, lying peacefully beside her. She snuggled into the pillow and lay there, taking in every feature. She became so transfixed she lost track of time.

"What?" Alex mumbled, and Mel blushed. "I can feel your eyes on me Jellybean." He opened one eye blearily to confirm his suspicions, and was gifted with a glance of Mel looking serene yet blushed with colour at being caught out. He opened both eyes to take her in properly. "Good morning Miss Anderson." He grinned.

"Good morning Mr Matthews." She smirked back. He moved in to kiss her and she pushed him back. "No! I've got morning breath, get lost!" She giggled as he continued to push himself up against her.

"Ohh shut up woman!" He scolded, brushing his lips against her, running his tongue against her bottom lip, begging for entry. She pushed her hands against his chest, trying to pry him off her, but he slid his tongue over her top lip, and she melted against him, opening her mouth and allowing him to access. He wrapped his arms around her and pulled her tight against him. He kissed her long and leisurely, like he had all the time in the world to savour her and he was in no hurry to rush the experience. Her hands moved from his chest to his arms, and gripped his biceps, pressing herself against him. He moaned against her mouth. "Jellybean." He growled in a way that warned her if it went much further he wouldn't be able to stop and would need to feel her under him. As she was about to ignore his warning her stomach spoke for her, erupting with a long growl of its own.

Alex stopped and looked at her. "What was that? Speak up, I didn't quite catch that?" He laughed, and she went red.

"Yes, okay, hilarious. I'm starving! So before you feast on me, you might want to let me feast on some breakfast."

"Your wish is my command M'Lady." He smirked.

"You're going to cook for me in my own house?" She laughed.

"Why the hell not!" He winked. He kissed her on the tip of her nose and moved to get up out of bed.

Mel stretched out across the side of the bed that Alex was departing. He looked over his shoulder at her as he stood. Her eyes roamed over all of him before settling on his naked backside. "Like what you see?" He grinned over his shoulder. She frowned at him and dropped her face into the bed, groaning. "Dear God yes!" she smirked raising an eyebrow at him.

"Stop it!" He reprimanded. "No making come to bed eyes at the chef, Jellybean. Play fair." He grinned. Mel laughed and rolled her eyes while Alex bent to put his feet into his lounge pants and drew them up his legs. He shot her a seductive look over his shoulder as he pulled them over his backside, finally blocking it from her view. She groaned, "It still has an affect on me even when it's covered you know." Alex laughed as he strutted towards the bedroom door.

"Just how I like it Jellybean, I always want to have an affect on you." He said with a wink and walked out. *Always?* His critic started. *Talking about always now are we?* Alex ran his hand through his hair and snorted while shaking his head, he was going to have to kick his critic's ass at some point; this was getting ridiculous!

~ ~ ~

Mel's phone ran as she lay sprawled out on her bed, she glanced at the display and saw Jonny's face on her phone's display. She pressed answer and put the phone to her ear. "Hey butthead, what's up?" She smiled.

"Baby I have a BIG problem!" came Jonny's voice down the line.

Mel laughed. "I've told you before, whip it out and prove it or you're just telling lies!"

Jonny groaned. "No, Mel, seriously, Nate and the guys are doing that gig for me tonight, and my sound desk just fucked up."

"You have a spare." Mel said, she had listened to Jonny talk about the volunteer work that he did with a music and media group to know that he had recently bought more than one sound desk.

"Yes, but guess where that is?" Jonny sighed.

"Are you asking me for a lift home to collect your sound desk and then to bring you and it back up to Belfast again Mr Tyler." Mel asked.

"Please, Mel?" Jonny pleaded.

She let out an exasperated sound. "Fine, if I collect you at two is that enough time? You were setting up at six right?"

Jonny agreed.

"Okay." Mel confirmed.

"You're still coming tonight aren't you?" He asked.

"Wouldn't miss it! Nate would kill me if I did!" She laughed. "Dylan and Jacob going too?" She asked.

"I think so Baby. So you'll be here at about two o'clock?" Jonny checked.

Mel sighed, she was going to have to cut her time with Alex short. "Yeah sweetie, I'll see you then!"

"Bye!" Jonny said, and Mel hung up the call. She groaned again, rolling her eyes, before wriggling out of the bed, grabbing her robe, and heading to the kitchen.

~ ~ ~

The smell of coffee and bacon filled her nostrils as she settled herself against the door frame, admiring Alex's body flex and twist as he moved around the kitchen preparing bacon and warm croissants with tea and coffee for breakfast. "You're ogling again Mel!" He said smirking and lifting an eyebrow when she snapped out of her daydream and looked at him.

She grinned back. "Stop saying it like you don't love my eyes on you!"

Alex stalked towards her, pushing his body up against hers, pinning her against the doorframe gently with his form. "Oh, I love your eyes on me Jellybean. I love your lips on me too, every last inch of me." Mel clenched her thighs together in response to the effect that Alex had on her body. He tugged on the tie of the robe, flicking it open, and cupping her exposed breast, kneading it as his lips went to her cheek, and kissed down her to her neck. His other hand stroked her face. Mel moaned, one hand going to the arm of the hand he had on her breast, the other to his waist, pulling him harder against her.

He lifted his lips from her neck and crushed his lips against hers, moaning into her mouth, the need to have her building, he wanted to be inside her, and sooner rather than later. Her hand went from his ass, stroking over his hip, and found its way to his cock, a growl erupted from him when she touched his hard cock through his thin jersey pants. He ground his dick against her hand and a pulsing shriek sounded, snapping them both out of their embrace.

"SHIT! The bacon!" Alex cursed, moving back to the cooker to rescue the bacon from under the grill. Mel winced and put her fingers in her ears, looking around for the smoke detector. Alex set the grill pan on the stovetop, and grabbed a brush from nearby, using the end of the handle to press the large reset button in the middle of the alarm. He moved across the kitchen to let some of the smoke out.

Mel fastened the robe around herself and started to laugh. "Have you burned my breakfast because you're too damn insatiable?" She accused.

Alex scowled at her with a smirk. "It's just the fat in the bottom of the pan burning, the bacon is fine, cheeky!" He pulled her against him again, his lips brushing over hers briefly before he added, "And if I'm insatiable, that would be all your fault!" and pressed his mouth on hers again. Mel giggled in between nibbling kisses against his mouth.

"Oh sure, all my fault." She breathed.

"Mmmm..." Alex agreed. "Definitely..." punctuating each word with a kiss towards Mel's neck. A second alarm started to go off, and Alex pulled away from Mel with a sigh, turning off the oven and lifting out hot croissants. Mel laughed and moved around the breakfast counter away from Alex. She settled into one of the stools and looked at him. "I'd like my breakfast now please, slave, I'm starved!" She cooed in a fake posh accent.

Alex looked over is shoulder with a raised eyebrow. "Oh, yes M'Lady." He said as he gathered bacon and fresh baked goods onto a plate, and set it in front of Mel. He walked back and lifted the pot of tea that was waiting, pouring it out into a cup that he had sat at the place setting he had laid out. "Anything else M'Lady?" he said as he bowed.

"No thank you servant that will be all." She said smirking.

"You'll pay for this later." Alex growled and straightened from his bow.

"I'm counting on it." Mel with a wolfish grin.

Alex rounded the counter from Mel, and lifted his own breakfast plate and cafetiere, and returned to sit beside her. "So what have you planned today? I know you have your friend's concert tonight right?" Alex asked before taking a bite out his croissant.

"It's just a small gig, not really a concert, and funny you should mention that." She cleared her throat and took a sip from her tea. "Jonny called when you went to the kitchen, his sound desk died, and he needs me to take him home and bring him and the spare desk to the gig." She watched as Alex's jaw twitched, and his mouth formed a grim line.

"What time do you need to go?"

Mel's brow furrowed as if she was suspicious about something as she looked at Alex's reaction. "I need to get him at about two, so I guess about half one, gives me time to get over to his house, collect him, wait for him while he fucks about looking for his keys. That kind of thing."

Alex swallowed and breathed deeply.

Mel touched his arm. "Are you okay?"

Alex stared at her hand. "Yes." He answered gruffly.

Her eyes widened, and a notion formed in her mind. *He's jealous!* She thought, and she felt her heart skip at the thought that he cared enough about her to be jealous. *Oh, don't be so ridiculous Mel, maybe you just spoiled his plans for an afternoon of fucking!* She chided herself. She lifted her hand from his arm, and the pair continued to have their breakfast in awkward silence.

Mel lifted her empty plate and cup and put them into the dishwasher, turned and moved to Alex's side to move his plate and cup to the dishwasher. He grabbed her wrist when she did, and pulled her against him, crushing his mouth to hers, bruising her lips with his. She grabbed his hair, pulling herself tight against him, her tongue duelling with his between their two mouths. Alex reached down and scooped her up in his arms, and carried her upstairs.

CHAPTER 13

Alex pushed the door of the bathroom open with his foot and set Mel back on her feet so he could turn on the shower. He pulled the belt around her waist and pushed the robe back off her shoulders, letting it pool on the floor at her feet. His lips were on her again, his mouth in a fiercely passionate kiss against hers, he grabbed a hold of her wrists and he pushed them behind her back, holding them there. He kissed her long and hard, needing to set her on fire, needing her to yield to him. When she moaned against his mouth, he pulls his lips from hers. "Shower. Now." He commanded, pulling down his leisure pants and kicking them into a corner. Mel blinked at him, her eyes wide with desire.

"You're not fucking me in the shower out of jealousy!" She said softly.

"You think I'm jealous?" He challenged.

Mel smiled. "I *know* you're jealous!"

Alex took her hand and pulled her to the glass door of the shower. "Jellybean, I'm more than jealous. Get. In. That. Shower." He growled.

Mel leaned forward and moved her mouth to his, he bent to receive her kiss and at the last minute Mel turned her mouth to the side of his face instead of his lips. "Ask nicely then." She breathed against his ear.

Alex took advantage of her position, his lips meeting with her neck, and she wrapped her arms around him and he nibbled her there. He kissed her shoulder and bit it. When she moaned he sucked and bit harder on that point on her shoulder, lifting her off her feet. Mel lifted her legs, wrapping them around Alex's hips, holding on to him as he marked her shoulder. He stepped into the shower with her clinging to him, his lips returning to hers. He held her tight against him, lifting her up slightly, his cock springing free from being trapped between them, and he lined himself up with her wet pussy. He loosened his grip, letting her slide slowly down just enough for her wet warm tightness to be conquered by his hardness. Mel moaned out as she felt Alex fill her, her head falling back as he started to bounce her on his dick. Alex thrust up hard with every bounce, making sure Mel felt every last inch of him. She held on tight to his shoulders, pressed tight against him, digging her nails into his back as he fucked her hard. The warm water splashed off their bodies as Alex pounded hard into her, focusing all his possessiveness and jealousy into making her his, claiming her, reminding her of what she was to him. *She can't know what she is to you, you haven't told her you dumbass!* His inner critic reminded him. Alex sighed out a groan. "Look at me!" he instructed.

Mel's head lifted up and she opened her eyes, looking deep into the chocolate brown pools of desire that were blazing into her.

"You. Are. Mine." He breathed, punctuating each word with a thrust. "Mine Jellybean." He moaned, and she sighed at his words.

She held his gaze as he thrust into her again. "Oh god!" She moaned. "Yes, yours."

He felt her body start to tighten and he knew that her orgasm was coming. She tried to grind her hips against him, seeking the last bit of friction to send her over. Alex bit into the mark he had left on her shoulder, and she cried out as her climax flooded her senses. "Oh God!" She called out. "Mmmm ALEX!" He kept thrusting encouraging every last shiver of pleasure out of her body. He moved slightly, allowing him to let Mel's back make contact with the tiles of the shower wall. She clenched everything when she felt the cold on her heated skin, and Alex thrust into her harder, using the contact with the wall to stop her from moving too far from him, allowing him to drive deeper inside her than he had been. The extra depth, and the sensory overload from the cold tiles and her recent orgasm had Mel ready to come again.

Alex felt his own climax building, he growled, staring at Mel's closed eyes. "Open." He barked as he thrust back into her roughly. Her eyes jolted open and looked deep into his. "You. Are. Mine." He rumbled at her again, every word a thrust. "Say it!"

Mel's mouth fell open but her orgasm was too close and the words wouldn't come.

"Say. It." Alex snarled, fighting back his own climax for just a few more precious seconds.

"I'm yours Alex!" She cried out as her second orgasm washed over her body like a tsunami. "FUCK! I'm always going to be yours!" The weight of her words washed over him, and he drove his cock deep inside her one last time as he filled her pussy deeply, erupting inside her with his own climax.

Alex held Mel against him, as they both trembled in a post orgasmic haze. He moved back, drawing them back under the warm water, waiting until Mel's legs were capable of holding her up again. She nuzzled against his neck. "Can you stand Jellybean?" He said softly against her cheek. Mel let go of her vice like hold around Alex's hips, he lifted her up a little, allowing his semi erect cock to slide free from her pussy. She hissed at the loss of him and let her legs slide down until her feet touched the bottom of the shower. Alex held her close in case she wobbled. She tested her legs, slowly taking her full weight on them. She let Alex keep his close hold of her, and drank in the sensation of having been thoroughly marked by him, and yet, be standing held tenderly in his arms.

They finished their shower by taking it in turns to wash each other in silence. Alex paused over the mark he had left on her shoulder, he winced inwardly, he hadn't meant to be so aggressive with her, but he couldn't suppress the need to claim her. *Smooth moves for the caveman. What are you going to do next time she mentions her mates, club her on the head and drag her back to your cave?* The critic jeered. Alex closed his eyes, shutting out that voice inside that was always berating him. He kissed her shoulder softly and continued to run his soapy hands over her body.

Alex got out first, wrapping himself in a towel while Mel finished rinsing the shampoo from her long brown locks. When she shut off the water and stepped out, Alex wrapped her in a towel tightly and kissed the end of her nose. Mel walked out of the bathroom, and headed for her bedroom, Alex followed quietly behind her. She looked at the clock on her bedside table. His eyes followed hers, and he pulled her in against him, nuzzling into her neck. "You still have time." He whispered softly against her bare shoulder.

"For what?" She grinned at him.

Alex laughed. "Not that Jellybean! You'll kill me!" He told her, even though his cock was trying to encourage him to follow Mel's suggestion. Mel looked at him in exasperation and swotted at his backside as she walked away from him to her closet.

"I don't think you'll die from it Mister!" She said with mock offence.

He smirked and shook his head. "It'd make a damn fine way to go, let me tell you!"

She sighed and rolled her eyes at him. He walked over to her at her closet and draped himself around her back, his arms hanging round her waist. "Sorry, if I was a bit of an ass in the shower." He murmured and kissed her neck.

She elbowed him playfully in the ribs. "I don't remember complaining. In fact, I think I damn well encouraged you!" She smiled, turning in his arms to face him.

"Okay." He sighed. "I know that you have this gig with your friends tonight, but I don't want you arranging anything for next weekend okay?" He said, putting his forehead against hers.

Mel looked at him. "What are you scheming Mr Matthews?"

Alex looked at her with pretend insult at her suggestion. "Moi? Scheming? Oh Jellybean, don't you trust me?"

"Ohhh!" She exclaimed. "Playing the trust card with me now huh? It's a good job I like you so much or you'd be out that door!" She said, pointing at the doorway she was threatening to expel him through.

He stood staring at her with a goofy grin on his face. Her words had warmed his soul, and he couldn't hide it. "What's that look for?" She laughed.

He lifted her up in his arms, squeezing her tight as she shrieked in surprise flinging her arms around his neck to hold on tight. "You *like* me?" He asked.

"Mmmm." She grinned. "Very much."

His lips were on hers in a split second. Brushing against her mouth with his own, tenderly and unhurried, as he set her back down on her own feet again. He pulled his lips from hers and she sighed. "I like you too." He said softly and licked his lips.

Mel grinned and kissed his cheek. "So, what are you planning next weekend?" She smirked.

Alex laughed, shaking his head, and moving back to sit on her bed so she could get ready to go to Jonny's rescue. "Ohh no, Miss Anderson, a surprise, is a surprise!" He said and winked.

Mel huffed in protest as dramatically as she could and turned on her heel back to the open closet. Alex continued to laugh behind her. "You're heading to Italy this week aren't you?" She asked as she looked through the clothing hanging in front of her.

"Yeah, Tuscany for the Eco-Architecture conference."

Mel looked over at him. "You mean how buildings are meant to blend into their natural surroundings?"

Alex raised an eyebrow at her. "Very good Miss Anderson, yes, that's the basics of it, although there's a lot more to it than just that." He grinned. She shrugged and turned back to the clothes. "Why do you ask?" he queried.

Mel lifted out a top and a pair of jeans from her wardrobe. "Just thinking of it in terms of my ability to see you this week."

He grinned more. "Are you saying you'll miss me?"

She stopped what she was doing, and looked at him. "Fishing Mr Matthews?" She sighed. "Isn't 'I like you' enough of a compliment for one day?" She smirked.

Alex just raised an eyebrow.

"Perhaps you would like, my, what a big dick you have? Or you give me the best orgasms of my life? No?" She grinned at him.

Alex reached for Mel's wrist and in an instant, pulled her across his knee, pulling the towel up, baring her ass in the process. Mel squealed and tried to wriggle free from his grasp. He held his hand firmly on her shoulders, keeping her in place. His hand cracked down on her backside and she jumped with a gasp. "Such cheek Miss Anderson!" He laughed. He swatted her again. "Admit you'll miss me." He said, pausing for her answer, when none came he spanked her buttocks again.

"No!" Mel said, sounding petulant, she wriggled more, feeling his cock harden at her side.

Again his hand connected with her backside. "Say it." He growled.

She glanced over her shoulder and with a cheeky defiance reinforced her previous answer.

"I said, no." She smirked. Alex loved her defiance. He loved that she challenged him, that she didn't just take everything he was willing to give her without playing her own part in how things happened. He held her tight and raised his hand over her rear end again. He slapped each cheek of her ass three times, in quick succession. Instead of crying out, Mel tilted her hips in need and gasped before letting out a moan.

He couldn't resist. He rubbed his hand soothingly over her heated backside and allowed his middle finger to skim down the crevice of her cheeks to her heated sex. He groaned when he found her wet and ready for him. He pressed his finger into her, feeling her pussy hug him greedily. She moaned again, grinding herself against him. "Tell me what I want to hear, and I'll give you what you need Jellybean." He teased. She shook her head and bit her bottom lip. Alex pulled his finger from her warmth and spanked her ass again, striking both cheeks one after the other. Alex's hand roamed over her skin and found its way back to her pussy, this time sliding two fingers inside her, fucking her, making her want more.

"Oh please!" She sighed.

Alex removed his fingers from her pussy and slid her slick juices over her asshole. He pushed his thumb against the ring of muscle and grinned as she relaxed and he entered her. He twisted his wrist, turning his thumb in her ass as he fucked her ever so slowly with it. She groaned at his intrusion, and tried to lift her hips to get what she wanted. "Say it Mel!" He warned her again.

"Mmmm." Was her only reply.

Alex stilled his hand, a frustrated hiss passed Mel's lips when he did. He lifted the hand that had been previously holding her across his lap, and he smacked her ass again.

"Melody." He growled in warning.

He moved his hand once, pressing his thumb deep in her ass, and grazing her clit with his fingertip as he did. A long groan arose from Mel's throat. "Ohhh God, okay okay! I'll miss you!" She moaned. A giant grin broke out across Alex's face. He pulled his thumb out of her and smacked he backside again.

"See was that really so difficult?" He asked as he helped her up from his lap. Mel stared at him with a thunderous expression.

"You're stopping?"

He grinned and raised an eyebrow, wiping his thumb on the towel that was around him.

"Oh no!" Mel warned, pushing him back on the bed. "You don't get to tease me like that, and not finish the job you started buster!" She dropped the towel she had around her, and crushed her mouth against his, pushing until he was lying flat on his back with her straddling him. When her tongue penetrated his mouth, his hands immediately went to her hips, grabbing her roughly, pulling her against him. She reached between them and flicked the towel away from his body, his cock springing up to greet her. She let her fingers glide over the soft underside of his erection. He moaned into her mouth, and she lifted her lips from his.

"Okay, you make a convincing argument for finishing what I started." He smirked, his eyes sienna pools of desire.

She smirked back at him, lifted his cock, and once lined up between her labia, sank herself down on it to the hilt. Alex's eyes rolled back in his head, and a long growl rumbled in his chest at the sensation of filling her tight pussy so completely.

Mel lifted herself so she was sitting up astride Alex, instead of leaning over him. She put her hands out of his broad chest to steady herself, she ground her hips against him in a circle before starting to move up and down his shaft in a slow and sensual way. His fingers dug into her hips. "Jesus Jellybean." He hissed at her. He needed more, he wanted more, but he needed it to be on his terms. He lifted his hips against her as she moved on a down stroke, and pulled her hands from his chest, rolling to the side so she was beneath him. He drew her hands over her head, holding her wrists there. He began to thrust deep and fast into her, pushing her frantically to orgasm. She moaned out, writhing beneath him, needing to touch him and needing to feel the perspiration on his skin. He caressed her skin with his lips, on her neck, over her shoulder, against her mouth. Mel's pussy began to clench and pulse around Alex's hard cock. He kissed the tip of her nose. "Come for me Jellybean." He told her and thrust hard and deep inside her. She screamed out as the world around her fell away and she was left floating on a wave of pleasure. As her body gripped him, he growled, his own orgasm ripping through him as he pumped deep into her pussy.

He left go of her hands, and she pulled him into an embrace both of them lying together, panting in the aftermath of another passionate clinch. Alex pushed himself up on his elbows, and moved his body, withdrawing his cock from Mel, and she shivered as he did. He rolled to beside her and smiled. "You okay?" He asked.

She smiled weakly and nodded. "Uh huh." Was all she could manage at that moment. He glanced over at her alarm clock checking what time it was.

"It's one o'clock." He said, running a finger down her upper arm.

"Dammit." She sighed, groaning as she moved to get off the bed. She moved to her chest of drawers and pulled on panties and found a matching bra to go with them.

Alex lay on the bed watching her, propped up on his elbows to see what Mel was doing. She pulled on the jeans that she had picked out earlier, heaving them up her legs, and up over her backside. She looked over to where he was relaxing on her bed. "Alex! Get dressed!" she told him.

Alex sighed as he moved off the bed. "Ohh, she's had her way with me, and now she's kicking me out... I feel so used." He grumbled. Mel stopped dead and looked at him, her arms in her top, paused in the middle of putting it on. She shot him a look that could kill and he burst out laughing. "Jellybean, you should know by now, you can use me anytime!" He said and winked at her before getting up and finding his clothes.

Mel watched his body move and flex as he put on his clothes. She couldn't help but let her eyes roam over his body, a clenching happening in her pussy at the same time as a fluttering in her chest.

"I can feel your eyes Mel!" He laughed. She lifted the cushion from the chair beside her closet and threw it across the room, hitting him on the back. Alex laughed. "Tsk tsk Miss Anderson. I'll have to correct your manners later!" He threatened with a raised eyebrow. Mel grinned and grabbed her trainers before sitting on the bed to put them on.

"So, this gig tonight, it is a late thing?" Alex asked trying to sound casual.

Mel rolled her eyes. "Not too late, but since I'm now helping Jonny bring stuff there, I might have to drag it back away again after." His jaw tightened into that tell-tale tight line again.

"Be careful out that late at night on the roads." He advised.

Mel smiled. "I will."

Alex finished dressing and stood by the door as Mel finished tying her shoe laces. It wasn't long before they were both in her car. She dropped Alex off at his sister's so that he could collect his car, promising to keep next weekend plan free, and then she headed over to collect Jonny.

CHAPTER 14

It was just after two when Jonny slammed his front door and headed for Mel's car parked at the end of his street. He opened the passenger door and bounced into the seat beside Mel. "Hey sweetie." She greeted him.

"Hey baby. Thank you so more for this!" He grinned back, putting on his seat belt. He lifted his phone out of his pocket and reached for the Aux cable attached to her car stereo.

Mel glanced over at him. "You owe me Jonny!"

"Did you miss out on an afternoon of sex?" He smirked.

"Nope! Had plenty before I came to get you!" Mel grinned waggling her eyebrows up and down.

"Should have known!" He laughed. Mel laughed with him and pulled out kerb, setting off on their two-hour round trip to Jonny's home town.

Jonny tapped on his phone, opening Spotify as he always did in Mel's car. "What are we listening to today?" She asked.

"You'll see." He grinned back.

The sounds of 'Gimme Shelter' by The Rolling Stones played out through her car stereo and she started to laugh. "Oh, bloody hell Jonny, good choice!" She giggled, before putting on her sunglasses and settling into the long drive to collect the other sound desk. The passenger side window went down, and a lighter and packet of cigarettes came out of Jonny's pocket. He made himself comfortable in the seat, resting one foot on the knee of his other leg, and took a long drag of his freshly lit cigarette.

"So what's new in the world of Mr Tyler?" Mel asked.

Jonny shook his head. "Just the usual.... Housemates are being dicks again."

She asked what had happened and Jonny told her what was becoming a regular story about the housemates that were a bit too fond of partying, without going to the effort of tidying up the mess that a party involved. It was the one part of student life that Mel was glad she had managed to avoid. When Mel's dad had died when she was 14, her mum had invested a large amount from his life insurance in a trust for her. When she turned 21 that amount had been enough along with the earnings that she had been saving since 17 to put an 80% deposit on a house, leaving her with a tiny mortgage that she was able to pay even working part time as a student. She had a spare room, and had offered it to Jonny before, but he had always refused. "Well, you know I have a spare room if you need it sweetie." She reminded him.

He grinned at her. "I know baby, I'll get it sorted; it'll be okay." She rolled her eyes at her stubborn friend.

"So what time is this gig tonight?" She asked. Jonny flicked the last of his cigarette out the window of her car. "OI!" She shouted at him. He laughed and gave her a cheeky grin.

"No one saw!"

"I don't care! Litterbug!" She scolded.

Jonny just grinned back at her. "Nate and guys start at 9, but we have to be in and sound check by 7."

"Do you think that he'll get a contract eventually?" She asked. Jonny thought about it for a moment and glanced over to catch the look on his face. "You're scheming." She said recognising his look. "You know someone I take it?" She smiled, knowing that Jonny was plotting a way to help his friend out.

"No directly." He paused. "But I might know some people who know some people." He grinned.

Mel laughed. "Yeah, okay Huggy Bear."

Jonny looked at her pretending to be insulted, and extended his middle finger in her direction, causing even more laughter to erupt from her.

~ ~ ~

Alex took a sip of the coffee his brother in law had handed him. "God, this house is never this quiet!" Alex smirked.

Ben grinned. "Tell me about it mate. It's heaven on a Saturday. My mum's taking the kids tonight so Em and I get an evening to ourselves. I can't fucking wait." He shared.

Alex stopped mid-sip, the cup almost at his mouth. "Ben, you better not be talking about sex with my sister!"

Ben burst out laughing. "Alex, I'm happy to have a night of uninterrupted sleep these days!" Alex eyed his brother suspiciously, only causing more laughter to erupt from Ben.

The two men sat on the sofa, and drank their coffee making small talk about the rugby that was on later in the afternoon. "Emily tells me there's a new woman in your life?" Ben started. "I hope she's not like that Naomi, Jesus she had me worried mate, she's a bunny boiler that one!"

Alex smirked. "Nah, not so much a bunny boiler, she just hasn't the ability to keep her mouth shut."

Ben grinned. "Yeah, Em mentioned something about that too."

Alex felt his face turn red and rubbed his hand over it. "Is there nothing my sister can keep secret?"

Ben shrugged. "She loves you, she worries about you as her baby brother, and she confides in her husband. Besides, it's nothing you haven't mentioned yourself." Ben smirked.

Alex shook his head. "Yeah, but she doesn't know that! That was man to man!"

Ben laughed. "So am I going to hear your version of what's happening with you and this new girl?" He asked.

Alex took one last sip of his coffee, and thought about how he was going to explain what was happening between Mel and him. "I'm not sure I know how to explain it." Alex began. "I was on a dating site..." Ben raised an eyebrow in silent questions. "No." Alex answered before his brother-in-law got to ask anything more. "I don't know what I was doing on a dating site either. It's not like a date anymore." He explained. "But I did it, and there she was. We met up, liked the look of one another, and started to see each other."

"Seeing?" Ben laughed. "I assume you mean shagging?"

Alex rolled his eyes. "Yes! You know that's what I meant!" He sighed. "But lately I have been thinking of her..." His voice trailed off, unwilling to say the actual words.

"You like her." Ben stated. "A lot from the looks of it."

Alex nodded.

"But you're still worried about a repeat of the whole Natalie thing yeah?" His friend asked.

"Yeah." Alex confirmed.

Ben shrugged. "Alex, I love you like a brother, but no matter what Natalie did, is she really worth leaving your balls in a vice for?"

Alex looked confused. "A vice?" he asked.

Ben started to explain. "Natalie was a manipulative, nasty, backstabbing bitch, I understand the affect that can have on a man. But the longer you're not out there, the longer you're leaving your nads hanging where she can crush 'em and still control you." He finished.

Alex shook his head with a smile. "Bro, you have a seriously fucked up way of describing things!" Ben laughed, and some of what he'd said started to sink in with Alex. "Thing is Ben, what if I don't want her to win anymore, but fear has me stuck to doing what I've always done?"

Ben put his hand on his brother-in-law's shoulder. "Do what you've always done, and you'll get what you've always got." He advised. "Now... Beer and rugby?" He asked.

Alex nodded his head. "Yeah mate, thanks."

~ ~ ~

Mel closed the truck of her car and she and Jonny got back in. "Sorry, that took so long." Jonny apologised.

Mel laughed. "Wouldn't be like you to be on time Jonny!"

"Cheers dipshit." He smirked.

"You're welcome asshat." She laughed as she started her car and pulled back into traffic.

"So are we going to talk about the elephant in the room?" Jonny asked her after a few miles of driving. Mel looked at him like she had no idea what he was talking about. "Alex?" He prompted.

"Oh!" Mel said finally understanding where the conversation was heading. "What about him?" She asked.

Jonny went for his cigarettes again, putting down the car window before lighting up and taking a long drag. "Are you still 'just friends' with him?" He asked making speech marks with his fingers at the appropriate phrase, his cigarette bobbing in his mouth as he spoke.

"I don't know." Mel answered honestly. "I'm not sure that I can stop myself from wanting more, even if it isn't meant to go any further."

Jonny nodded.

"I'm not sure what he thinks. Reading men hasn't been something I've even done well. You know that." She explained.

"Well, no matter what you end up doing, I got your back. And it's nice to see you genuinely happy. I know that me and the lads keep you contented and all that shit, but you're different with him around. It's nice to see, baby." Jonny smiled. "But if he hurts you and you spend even one tear on him, I'm going to have a lot of fun fucking with him." Jonny warned.

Mel smiled. "I know sweetie. Nate said pretty much the same thing!" she admitted.

"That's because we love you Mel. You're our girl, and God help anyone who fucks with you!" Jonny smiled at her fondly.

"I love you guys too." Mel smiled. "And you know I'll deal with any bitch I find trampling all over any of you."

Jonny reached for Mel's hand on the gear stick and gave it a squeeze. "That's friendship for you baby, we look after each other... Now what music would you like this time?" He smiled opening the Spotify app on his phone.

"80s." Mel grinned.

Jonny groaned. "Fine..."

~ ~ ~

Nate looked around the empty club as they set up their instruments, thinking about what was to come that evening. The band had come a long way since he started it 21 months ago. From the small time gigs that they had played in all the dive bars, to finally make it to the club in Belfast that had hosted Blur, Oasis, and The Strokes.

They had started as just Nate and his friend and fellow guitarist Ian Hughes, a now 21 year old muscular blonde with long hair, a long beard, green eyes and amazing abs. They would jam together in Nate's garage, writing lyrics, and practicing on Nate's bass and Ian's Fender. Then Cassidy Jenkins had joined them. She joined as their drummer, a striking 24 year old with long bright pink hair that hung in ringlets, and striking blue eyes with long thick eyelashes. She had tattooed sleeves on both arms and across her shoulders and back which she loved to show off in vest tops as she drummed. Cassidy had introduced her twin brother Cody to the group, and he had become the final member on a second guitar. His raven hair, and eyes which were almost as black as his hair really setting him apart from the others in the group. And yet, here they all stood, together, for the first gig in a long line of potential bigger and better gigs.

Jonny and Mel finally arrived in through the door at half five. "Where the fuck have you been?" Cassidy asked laughing and pointing at Nate. "He's been prowling about like the world was going to end!"

Mel laughed. "Hey Cass!" She said as she walked over and hugged Nate. "Have you really been that bad sweetie?" She grinned at him.

"NO!" Ian yelled from the side of the stage. "The bastard has been worse!"

Nate rolled his eyes and returned Mel's hug tight. "Thank you so much for rescuing this." He murmured next to her ear.

"Hey, I know Jonny can be a disaster at times, but you know he'll never let you down."

Jonny sighed from over their shoulders. "Guys, I'm in the fucking room." Nate pulled on Jonny's arm as he passed, tugging him into the hug with Mel. Cassidy ran over to the hugging trio and threw her arms around everyone.

"Ian! Cody! Group hug!" She called, jumping up and down, trying to wrap her arms round as many of the others as she could manage. The last two members of Remembering Tomorrow joined the hugging mass of friends laughing. From the middle of the pack, Mel called out. "Here's to the first of many amazing gigs! Wooo!" Everyone echoed her finishing cheer, and the bodies around her moved away, ready to get stuck in. They had a gig to prepare for, and it was going to be amazing.

CHAPTER 15

The gig for Nate's band had been a roaring success, and the manager of the bar had promised him more gigs in the not too distant future. On Sunday night, they all went out to celebrate, and on Monday morning, Mel was feeling just a little bit sorry for herself. The rest of the week passed slowly. Mel hated to admit it, but she was genuinely missing Alex, his occasional texts from Tuscany were not making up for the fact that he wasn't there with her.

Mel woke on Saturday morning excited. Alex was home and had asked her to keep this weekend free for him. She kept a look out at her window for 20 minutes before Alex was due to actually arrive. Finally, she watched as he drove into her driveway at noon, just as he had promised. She locked her front door and walked to the passenger side of his car. "Are you still not going to tell me where you're taking me?" She asked once in the car and fastening her seatbelt. Alex grinned over at her. "What kind of surprise would it be if I told you where we were going?" Mel rolled her eyes in reply. He just continued to smirk at her, opened Spotify on his iPhone and put his Range Rover into reverse and pulled out into the street.

It was a beautiful day, with a crystal clear blue sky above them. Alex had his car's air conditioning up and had a cooler and blanket in the back. "So how long is it going to take us to get there?" Mel asked him. He laughed at her and pulled his sunglasses down to the end of his nose so that he could look at her over the top of them. "Melody Anderson... It's a surprise you wicked woman. Cut it out!" He scolded and smirked at her as he pushed his glasses back in place, signalled, and pulled out onto the main road.

Mel folded her arms in a huff. She wasn't great with surprises. It wasn't that she didn't like someone doing something nice for her, it was just that she liked to know what was happening; she liked to be prepared. For the first few miles, she cast glares in Alex's direction as he drove along, receiving nothing but smirks in reply. They had covered about 3 miles when she fired off another dirty look at him, and he responded by sticking his tongue out at her and laughing. She sniggered at him in spite of herself, and when he grinned at her she couldn't help but return the grin to the cheeky boyish charm radiating from Alex. "I can't believe you just stuck your tongue out at me! You're such a big kid!" She said softly shaking her head. "Jellybean, you ain't seen nothing yet!" He grinned wickedly at her, raising his eyebrows. Mel burst out into a full laugh and looked out of the window.

It was 30 minutes before they arrived somewhere that Melody recognised. A puzzled expression grew across her face and Alex caught it when he glanced over at her. "What's up?" he asked her. She turned in her seat to look at him. "I was born in this town. I come out this way when I want to escape, there's a nice beach just round the coast from here, it's deserted most evenings, and it's nice to just stand on the shore." She said, looking over at him, watching to see if he gave anything away when she looked at him. He looked over at her catching her gaze for a moment. "I didn't know that." He said softly. "But I wasn't bringing you here, we're just passing through." He told her, his eyes focusing back on the road. "Oh... Hmmm..." Mel said, the gears turning in her head as she put together where it was that they were going, thinking of all the places that lay further out than the town she was born in.

Alex followed the one-way system around the town, and headed out the other side, along the coast road that Melody had spoken about. "You'll have to tell me where this beach of yours is when we pass it." He smiled. Mel smiled back. "It's about 5 or 10 minutes further along, at a little place called Cunningburn." She smiled, remembering the last time she had been on that beach just the week before. "Is that where you went when you sent me that picture message last week from the beach?" Alex asked her. Mel shifted in the seat, sinking into it and relaxing. "Yip, that's the one." She sighed contently. "Alex?" she asked.

"Yeah?" he replied.

"There're only two places I can think of out this road, and you just passed one of them." She stated, glancing at him. He just smiled at her and shrugged. "Plenty of nice places along this peninsula you know." He told her. Mel rolled her eyes again and sat in silence looking out at the sun shining off the waves out on the water in the lough. It was a stunning sight. Sailboats could be seen skimming over the water, children and dogs played in the water and on the beaches that they passed along the way. "God, it's just stunning out here." She mused. "Not as stunning as you." Alex replied gently. Mel blushed and bit her bottom lip, not sure how to reply to his compliment.

An hour and 20 minutes after leaving Mel's house, Alex drove into the last town along the peninsula. There was nowhere else to go after this, unless he intended to just drive back up the other side of the coastline. Mel frowned again. Alex caught her with just a glance as he manoeuvred the streets of the small coastal town. "What's that look for Jellybean?" He asked her. "I think I know where you're going now!" She told him, looking smug as she folded her arms across her. "To the ferry?" He asked her teasingly. She glared at him again. "You won't have driven all the way down here just to use the ferry to get to the side of the lough we started on!" She was huffing with him again, and he laughed. "Just wait and see you infuriating woman!" He smiled. They pulled along the sea front and Mel was distracted by how gorgeous the scenery was. The sun shimmering on the water, the lush dark green of the woodland on the other side of the narrow strip of water, the children playing off the end of the jetty, swimming in the cool blue sea. Alex pulled into a space outside the hotel on the sea front and turned off the engine. Mel turned to look at him. The engine being silenced had distracted her from the view. "Are we here?" She asked, looking at the hotel. Alex grinned at her when he followed where her eyes were looking. "No Jellybean, not a hotel. But I like how your mind works." He laughed and winked at her. "Let's go." He commanded and got out of the car. Mel opened the door and climbed out just as Alex arrived at her side of the car. He took her by the hand, kissed her knuckles, and pulled her back to the pavement, locking his car as they walked away.

They walked up a side street, away from the sea front and turned a corner. Mel knew instantly where she was, it was the very place that she had almost accused him of moments before. "The aquarium?" She grinned. Alex only nodded and grinned when Mel said, "I knew it!" Hand in hand they walked through the gates, and into the building that housed the aquarium. "We have 7 seals in the sanctuary at the minute if you're interested in having

a look. They're all pups, mostly less than 3 months old."
The receptionist told them as Alex paid the admission for
them both. She handed Mel a guide to the exhibits, and
handed a receipt to Alex. "Enjoy your visit. The next
demonstration is in 50 minutes." She smiled at them.
"Thank you." Mel smiled sincerely.

They entered the first hall, a huge demonstration tank
filled the centre of the room, and lots of smaller tanks
with observation portholes lined the walls. Alex watched
as Mel's face lit up, and she wandered slowly from tank to
tank. "Have you ever been here before?" She turned to
ask him while she was looking at a tank full of squat
lobsters. Alex shook his head, "Not since I was a child,
and I don't remember much of it. It was a school trip."
Mel smiled and led him over to the demonstration tank
in the middle of the room. She pointed out all the
varieties of fish and other sea life that they had in the
tank and explained to Alex how in 50 minutes they would
come back here, because the staff of the aquarium put on
a kind of show and tell where they let visitors touch, and
hold the creatures in the tank. She was so animated about
the types of fish, and how to handle the starfish and sea
urchins. A warmth started in Alex's chest, radiating out to
every last inch of him, reaching his fingertips and toes.
The more he listened to Mel and looked at her, the more
he felt it. It consumed him, filled him completely. He had
never known anyone like her in his life, and at that

moment he knew that he never would again. She pulled him round the next corner in the exhibition, passing a dark little nook. He couldn't resist it, he pulled her back into it, pulling her tight against him and kissed her slowly, tenderly, and completely. Their lips parted and she looked deep into his eyes. "What was that for?" She asked. Alex blushed and shrugged his shoulders. "I just felt like it." She smiled at him tenderly and brushed her lips against his gently before taking his hand again. "Come on." She beckoned, pulling him back towards the displays.

They toured around the tanks, Mel smiling when she heard kids exclaiming in delight about the fish in the tanks. Alex smiled just watching Melody, how she became enraptured by the exhibits, how much she knew about the tanks and what was in them, how she smiled at children and parents alike. *She's under your skin now!* His inner voice chided. He wasn't sure how he would deal with that in the long term. The thought terrified him to think beyond this moment. But at this moment she was amazing, she was indeed under his skin, and he never wanted her to not be there. He was distracted by his thoughts again as she took his hand and led him out to the seal sanctuary. He stood in awe looking at the adorable little puppy dog faces looking out of individual pens, and at all the orphaned seal pups which had been given names like Birch, Fern and Larch. Mel was caught up looking at their "adorable little faces", and Alex was caught up looking at her.

True to her word, when 50 minutes had passed, she led the way back through all the displays to the beginning where the demonstration tank was. She told Alex to roll up his sleeves so that he could touch the fish, and hold a starfish. The member of staff came out and talked to the crowd about the sea life in the lough, how the fresh salt water from the lough was pumped around the aquarium, and talked about all the creatures that they had in the tank in front of them. Melody watched, listened, and smiled when a horn backed ray appeared from the water at her hand and poked its nose against her. She grinned and turned to Alex as she ran her fingers over the fish. "See, they love the attention." She told him. He put his own hand over the water, and just as Mel had said, the same ray nudged at his hand too. They enjoyed the presentation, and touched and held all the creatures that were offered, including the small bottom feeding sharks that were in the tank, and seemed just as keen on a petting as the rays. When the presentation was over, and the other visitors had started to walk away, Mel asked the demonstrator about the closure of the aquarium that had been threatened by the local council. Alex just stood and watched her in awe, discussing what she knew with the staff member, asking if they were in fact closing, listening to him explain the current financial promised from local government. She thanked the staff member, and wished him luck, then turned to Alex. "What?" she smiled, catching the look on his face as he watched her. He beamed and shook his head, giving her another soft kiss on her lips. "You're amazing." He smiled and took her hand pulling her towards the area they could wash their hands in after contact with the fish before leading her into the gift shop.

They walked out of the gates at the front of the aquarium with a cuddly seal, a cuddly ray, and a key ring. Mel cuddled the seal, and Alex had the ray. She paused looking at him. "Thank you." She smiled gazing at him. He leaned over and kissed her briefly, brushing his lips on hers, and as he went to pull back, she grabbed him by the front of his shirt and pulled him back, kissing him for that little bit longer. He finished their kiss with a little peck on the tip of her nose and a contented look settled across her face. He took a step back and held up the cuddly ray, starting to make it swim through the air. "Look Mel, I'm swimmin'!" he grinned, dipping and raising the ray as it "swam" around in the air in front of her. She burst out laughing and nudged him in the arm. "You are such a kid. Can't take you anywhere!" She scolded trying not to keep laughing. "Pffft!" He replied. "You're just jealous because Larry's a great air swimmer!" Mel shook her head laughing, linked her arm with Alex's and they started to walk back to the sea front.

They walked past the car, and over to the sea wall, settling themselves on a bench that faced out over the water. Alex was still swimming Larry through the air and bumped him softly into the tip of Mel's nose. She laughed at him and snatched the toy out of his hand, hiding it behind her back. Alex gasp and dived his arm around her, trying to get to the toy behind her back. Their faces were just inches apart, and his rescue mission for Larry was swiftly forgotten as he dipped his lips towards hers and used the arm he had around her to pull her tight against him instead. His tongue dipped between her lips and teased with her own. Before she knew what he was up to he suddenly yanked Larry out of her unsuspecting hand and pulled back waving the toy in front of her. "Hahaha! I got him!" He laughed, clutching the toy to his chest and stroking it. "There, there Larry, I've got you, she'll not hurt you again!" Shooting a crazed look in Melody's direction. A hearty laughter erupted from Mel's throat as she watched what he was doing. "You're crazy!" she giggled. "I'm not sure if I'm safe with you!" Alex smirked at her and wiggled his eyebrows at her. "Come on!" He said getting up. "Let's find somewhere to get something to eat. Larry says he's starving." He smirked, holding his hand out to her. She accepted it and they strolled back to the car.

CHAPTER 16

45 minutes later Alex pulled up in the deserted picnic area attached to the beach where Mel liked to go to escape. She got out of the car, crossed the grass, and walked out the concrete slipway onto the pebbled beach beyond. Alex watched her for a moment, before getting out, locking the Range Rover, and following Mel out across the pebbles. She had stopped on the water's edge, looking out over the rippling waves, watching a few people on sailboats as they sailed up and down the lough. She closed her eyes and took an extra deep breath, savouring the fresh smell of the salt water. "I love it here." She said, knowing Alex was right behind her even with her eyes closed. He looked around, taking in the view spread out before them. "I can see why." He said softly over her shoulder. He moved forward a fraction so he could wrap his arms around her waist, and nuzzle his face at her neck. She opened her eyes and sighed out in satisfaction. One hand stroked where Alex's arms embraced her, and her other hand reached up to her shoulder, and ran through his hair turning her mouth to his. "Better with you here I have to admit." She smiled at him. He crushed his lips against hers and turned her in his arms, pulling her tight against him. Her arms lifted to wrap around his neck, and his hands moved from her

waist to have one spanning her backside, and one tangling itself in her long hair. Her chest was tight against his, rubbing against him as their breathing became ragged, her nipples pebbling with the friction. Their tongues dipped in and out of each other's mouths, mimicking the passionate love making that they had frequently experienced. Alex felt her nipples brushing against him through his thin cotton shirt, his hand slipped from her hair and he took the fullness of her breast into his hand. Mel moaned against his mouth, her hands tangling in his hair at the nape of his neck, pulling on it, moulding herself against his body. He broke their kiss with a groan and stared intently into her eyes. "I suggest if you don't want to be taken here, now at the water's edge, you and I go back up to the Range Rover. I have a picnic in the back." She looked up at him with lust filled eyes. "The back of the Rover has tinted windows doesn't it?" Alex looked down at her and raised an eyebrow, a full smile grew over his lips and he took her hand leading her back up the beach towards his car.

As soon as Alex closed the car door behind her making sure it was locked, Mel started to shimmy out of her jeans. Leaving them lying on the floor, she turned to Alex, straddling him in the back seat. She crushed her lips to his in a bruising assault on his mouth, needing to show him just how much she desired him, how wet she was, and how much she needed him deep inside her. He pushed her hips up off him as he fucked her mouth with his tongue, just far enough so that he could get his own jeans down until they hung at his knees along with his boxers. Mel wrapped her arms around his neck, nipping on his bottom lip, sucking on his tongue, teasing him and encouraging him to give her what she hungered for. He pulled the lace of her panties to the side and lined himself up against her wet pussy. As soon as she felt the tip of his cock applying tempting friction to her moist opening she let her hips drop, and she sank down onto him in one swift move. The delicious fullness that she got from sinking down on Alex's hard prick to the hilt making her lips part from his and a long low moan sound deep in her throat. "Fuck Mel!" Alex hissed feeling her heated sex grabbing his cock all at once. He grabbed her hips to stop her from moving. "Just fucking wait…" he rasped against her ear. Mel groaned at his stillness, she couldn't take it, she didn't want to wait. "I can't, Alex, I need you." She pleaded, trying to move her hips, grinding her pelvis against his. Alex exhaled in bliss as she did, and he bucked his hips, thrusting himself deeper within her, hitting that one secret spot deep inside that no one else had ever managed. He felt her spasm around him as he continued to buck his hips up, his short but deep thrusts causing the perfect amount of friction within her. He grabbed her t-shirt pulling it over her head, and undid her bra, his hands slipped back to her hips, and his mouth covered a nipple, sucking it into his mouth. That was all she needed, Mel's whole body tensed and she cried out, he felt a sudden gush of wetness covering his penis and moaned as her walls tightened over him, creating exquisite friction holding him in a firm grip inside her. Her nipple was pulled from his mouth as her head sagged forward against his shoulder, and he continued to thrust short and hard into her as he felt her ragged breathing against his neck. He was close, but he was greedy, and he wanted to hear her crying out again as they reached a climax together. His hand slid between their bodies and his fingers rubbed over her swollen clit. It only took a matter of seconds before Melody was coming again. She bit his shoulder as she cried out for a second time, the pain of teeth on his hard muscle proving to be a trigger for his own release. "FUCK MEL!!!!" he bellowed as he exploded deep inside her. They both lay there on the back seat, Mel folded over Alex as they waited for their hearts to stop pounding, and their panting breath to calm. He lifted his hand to her cheek, caressing her face. "You undo me Jellybean." He whispered in her ear before nuzzling into her neck.

Melody sighed. "I should really move and put my clothes back on before some nice policeman comes." Alex smiled at her before kissing the tip of her nose and helping her move off his lap. "Still hungry?" He asked as he wriggled his boxers and jeans back over his hips. Mel pulled her T-shirt over her head and stared at Alex. "Ahh, definitely!" She said looking shocked. Alex grinned, leaned over to give her a kiss on the cheek and said, "Well hurry up then. I have a cooler of goodies in the back!"

By the time he had finished, there was a selection of treats spread across the picnic table, and an ice box with a bottle of non-alcoholic wine chilled to perfection. "Wow!" Mel exclaimed when she saw all of the effort, bumping her hip against Alex while she placed an arm around his waist and asked, "Remind me again why some woman hasn't kept you all to herself?" She was being playful and teasing him, but she couldn't help the sudden look of fear on his face. "It looks amazing." She said as she kissed his cheek. "Thank you, I'm having an incredible day." She smiled at him, hoping to put him at ease, taking his hand in hers and giving it a squeeze. Alex looked at her and forced a smile, lifting her hand to his lips and kissing her knuckles. "I'm glad." He replied. "Let's munch." He said, his sagging shoulders giving her cause for concern, no matter what his smile tried to convince her of.

They sat in their peaceful surroundings, enjoying the food, wine, and each other's company, chatting about their day, about the weather, the gorgeous views over the lough that they had seen. By the time, they had finished the sun was starting to cast long shadows around them. Mel helped Alex clear up after the picnic and put everything back into the Range Rover. "Take a walk with me?" She asked, holding out her hand to him. He closed the back hatch of the car, locked it and took Mel's hand in his. She smiled at him and pulled him back towards the concrete jetty. Mel coaxed Alex down towards the water's edge again, starting to follow the coastline north as she did. He squeezed his hand in hers and spoke. "I'm sorry I was a bit off earlier." She didn't look at him and kept walking, staring out over the waves as she did. "I'm listening." She stated, and Alex sighed. "I know you are... I've just got a history Mel, it didn't work out the way I expected, and that's all I want to say on the matter." He tugged her hand to get her to stop and turn towards him. She sighed and turned to him, her hand going to his face, caressing his cheek as she spoke. "Alex, everyone has a history. It's how we let it sway us that's the real test of our character." He leaned over and quickly seized her mouth with his own, crushing against her lips for a brief yet unmistakably passionate kiss. "How did you get to be so fucking wise?" He whispered against her lips, his hands on either side of her jaw, keeping her face prisoner, locked just inches from his. His eyes staring deep into hers. She stared back into the dark chocolate pools, and while she didn't yet understand where it had come from, or how much control it had over him, she saw his pain and his fear, she saw the love that he had for her, and she was overwhelmed. She needed to soothe him, she needed to help him let go of his fear, and she longed to tell him that she loved him too. Instead, she did the only thing she could at that moment, something that she hoped did all of those things for him anyway. She tilted her mouth up to his, bruising her lips against his claiming his mouth, pouring all the love and support she had for him out in that one intimate and passionate act as they stood there in complete isolation on a deserted beach.

Until the sun finally started to sink down below the surrounding hills they remained hand in hand out on the pebbles and sand of the beach. Alex's mood seemed to have lifted, and Mel didn't push any further about the wounds from his past. They kissed, they skimmed stones and eventually turned around to walk back to the jetty. "Mel?" Alex called to her as she started up the walkway. "Yeah?" She asked as she stopped and turned back to him. "Thank you. I've had an incredible day with you." Her smile started at the corners of her mouth and grew until she was beaming back at him. "And I have too." She held her hand out to him again. "Come on, it's getting chilly, let's go home." She smiled down at him. Alex took the hand she offered out to him, pulling himself up the jetty and preventing her from walking away from him. He kept her hand in his as he wrapped his other arm around her and pulled her tight against him. "You're perfection." He whispered pressing his lips against hers, drinking her in, dancing his tongue in and out of her mouth, drawing her ever tighter against him. Mel pushed him, breaking their kiss. "Jesus Alex, if you keep that up I'll be begging you to fuck me here on the jetty!" She panted against his lips, her forehead pressed against his. "Jellybean, you keep talking like that, and you won't need to beg! Come on, pumpkin time!" He smiled, tugging her back to over to the car and placing her safely in the passenger seat before he got them both into trouble and did exactly what she had hinted at.

Mel snuggled into her seat, and Alex started the car, "Broken Stones" by Paul Weller playing on the car stereo. It wasn't long before she dozed off, her head resting on the glass window. Before she knew it, Alex had pulled into her driveway and turned off the Range Rover. He rubbed his hand on her knee and called her name softly a few times before her eyelids fluttered open. His face was the first thing that she saw when she opened her eyes, and she couldn't help but grin. "Hey you." She whispered, still smiling. He smiled back, "Hey *you*. You're home sleepy head." He told her softly. "Okay." She breathed, her eyelids fluttering closed again. Alex sniggered to himself, grabbed her small bag from the floor, and fished out her keys. He went over and unlocked her front door, leaving her bag hanging on the banister, and went out to retrieve Mel from the car. He opened the passenger door and scooped her up into his arms, her arms naturally holding onto his neck as she nuzzled into his chest. He pushed the car door closed with his foot and carried Mel into the house. Once inside, he managed to close the front door with his foot too, and then started to take Melody upstairs to her bedroom.

Alex placed her softly to sit on the edge of her bed. In her semi-conscious state, she was almost co-operative with him while he stripped her down to her lacy panties, pulled back the covers and tucked her into bed. Once his precious cargo was safely in bed, he walked to the other side of the room and pulled the curtains, slipped off his own clothes, and got under the covers beside her. He pulled her in against him and kissed her bare shoulder. "Goodnight Jellybean." He whispered on her skin. He heard her sigh out a satisfied little sleepy noise. "Goodnight my Alex." She murmured. *My Alex!* The words replayed on repeat in his head. That's exactly what he was now, body and soul she had possessed him. He was hers, completely and utterly hers. And with those thoughts running through his head, Alex drifted off to sleep with Melody wrapped in his arms.

CHAPTER 17

"I can't believe you haven't fucking told him yet Natalie." Malcolm shouted.

"Keep your damn voice down." Natalie hissed. "You don't think that I might have been a bit more concerned about the fact that I was losing our baby Malc?"

Alex stood at the door and listened. Natalie and his best friend Malcolm seemed to be completely unaware that he had been slamming the front door shut just moments before. "I lost our son." She told Malcolm.

"I know you did." His voice barely audible through the partially open door. Alex could hear the sounds of Natalie sobbing, and the soothing sounds that his friend was making.

"I promise I'll tell him soon, I just can't face it so soon after this." She cried.

"Shhhhh!" Malcolm soothed.

Alex pushed the door gently, letting it open wide enough to get a clearer view of the pair. His stomach turned to lead and sank to his feet in an instant that he saw his fiancée nuzzling into his best friend's chest. When he saw the tears silently falling down

Malcolm's face, Alex's last shred of patience disappeared.

"Am I interrupting?" He asked, announcing his arrival to the embracing couple. Alex watched as the colour drained instantly from Malcolm's face, and Natalie turned with a look of horror to look at him.

She pushed herself off Malcolm's chest. "It's not what it looks like Lexy." She cooed at him, her tears forgotten in an instant.

"You'll be telling me that it wasn't what it sounds like either." Alex snapped. "I fucking heard you Natalie! I heard what you said!" He shouted. Natalie's face dropped and she glanced over at Malcolm for back up. Malcolm looked at her, and then at his friend, and hung his head.

"I'm sorry mate." He started. "I wanted to tell you sooner, but I believed Natalie when she said that she was handling it." He explained. Natalie's previously blank expression had changed to one of quietly simmering rage.

"Shut up Malcolm!" She said, raising her hands and turning to shove him away from her. It was almost as if she believed that if she distanced herself from Malcolm, she could distance herself from the web of lies that she found herself trapped in. "I wanted to tell you Alex." She whined. "Honestly. But I just couldn't find the right words, or the right time to bring it up, and then I found I *was pregnant, and it could have been yours, I mean, I wan ted him to have been yours." She told him.*

Alex glanced at the expression on his soon to be ex-friend's face, and just how much he cared for Natalie was apparent, as was the kick in the guts that she had just delivered to him with her previous comment. Malcolm reached to grab Natalie by the arm, and any sympathy Alex might have been experiencing for him evaporated in a fraction of a second. Jealousy, hurt, and betrayal coursed through his veins, and in an instant, his balled fist had been pulled back, and launched at Malcolm's face. It caught him square on his nose with a sickening crack, and blood poured down his face.

"Oh my God! Alex, I think you broke his nose!" Natalie screamed, holding on to Malcolm, trying to direct him back so he could sit on the bed behind him.

"Yeah?" Alex asked sarcastically. "Well, you and he have broken my fucking heart. So don't expect any sympathy from me!" He said, and turned to walk out. He couldn't look at either of them anymore, he couldn't breathe the same air as them, and he needed to escape. He stormed through his and Natalie's apartment and slammed the front door. His life as he knew it, in tatters.

~ ~ ~

Alex woke with a start. Sweat was pouring down his face and neck. His heart was pounding in his chest, fear was gripping his throat and he could barely breathe.

Panic attack, buddy. His inner voice informed him. *Just a panic attack from your nightmare.* He needed to get up, he needed to run. He glanced over to find Mel still deep asleep beside him. Making sure he didn't wake her, he got up and crept out of the room.

He just made it to the bathroom before his stomach ejected its contents. He retched repeatedly until there was nothing left. He slumped onto the cold floor beside the toilet, wiping his mouth with the washcloth that had been sitting by the sink. He sat there, leaning on the wall, and tried to calm his breathing. He closed his eyes, leaning his head back against the wall, focusing only on the deep breath in, deep breath out technique that he had been taught to help deal with his panic attacks. He couldn't believe that after all this time she was still affecting his life like this. *Perhaps Ben is right?* He thought to himself. He thought about it and realised that he had only two possible options. One, give into the fears, and run from Mel, or two, fight back, overcome his fears, and move forward with Mel. He thought about which of those two options make him less sick. He decided it was option two. The thought of being without Mel filled him with more dread than being with her.

As his breathing calmed and his head cleared, he replayed his dream, thinking about what had happened. Thinking about what he remembered. He remembered hitting Malcolm and how it didn't come close to relieving even a fraction of the pain he had been caused by the pair. He remembered the incredulous feeling that had washed over him when Natalie said that she had wanted the baby to be his, knowing full well that she had been lying. That it had just been more of her manipulation of him.

Alex sighed and got up from the floor. He leaned over the sink, splashing water over this face and around his mouth. He grabbed some toothpaste on his finger and ran it over his teeth, to freshen up before crawling back into bed with Mel. He took a deep breath, calming himself completely before turning the light off in the bathroom and heading back into Mel's room.

As Alex got under the covers, Mel stirred. "Are you okay?" She murmured sleepily.

"I'm okay Jellybean." He whispered. "Just at the bathroom." He offered. Mel snuggled back against him in bed, putting her hand behind her pulling him against her. Alex wrapped his arms around Mel and pressed himself against her back. He kissed her bare shoulder and went back to sleep. Mel lay there in the darkness. She knew that a dream had troubled him and a dozen scenarios played over in her mind as she fell asleep into a troubled restless sleep herself.

~ ~ ~

Mel woke the next morning to find her bed empty and the smell of bacon wafting through her house. She stretched, trying to shake the fatigue from her body. Her sleep had been far from peaceful, her worries about Alex robbing her from rest even wrapped in his arms. She got up, tucked her robe around herself, and followed the delicious smells downstairs.

Alex grinned a full smile when he saw Mel standing in the doorway behind him. "Morning Jellybean." He smiled at her, his eyes twinkling. "Fancy some breakfast?" He asked as he held up the frying pan full of scrambled eggs.

A wash of warmth flooded Mel's body, and she couldn't help but smile back at him. "I could get used to waking up to find you busy in my kitchen." She grinned. Alex smiled, intensity shining in this look. He took the pan off the heat and stalked towards her.

"I could get used to having breakfast with you every morning." He murmured, before he lowered his mouth and claimed hers. His arms wrapped around her and pulled her tight against him. Her arms went around his neck, her fingers entwining in his hair, pulling on it. He let out a moan against her lips.

"God Mel, how is it every time I see you I just have to claim you." He breathed against her mouth, their foreheads still touching. He took a step back and flicked off the ring on the cooker, before pulling Mel back in against him and directing her to the other side of the kitchen. She felt the counter top behind her, and Alex lifted her setting her on it. He tugged on her robe, the front of it falling open. He reached his hand up and cupped her breast, her eyes following his hand's movements. She purred when he kneaded her flesh. When his fingers traced over the stiff little peak her nipple had become, her heavy lidded lust filled gaze looking deep into his eyes. He crushed his mouth against hers, hungry to claim her.

After a few heated moments, Alex pried his lips from hers and dipped his head towards the hand he had on her breast. His mouth covered her nipple and he sucked it harshly. Mel moaned, grabbing at Alex's hair, encouraging him to continue. He stopped sucking and let her nipple fall from his mouth, before grabbing it between his thumb and forefinger, and moving his mouth to the opposite nipple.

"What about breakfast?" She murmured between lusty sighs.

"I will finish making your breakfast once I've eaten." He said, and dropped to his knees in front of Mel. He pushed her thighs apart. "You need to hold on to the countertop okay?" He asked.

Mel looked down at him and nodded. And Alex's face disappeared between her thighs. His hands held onto her inner thighs, and his tongue lapped through her labia, teasing her. He gripped her thighs and pulled her closer to the edge of the countertop where he had better access to her.

220

"Rest your legs on my shoulders if you need to." He commanded before dipping his tongue back into her wetness. Mel lifted her legs and put her feet sole to sole at the back of Alex's shoulders, allowing her legs to spread wider and give him as much access as she could. She groaned loudly, her knuckles white trying to keep her balance and stop herself from slipping off the kitchen surface.

Alex mouth cupped over her pussy and he hummed as he rubbed his lips in her wetness. He flicked his tongue in, finding her clit, his mouth closing in around the soft little nub, and sucking on it gently. A loud gasp escaped from Mel and her grip tightened. He skimmed over her labia with a finger, and slid it into her as he sucked. He felt her tensing above him, and he slid another finger in with the first, slowly fucking her while he licked, nibbled and sucked on her clit, driving her to orgasm. Her breathing turned into an erratic pant, and he felt her pussy clenching. He sped up the tempo of his fingers, and focussed on flicking his tongue in circles over her clit. Her heels dug into his shoulders as her back arched and she let out a long moan, signalling her climax out loud. Alex sucked on her tender clit, coaxing every last shiver from her body. He slid his fingers from her, and looked up at her with a lust filled expression and licked his soaked digits. She shuffled back from the edge of the kitchen counter and beckoned him to stand. When he did, she pulled him in against her, claiming his mouth with hers, savouring her own flavour on his lips, and showing her complete appreciation in her kiss. Alex broke his lips from hers, kissed the tip of her nose with a big grin.

"Don't move." He warned as he washed his hands and moved back to the cooker, turning the heat back on and retrieving his previously forgotten scrambled eggs and putting them back onto the heat.

Mel did exactly what she had been told the entire time. She didn't move from where she was perched on the counter. Instead she watched with a smile as Alex moved around in her kitchen preparing breakfast for them both, occasionally asking where in the kitchen various things were located, a smile on his face the entire time. When the food was finally ready, she was allowed to remove herself from the kitchen and sit at the dining room table instead.

Alex walked out of the kitchen with two plates in his hand and set a feast of scrambled eggs and toast down in front of her, before disappearing back into the kitchen and returning with a mug of tea for her, and a mug of coffee from himself. The pair sat in silence for a while enjoying each others company and delighting in the food.

After a long silence, Alex looked up at Mel with a frown. "What are you doing next weekend?" Alex asked her.

She looked at him suspiciously. "You're planning something!" She declared.

Alex grinned. "I might be." He smirked as he took a sip of his coffee. "So are you doing anything or not?" He repeated.

"I'm not at the minute." She grinned back. "What are you scheming?" She said as she put a forkful of eggs into her mouth.

Alex leaned over and kissed the tip of her nose. "Jellybean, you are so sceptical!" He smirked. Mel glared at him suspiciously. "Okay! Okay!" He laughed. "I was thinking of taking you to Dublin for the weekend. But I was also thinking about that third scenario you emailed me about back in the beginning."

Mel thought for a second, trying to remember which scene he had been talking about. "Hotel maid?" She asked with a faint blush rising in her cheeks.

Alex grinned. "Yes. But you should know that I want to push your limits, I want to see just how much you're capable of." Alex looked at the expression on her face, reading her reaction. "Do you trust me Mel?" He asked.

Mel touched his cheek. "You know I do."

"So you're up for an extra dirty weekend in Dublin then?" He grinned.

"Looks like it." She smiled back. Alex grinned a full smile and leaned in, placing his lips against hers briefly before grinning at her again.

"Eat your breakfast!" He smirked.

"Yes Sir!" She grinned with a mock salute before taking another bite of toast.

They chatted over the arrangements for the weekend. Alex suggested driving them both down on Saturday morning, but Mel told him that she had work, and wouldn't be free until four o'clock.

"Why don't I take you to work on Saturday, you leave your bags with me, I'll take them down, and you can meet me down there, I'll get you a first class ticket for the Enterprise train?" Alex suggested.

Mel paused thinking about it for a moment, then a grin broke out across her face. "I can see how that might let me turn up at your hotel room door looking more like a member of hotel staff without a bag and everything." She grinned.

"God I love how sneaky your mind is!" He grinned back at her. "So that works for you then?" He asked.

Mel nodded with a grin. "I quite like the idea of heading down on the train in first class." She smiled at him with a wink. Alex laughed and leaned over and kissed her.

~ ~ ~

They hadn't had much time together in the week that followed. Alex had spent the night with her on Wednesday, and they had as usual, texted daily. On Saturday afternoon, Alex dropped Mel to work before heading to Dublin in his Range Rover, taking her things with him. When work was over, Mel jumped into the taxi that was waiting to take her to the other side of the city centre, so she could catch the next 'Enterprise' service to Dublin's Connolly Street Station. She enjoyed the trip down in relaxed comfort, and when she arrived she got herself another taxi and headed for The Shelbourne Dublin, an amazing renaissance hotel situated in the city's Saint Stephen's Green area. She walked in and crossed the marble floor, admiring the chandelier's, regal columns, and guilt detailing around the ceiling. She walked up the stairs, her hand skimming along the banister that sat on top of the ornate railings and heading for the room number that Alex had texted her with earlier.

CHAPTER 18

Mel smoothed out her skirt and hair, and knocked on the door of the hotel room. The door opened and he stood there for a second looking her up and down. She felt that familiar feeling start in her stomach and spread down to her groin.

She gathered herself together, and prepared to play her part. She put her hand out for him to shake. "Mr Matthews?" She began. "I'm Miss Anderson, I'm an assistant manager here at the hotel." Alex stood aside and gestured for her to enter the room. "I understand you had some issues, Sir?" She finished, standing with her back straight, and glancing around the room.

"Yes, Miss Anderson. I do." Alex said, staring at her intently, opening the door of the bathroom and turning on the light. "The bathroom is filthy." He said pointing at the sink and the shower.

"I'm not sure that I see the dirt that you're talking about Mr Matthews, it all seems very acceptable to me." She smiled politely at him.

Alex glared at her. "Look at the bottom of the shower tray Miss Anderson, and tell me if you think that looks acceptable to you?" He said, pointing at the bottom of the shower. Mel walked in to the bathroom, and bent over to look at the bottom of the shower cubicle. Her pencil skirt tightened over her backside as she did. She glanced over her shoulder at him.

"I'm not sure I see what you mean Mr Matthews." She told him. Alex moved into position behind her. His hips moved against hers, and he leaned over her slightly, pointing into the far corner of the shower.

"There! Miss Anderson!" He said, directing her attention. One of his hands skimmed her hip, as the other indicated into the corner.

Mel stood up straight looking at Alex's hand on her hip. "Excuse me?" She asked in shock. He slid his hand from her and held both of them up in apology.

"Sorry! I didn't mean to offend you or make you uncomfortable." He smirked. "But tell me, did that look clean to you?" Alex's hands went back down to his sides and Mel glanced from them and back up to his face.

"Well..." She said, leaning back over to take a look. "I suppose it is a little grubby." She admitted from where she was, she glanced over her shoulder to look at him as she straightened her body, and stood up in front of him again.

"What about that?" Alex asked pointing in the direction of behind the toilet.

"Where?" Mel asked.

Alex sighed. "Right there Miss Anderson. In behind the toilet by the wall." He told her, directing her once again to the 'dirt' that he had discovered in his room.

Mel again leaned over, and looked towards where Alex had instructed. She put her hands on the closed toilet lid for support and this time, bent over completely, her ass in the air, her skirt stretched tight over it as it rode up her thighs. Alex moved in behind her in a heartbeat, and a second later she gasped as he connected his palm with her ass.

She moved to stand up, and as she did Alex put a hand on her upper back, pushing down on her so that she was unable to straighten. He slapped her backside again. "What do you think you're doing?" She shrieked. "Mr Matthews! Get off me!" She pleaded.

Alex leaned over her his mouth just over her head. "Miss Anderson, your employer told me that I could talk to you about the issues I found with the room, and that you would be only too happy to help me resolve them." He said, and smacked her ass again. "Of course, if that's not the case, I'm happy to go back to your boss, and tell him that you were not interested in resolving this with me." Alex said, and paused with his hand ready to swat Mel's butt again. "Is that what you want Miss Anderson? I'm pretty sure that your boss wouldn't be happy with that at all. What do you think?" He asked her sardonically.

Mel paused. She would never have guessed that this was how the scene would play out for her. They hadn't discussed the finer points of the scene, she trusted Alex.

"Let me up!" She demanded, and the pressure Alex was placing on her shoulders to keep her bent over was released. She pushed off the toilet cover and stood in front of him with her back perfectly straight as in defiance. Her breathing quickened. "Surely you don't mean that I should let you do whatever you want?" She asked him, looking concerned at what his answer would be.

"What else would you suggest?" He asked with a hard stare.

"Surely we could arrange for a new room, or a complimentary meal. I can assure you, I'm not part of the service at the hotel Mr Matthews." She advised him.

A wicked grin formed across his face, and she felt her pussy clench in response to the gleam in his eyes. "None of those things would satisfy me Miss Anderson." He looked at her like he was a predator sizing up its prey. She swallowed hard at the look and licked her lips, her mouth suddenly dry. Alex closed the small space between them, wrapping her wrists with his hands, and pulling her hands behind her back. He pressed his chest against hers, causing her nipples to pebble from the contact.

Before Mel knew what was happening, Alex had looped a cable tie around her wrists and pulled it tight. Suddenly she felt very helpless, she swallowed again, looking deep into the dark pools of almost black that were looking down on her. "Please Mr Matthews, this is highly inappropriate!" She protested.

She felt Alex's body tense as she said it, and as she stared at him, his lips crushed against hers. His tongue pushing between her lips and demanding she let him in. She almost instantly parted her lips for him, her tongue seeking out his as they rolled together switching between his mouth and hers. Mel leaned her body against his even more, feeling the heat of his skin coming through her shirt and his, radiating into her, making her warm. She clenched her thighs together and instantly realised just how wet her knickers were from Alex's treatment of her. She moaned against his mouth, and he pulled away from her.

"I think you're going be very agreeable to the notion of helping me with the issues that I have about the room. Aren't you Miss Anderson?" He smirked.

"There are other issues?" She asked tentatively.

He led her out of the bathroom, hands still cable tied behind her back, and flicked back the corner of the bedspread revealing an unmade bed. He moved over to the windowsill and ran his finger over it before showing it to Mel and explaining that he was completely dissatisfied with the room.

"I'm sorry Mr Matthews." She said softly.

"I'm glad to hear that Miss Anderson, because I need you to be accountable for this, and make it up to me big time." He said, moving back towards her, so close that he was looking down on her.

She swallowed hard and looked up at him. "Yes Mr Matthews." She mumbled.

"I think you should call me Master Lex, don't you?" He smirked staring down at her.

She licked her lips. "Yes Master Lex."

"You're going to do what I ask you to, aren't you Miss Anderson?" He asked.

She nodded, and he took her by the arm and led her over to the small wooden table in the room. "Bend over." He instructed her. Mel bent over the hard surface as she had been commanded. "Have you ever been paddled?" Alex asked her, walking over to the large holdall that he had brought with him.

"No Master Lex." Mel informed him and he lifted a long leather paddle out of the bag.

He cracked the paddle against his hand, and she jumped at the sound. Alex went back to the bag and pulled out leather restraints and moved to behind her, rubbing one hand across her ass and up her back to her hands.

He fastened a leather cuff around her left wrist and then her right, clipping them together. When his task was complete he snipped the cable tie that had originally bound her wrists.

He moved to her ankles, repeating the binding there with more leather restraints. He pulled chains from his pocket. There were four individual chains, connected at one end with a single ring, allowing them to form a large 'X' with the ring at the centre. Each of the 4 ends had a leash clip connector on it.

He clipped the ankle restraints to two of the chains. He stood, unclipped her wrists from behind her and pulled her arms down on either side of the table she was bent over. He lifted the last of the chains, and attached them to the cuffs on her wrists. Mel was left bent over the table, restrained, her ankles connected to her wrists as her arms dangled over the edge of the table.

Alex moved away from her. Mel flexed against her restraints, testing just how far she could move. If she tried to move her hands to help push herself up off the table, the chains tightened proving themselves too short. She couldn't get her hands up high enough to help herself off the table. She was well and truly trapped. Her chest and stomach flat against the table.

"You won't be able to get up from there until I want you to I'm afraid, Miss Anderson." Alex gloated.

"What are you going to do with me?" She asked sounding nervous. She had never been so turned on in her life. Every nerve in her body was on fire, and what she felt for Alex only seemed to intensify the experience. He walked back behind her, just out of her line of sight.

"I hope you're not attached to your outfit Miss Anderson." Alex smirked. Mel squirmed trying to see what he was doing behind her when she felt him touching the hem of her skirt.

The sound of fabric ripping echoed loudly in the hotel room and Mel gasped. "What are you doing?" She cried out, feeling her pussy clench at the thought of what was to come. "That's my uniform! My boss will kill me!" She exclaimed, tugging on her restraints. Alex took the scissors he had in his hand and cut through the waistband of her skirt. He wrapped his hand around her and lifted her slightly pulling the skirt from beneath her and putting her back down on the table. Alex threw the tattered skirt to the far side of the room.

He stooped and pulled her shirt cuff, popping the button off, the sleeve shredding as he tugged it hard.

"Master Lex! Please!" She pleaded. Her nipples pebbled hard against the hard top of the table. His forcefulness was turning her on more and more with each of his actions. Her panties were soaked, her pussy sopping from the dominant way he was treating her.

Alex grinned and shushed her, pulling on the other sleeve and the back of the shirt until it was in tatters like her skirt. He used the scissors again to finish removing that last parts of her top from her body. He threw it and it landed in the same place as her skirt.

Mel lay over the top of the table, her legs slightly parted, her ass in the air, and completely at his mercy. His cock strained at the flies of his jeans. He couldn't wait to bury his thick hard dick deep inside her tight ass. He adjusted his cock, and ran his hands over her lace covered backside. He let his fingers skim over the crotch of her panties, and finding them soaked he grinned.

"Well, well, well..." He crowed from behind her. "Look at the little slut all wet because she's going to be punished." Mel could hear her heart pounding in her ears. The more she thought of him taunting her, the wetter she became. If things carry on like this it'll be running down my thighs! She thought to herself, blushing at just how much this was turning her on.

Alex slipped a finger around her panties and sank it into her pussy in one movement. Mel sucked in a breath, jumping at the sensation of contact so intimately from him.

"You want to be fucked don't you Miss Anderson?" He teased as he thrust his finger deep inside her. She groaned, and he slid another finger inside her. Mel licked her lips at the delicious feeling that Alex was generating deep within her. He was right, she wanted to be fucked, and fucked hard as only he knew how, but she wasn't about to tell him that.

"Master Lex!" She panted. "You can't do this to me." She moaned.

Alex laughed. "I think you'll find, I can, and I am." He informed her while a smirk stretched across his face. He loved nothing more than seeing her spread out before him. He loved to find her wet and ready for him. He loved how her body responded to his. He slipped his fingers out of her warm core, grabbed at her panties and ripped them from her body. She gasped at how exposed she felt without them. He groaned when he moved his fingers through her wet sex again. His fingers were in his mouth before he had a chance to think about it.

"God I love how you taste." He moaned behind her, licking her juices from his fingers. "But you're not ready for a reward yet Miss Anderson." He said, moving away from her and back to where the paddle lay. He picked it up, and moved into the perfect position to make contact with her ass. He lifted the paddle up and away from her body, and brought it back down sharply until it made contact with her bare backside. Mel cried out, the burning in her ass cheeks from the crack of the paddle instantly transferring to a heat in her pussy, an aching need for Alex.

He pulled the paddle back again and cracked it down on her ass. "I am very unhappy with the quality of service in your hotel Miss Anderson." He scolded, as he brought the paddle down squarely on her ass again. "A dirty shower..." *Smack*. "... An unmade bed..." *Smack*. "... Dusty corners..." *Smack*. "... Not at all what I have come to expect from this hotel Miss Anderson." He pointed out, as he continued to smack the paddle against her bare flesh.

"Sorry Master Lex!" She panted, all of her nerve endings on burning with desire. Alex knew just how to work her into a frenzy, and he seemed to take a great pleasure in doing so.

"Oh, you're not sorry just yet Miss Anderson, but you will be soon enough." He said threateningly. Mel swallowed hard, he had promised her that if she agreed to this that he was going to push her limits, and see just how much she could take. The paddle was causing a sting in her rear that she hadn't quite experienced before. The sensation from it compared to Alex's hand was harsher, but that harshness just made Melody want even more. It excited her, it made her wince and want to cry out, but it drove her further into her own submission. She wanted more, she wanted to take whatever it was that Alex wanted to hand out to her. She needed it almost as much as she needed him.

Mel jumped when she felt Alex's hands move in a soft caress across her heated skin. She was sure that her backside would be a lovely shade of deep pink already. "Hmmm." Alex hummed. "That's a nice little warm up. You're already getting a nice pink glow on your sexy little ass Miss Anderson." He teased. He let his fingers dip into her sex as he stroked over her ass and smiled when he heard her moan in response.

"You know Miss Anderson, if behaviour like this is going to make you so turned on, perhaps I need to change how it is that you are punished. I think I might have to employ a different technique." He said. There was something in his voice that made the goose bumps rise over every inch of Mel's skin. Something deliciously threatening.

Mel didn't get the chance to ask anything more about it, because Alex's tongue was suddenly between her legs. He lapped at her pussy in long slow movements, making her moan, and long for him to take her hard. His slow lapping changed to circling of her clit, driving her forward to climax. He wrapped his lips around her clit and sucked gently, pulling it into his mouth, sliding two fingers deep inside her as he did.

Mel cried out as a blinding orgasm slammed into her. She arched her back, pressing her front hard against the table. Moaning loudly, crying out as the pleasure washed over every last inch of her body. Alex didn't stop curling his fingers inside her, pressing down onto that little bundle of nerves inside her, circling again on her clit, before she was soon erupting in a second climax. She grabbed the chains at her wrists, holding on as her second orgasm sent her spinning out into oblivion, coasting gently around the edges of reality. Alex gently kept up the attention that he was lavishing on her, coaxing every last moment of pleasure from her entire body, until she hung over the table limply.

He slid his fingers out of her tightness, and moved to undo the clips on her chains, freeing her ankles and wrists. He helped her to stand, and when she wobbled on her feet, he drew her into his arms and carried her to the bed. He placed her in the middle, and removed her bra and shoes. He laid her back on the bed, and moved to the bottom and her feet. He took one of her ankles in his hand and pulled it to the corner of the bed, before attaching it to a clip that he pulled out from under the mattress. He repeated the same action on her other ankle, followed by her wrists, until she was lying there on the bed. Spread eagled and completely naked, ready to receive whatever it was that Alex had in mind.

He stood looking at her exposed before him and smiled, before going back to his bag, and removing more from it. Mel lifted her head, curious to see what he would be bringing over to her next. Alex moved back towards the bed, and sat on the edge, looking at Mel.

"You Miss Anderson, are a very impressive submissive." He smiled. "But I don't think you know just how good a submissive you are." He smirked at her. "I know that you would like to know just how much you can handle, wouldn't you Miss Anderson." He asked with a sardonic smile.

Mel licked her lips and nodded. "I am truly your slut Master Lex, you're to do with as you see fit." She agreed. Alex leaned over her and crushed his lips against hers. He couldn't believe just how much she trusted him. But more than that, he couldn't believe just how much he trusted her. He let his tongue tangle with hers, enjoying how well she responded to his mouth against hers.

When Alex pried his lips from hers, she was panting. He longed to be inside her, he longed to have her arms and legs wrapped around him. But he couldn't lie to himself, he knew that right now his emotions were threatening to overwhelm him, and while he wasn't about to push her away, he did need to regain some control of the situation.

"Remember your safe words Jellybean." He said, and kissed the tip of her nose before pulling a blindfold from his pocket, and plunging her into blackness. From her face his hand slid slowly over the rest of her body, softly caressing her. Her breathing was erratic, and she flinched in anticipation of his touch. His hands cupped her breasts, one in each hand, and his thumb and forefinger teased her nipples into stiff little peaks. She moaned.

Alex dipped his head and sucked one of her nipples into his mouth. He pulled hard on the peak still between his fingers, while he drew her nipple into his mouth harshly catching it with his teeth, nipping it.

Mel gasped and arched her back, trying to pull her chest away from his rough attention. He growled at her. "Stay still!" He ordered. She stilled beneath him, goose bumps rising over her skin again. His mouth came down on her other nipple, and his thumb and forefinger returned to the moist peak that had just been in his mouth.

She groaned in response to his touch. She was beginning to think that Alex could make her come from just teasing her nipples. He removed his mouth from her breasts again, continuing to knead them with his hands as he spoke. "Your nipples are going to look great with clamps on them Miss Anderson." He told her, a moan escaped from her lips. "But not yet." He said, and she felt him moving on the bed beside her. He moved to between her legs and ran his hand over her thighs. She jumped slightly at the touch of his hands. Alex stroked lightly over the inside of her thighs, gently tickling the flesh between her knees and her pussy. She tried to pull her legs together, to prevent him from his teasing, and to gain some friction against her clit. Alex slapped her inner thigh, and Mel gasped. "Stay still Miss Anderson." He scolded again, rubbing his hand gently over where his smack had reddened the skin on her leg.

His hand moved in circles heading higher and higher on her thigh. He allowed his fingers to graze her exposed and glistening sex.

"So wet... And so needy." He taunted and plunged his finger deep inside her. A long moan escaped from her lips and her hips lifted up off the bed in a silent plea for more.

Alex let out a small laugh. "Such a greedy little slut aren't you Miss Anderson." He smirked, one hand still stroking along her thigh, the other encouraging her desire by sliding a second finger into her sopping wet depths.

He started to thrust into her with long deep strokes, pulling his fingers almost completely from her pussy before plunging them back into her as far as he possibly could.

Mel started to grind against his hand. She needed more, desperate to come again, her desire increasing monumentally with every touch, tease and taunt. Every time he called her a slut she felt her pussy clench. Every time he thrust his fingers into her she wanted to beg for more. Every time he pulled on her nipple or smacked her backside, she wanted to push him to more. She was an insatiable vixen, burning with a desire that only Alex would ever inspire in her. In that moment she knew that she belonged only to him, and understood that she had fallen completely in love with him.

CHAPTER 19

Mel sighed in frustrated pleasure as Alex's fingers dipped in and out of her soaked sex. "Mmmm... Please Master Lex!" She purred at him. He grinned, he loved how much she needed him, and how he was able to coax pleasure from her. *Almost like she was meant for you, huh buddy?* His inner voice reasoned. Alex's heart rate sped up, and he licked his lips and lowered his mouth to her wet pussy.

A long hiss rumbled in Mel's throat when she felt Alex's tongue lap through her slick labia. "Mmmm...." He sounded in appreciation. "I love how you taste. I love how wet you are for me." He breathed against her thigh, planting tiny kisses against the apex of her legs. "You are mine." He said and wrapped his lips around her clit, sucking and teasing her to the brink of orgasm. He felt her body tensing and pulled his mouth and fingers away from her sex, smirking as he watched her moving knowing she was so close.

"Please!" She moaned.

"Not yet Miss Anderson." He grinned. She felt him moving again on the bed. "Time to make those nipples look really pretty." He told her, moving to her breasts, his fingers caressing over her stiff little peaks.

Her breathing hitched at his contact and he roughly grabbed at her flesh, kneading her breasts in his hands. He lifted the nipple clamps from there he had left them on the bedside table. His mouth locked around her left nipple and he sucked it hard drawing it deeply into his mouth.

Mel groaned. She longed to run her fingers through his hair and hold him against her breast. Instead he sucked hard on her nipple popping it out of his mouth after a moment. She felt the harsh bite of a clamp as Alex attached it onto her super sensitive little peak.

Once Alex had the clamps secured on each of Mel's nipples he gave the chain that connected them a little tug. She cried out, arching her back, trying to ease the tug and bite in her skin.

"Mmmm..." Alex cooed. "Just perfect Miss Anderson!"

Mel felt Alex move off the bed and heard him moving around the room. She sighed and bit her bottom lip. She wriggled against her restraints, testing them to see just how much play was in them. She heard him laugh from somewhere at the bottom of the bed.

"You're not going to get very far Miss Anderson, I can assure you of that." He gloated as he stared at her naked form on the bed. His cock was throbbing in his jeans begging him to slide into her creamy tight depths.

Mel jumped when she felt Alex's lips wrap around her big toe, sucking it into his mouth and running his tongue over the fleshy pad underneath. A groan escaped from her lips and she felt her pussy pulse.

Alex grinned, lingering over each toe in turn, teasing them with his tongue while sucking on them gently. Mel had never realised how erotic such a thing could really be. Every caress of Alex's mouth caused her juices to run down the crack of her ass and into the sheet below. When he was done paying attention to her toes, his tongue trailed deliciously over the soul of her foot, from her heel, along the arch to the tip of her toes. He ran his hands up the inside and outside of her leg in a series of sensual caresses that she was sure were meant only to drive her to a fever pitch.

By the time Alex had kissed, caressed and nibbled his way to the inside of her knee, the throbbing in her clit and contact heat in her pussy made her think that she could come from what he was doing alone, and soon.

"Please Master Lex!" She begged him, writhing against her restraints, desperate for the connection she needed to come undone.

"Please what Miss Anderson?" He smirked. He loved just how intensely turned on she was for him; how greedy he had made her for his touch, for his control, for him.

"I need to come Master Lex!" She pleaded again. He could hear the desperation in her voice, he could smell her arousal, and he longed to taste her again. *Just not yet!* He reminded himself.

"Please!" She cried again when he didn't reply to her.

"Be careful what you wish for Miss Anderson!" He replied and she could hear the mischievous tone in his voice.

She felt the cool tip of a dildo being pushed slowly into her sex and she let out a hiss. Alex held the lubricated phallus and applied a constant pressure until it was seated as deeply as possible within Mel's hot pussy.

"Such a greedy little cunt you have Miss Anderson!" He teased.

Mel felt her face flush with colour at such a based word. She knew that she was mere moments away from splintering apart under Alex's long, deep thrusts with the dildo. Seconds later she did exactly that.

She cried out to him. "FUCK! Oh Master Lex!"

"Good!" He encouraged her. "Yes! That's it!" He grinned. "That's it Jellybean! Come for me."

Her body arched off the bed as much as her restraints allowed as she let the waves of orgasm roll over every inch of her body.

Alex continued to thrust the dildo in and out of her in long, fast strokes. He wanted to know just how far he could push her. Mel gasped for air as she returned from the stratosphere. She could feel another orgasm starting to build already.

"Oh God!" She moaned.

"You wanted to come Miss Anderson!" He reminded her, giving his wrist a little flick causing the dildo to twist around as it became buried deep inside her. A guttural grown sounded in her throat as Alex slid a finger between her wet labia and skimmed his fingertip across her clit. Almost instantly her hips bucked against his hand and the fake cock, and a second climax every bit as intense as the first slammed into her setting every nerve in her body burning.

Mel shook against her restraints and Alex slowed the thrusting of the dildo down to a slow leisurely pace allowing Mel to come back down without losing any momentum. She panted. Even without the blindfold her eyes would have been shut. Alex was teasing pleasure so intense out of every cell of her being. As her breathing deepened she already knew that she was on the climb up to another exquisite orgasm.

"Please!" She begged only this time she had no idea what she was begging him for. Her breathing began to grow erratic and a smile spread across Alex's face.

She sucked in a breath when she felt something push against her asshole, as the dildo was on an outward stroke.

"Ohhhh!" She cried out as he slid the butt plug inside deep enough for her ass to grip around the tapered base of the plug, securing it in place. She could feel her nipples burning under the clamps, she could feel her ass pulsing around the plug, and when Alex thrust the dildo inside her deep and hard, the universe exploded around her for the third time.

She barely made out his words through her post-orgasmic haze when he taunted her.

"You did say that you wanted to come Miss Anderson!" He reminded her.

She hissed, while each orgasm she experienced was slightly more intense than the last, how soon Alex could take her there became quicker and quicker. Every time she felt her body come down enough to have even the remotest notion of being capable of coherent thought, she was already on the ascent back up to climatic bliss.

Alex's thrusting never let up. He varied the speed and depth of the thrusts depending on how Mel was reacting, but in the constant thrusts of penetration he was relentless. Mel came repeatedly until no sooner was she ending on climax that she was starting another. She cried out in pleasure over and over again, until words no longer formed and animalistic grunts, moans and other guttural sounds were all she had the capacity to manage.

"One more." Alex coaxed, speeding his thrusting once again demanding Mel's body climb towards one more climax. She groaned loudly, hoping he would understand she was close. She felt his hand caress over her stomach and find the chain that connected her nipple clamps. She felt him tug them as her orgasm threatened to spill over her. Mel's breathing sped up; her body stiffened and just as she felt her climax rush through her Alex tugged hard on the chain and her nipples were freed with a rush of blood back into the tender peaks. A tsunami of pleasure ripped through her body. Her nipples burned, her pussy pulsed and her ass throbbed, and Mel became completely undone. She was so overwhelmed by the enormity of the pleasure that she felt that the world around her went black, and she almost passed out.

When she became remotely aware of her surroundings again, she found her arms and legs had been released. Alex moved on the bed beside her and pulled her into his arms, kissing her neck softly. She mewed at his touch.

"Shhhh Jellybean." He breathed in her ear. She leaned back against his chest, melting in against him. She drifted back out of consciousness, and when she stirred the next time, she found a naked Alex curled in behind her, his hands cupping her breasts, his lips nuzzling against her neck. She murmured as she felt heat building again in her core.

"Wake up Miss Anderson." he purred in her ear, "I'm not done with you yet." He pinched her nipple, making sure he was getting her attention. Mel groaned, and pushed herself back against him, pressing her still plugged ass against his hard cock. Alex pulled himself back from her and slapped her hard on the backside. "Ah! Ah! You will *not* tease me!"

She groaned again her ass stinging where his hand made contact, wetness pooling between her thighs again. Alex moved off the bed, and reached for her wrists, pulling her up off the bed.

"Time for another lesson I think." He told her, leading her away from the bed and over to the small wing backed armchair that stood in the corner. He clipped her wrist cuffs together and pushed her arms up above her head by the wrists. "Keep them there." He commanded, and walked over to the bag that he had with him. He lifted something out and walked back over to her. He showed her what he held in his hand, a pair of silver nipple rings, designed to stay in place by pinching the flesh. "These aren't as bad as the ones from before." He soothed before dipping his head and drawing a nipple into his mouth, making the stiff little peak rise just enough for him to secure the ring onto it. Once he had one in place, he repeated the process on the other breast. Mel looked down at the silver rings on her nipples; she was pleased with how they looked. "Maybe we will make arrangements for something more permanent since you seem to like the look of these." He purred at her, flicking the rings on her nipples. She hissed, the sensations running from her pinched nipples directly to her pussy and the plug in her ass.

Alex led her closer to the chair. "Put your knees on the chair and lean over, put your hands behind the back of it." Mel listened to his instructions; she knelt on the seat, and looped her arms and linked wrists over the back of the chair, leaning her collarbones against the backrest. Her nipples and adorning rings brushed against the back of the chair when she moved, sending the sensations directly to her wet pussy.

He moved away from her with a slap on the ass. He headed back to his bag of delights and lifted out two more items. He dropped one of them on the bed out of Mel's sight before returning to where she was spread out over the chair.

"Do you trust me Jellybean?" He asked her softly.

"Yes!" She confirmed without a seconds hesitation.

"Good." He smiled, letting his hand run over her soft backside.

"I have something that I want to use on you... Well two things. The first is a riding crop." Alex watched for Mel's reaction. Her eyes widening as she took in his words. "The second is a ball gag. If I use the crop you'll need to be gagged." He told her.

Mel squirmed what little she could in the position that she was in.

"Do you agree to that?" He asked her.

Mel swallowed hard. "I... yes."

"You still have your safe word Jellybean. I'll still understand it." He reassured her.

He stepped behind her, brought the simple ball gag down in front of her face, and popped it into her mouth when she opened it. He fastened the leather strap behind her head, pulling it just tight enough to stay in place.

Mel groaned into it and wriggled her backside against Alex's heavy erection that was pressed against the crack of her backside. Alex pushed a knee between her legs and pulled her head back by her hair.

"I suggest you stop teasing and tempting me Miss Anderson!" He warned her. He could feel the heat of her pussy against his balls, her juices already starting to coat them. He moved back and ran his hand over her ass again, allowing his fingers to skim through her wetness.

"So wet again Miss Anderson. Anyone would think you liked being punished for the indiscretions of your hotel is that what it is? You're a little slut who loves to have all her greedy little holes filled while she's taught a lesson. Is that what you are Miss Anderson?" He taunted her.

Mel moaned. "Yes!" She attempted to say around the gag. Alex grinned and smacked his hand against her porcelain buttock.

"Right answer Miss Anderson!" He crowed and smacked his hand down on her backside again. "The only problem is I only see two holes filled so far. One..." He said pulling on the strap of the gag. " And two..." He said, and pushed on to the plug still in Mel's ass causing another muffled moan to escape around the gag. "But three..." he said dipping two fingers deep into her sopping sex, "...needs filled properly I think." He stated. He palmed his cock, stroking over its length, wiping the pre-cum over the head to lubricate it slightly, before lining it up with the entrance of Mel's tight little cunt and pushing his hips against hers with one firm and demanding thrust.

Mel cried out against the gag. Her nipples were brushing on the back of the chair, tugging on the rings, sending sparks straight to her core. Her ass pulsed around the plug still firmly deep within her ass, and her pussy throbbing around Alex's thick cock as she adjusted to the size of him.

He grabbed a tight hold of her lips and slid himself almost all the way out before sinking back in deep, taking her hard and fast. Fucking her mercilessly the plug in her ass being pushed with every thrust. Mel's moans grew in pace with Alex's thrusts. She felt owned, she felt dominated, she felt something deep inside her let go and she gave into the wanton lust that was washing over her.

Mel ground her ass back on Alex with every fierce thrust. She moaned loudly and she salivated around the gag, her lips becoming wet. Mel felt her orgasm coming fast. She began to pant and Alex dug his fingers into her hips harshly, riding her hard. He felt her muscles tense and then begin to spasm as her climax started. Her pussy gripped him like a vice and he felt a sudden gush of juices flood around his cock and still he kept up his relentless pace. As soon as Mel was coming back to earth after her first wave of pleasure Alex was already building up the sensations for another.

After bringing Mel to three climaxes, Alex couldn't hold back any longer. He felt his balls tighten and the tingling pulse start in his cock; with a loud roar of Mel's name he emptied himself deep inside her. Encouraged by the feeling of his cock throbbing inside her as he came; yet another orgasm erupted from deep within her.

Alex's hand left her hips and he leaned across her back, his weight supported through his arms leaning on the arms of the chair. As his breathing slowed he kissed the middle of her back tenderly.

"God Jellybean.' He breathed against her back. Mel couldn't form words around her gag instead she hummed in agreement.

"Are you ready for more?" He asked her once his breathing had slowed.

Mel groaned nodding her head a little. Alex smiled at her and pushed himself off, allowing his semi-erect cock to slip from her warmth. He let his hands stroke over her back and she shifted against the chair, steading herself, back to the position that she had started in. Alex went to the bed and lifted the firm black riding crop that he had discarded there earlier.

"This will sting Miss Anderson. But I will not cause you any permanent damage, I'll warm you up first, but I think that ten lashes will be sufficient to encourage you to improve the standards around this hotel. Do you understand?" He stated behind her, his voice stern.

"Ummm Mhmm." Mel agreed around the ball in her mouth.

Alex stepped beside her and ran the end of the crop across the skin on her shoulder down over her back and flicked the end against the silky skin on the back of her creamy thighs. Mel jumped at the contact. *Shit!* She thought to herself. *This really is going to happen!* Alex ran his hand over her ass. A wave of apprehension flooded Mel's senses. She felt the muscles in her body all clench at once, and she involuntarily held her breath, waiting for the first strike of the crop.

Alex drew the moment out, savouring the anticipation. Finally he lifted his hand and brought the drop down on Mel's backside. Fire scorched her skin where the crop made contact, and she shrieked out against the gag. There was a harshness to the crop that she hadn't been expecting, the crop felt like it was slicing into her. It made her eyes prickle, and yet at the same time her clit throbbed and warmth radiated through her starting in her pussy.

He pulled his hand back again and brought it down on Mel's ass with a crack. She writhed in her position and let out another yelp at the shock of another harsh contact from the crop. Again the skin where the riding crop had made contact sizzled, scorched in the harshness of the meeting between her tender flesh and hard unyielding leather.

She jumped when his hands roamed over her burning skin. It felt like he was running his fingers directly across her clit. Nothing could ever have prepared her for the intensity the crop would bring.

Alex's hand left her skin and he lifted the crop again, cracking it down again, leaving another red angry welt across her otherwise pale backside. Mel cried out in pain and sexual frustration. Tears welled up in her eyes and threatened to spill out over her flushed cheeks. Every last inch of her was alive with sensations, the most overwhelming one of them desire. Her backside had three raised lines across both buttocks where the riding crop had made contact, each stroke connecting with both cheeks at once. She could feel the wetness all over her thighs. She was drenched, despite the harshness of the punishment, Mel couldn't help herself.

Again Alex's hand caressed her. Again the need burned through Mel and completely overwhelmed her. She was his. She would never deny it. She could never fight against it. No matter what, Alex Matthews owned every last inch of her. He had even laid down a claim to her heart. Mel's head began to spin. She had never been to aroused in her life, but the agony of each strike of the crop ignited something deep inside her that she never knew was possible. That pain drove her forward, it kept her focussed, it reminded her of how much she wanted to please Alex to serve him, to obey him. She would do whatever it took.

She was so entranced by her train of thought that Alex's movements didn't register with her until the crop connected again on a stripe of her exposed flesh. She let out a groaning yelp around her gag, and Alex's hand stroked over her skin again. She could feel the pulling in her nipples as they brushed against the chair she was leaning on. The tears that had been threatening to spill were now leaving soaked tracked down her cheeks. A sniff escaped from her and instantly Alex was at her side where she could see him. He made eye contact with her and wiped a tear from her cheek with his finger.

"Jellybean, are you okay?" He asked the concern resonating through his voice.

Mel nodded her head meekly.

"Do you need to stop?" He asked again.

Mel shook her head with stronger conviction this time.

Alex nodded and moved behind her. "You are doing amazingly!" He reassured her, gently stroking her angry skin. Once his touch was removed Mel prepared herself for the last six lashes. *You will do this!* She thought to herself.

Six more times the crop ripped at her skin. Six more times her head spun with a total overload of sensations. Six more times Alex's hands carefully smoothed over the angry welts. Mel's face was as wet as her pussy by the time everything was over.

Alex's fingers dipped into the warmth between Mel's legs and she found herself coming apart around his fingers. An orgasm like she had never experienced before shattered her into millions of fragments. As she was just starting to come down, she was vaguely aware of Alex's hands on her ass. She felt the sudden pop of her ass muscles allowing the butt plug to be pulled from her body, replaced soon after by the head of Alex's cock.

He stroked his hands across her buttocks before grabbing her hips and relentlessly pushing his dick deep inside her ass in one single slow movement. He held himself still allowing her body the time necessary to accommodate him. The feeling of Alex and his cock was enough to overload her senses again and she found herself quickly on the climb to another climax.

Alex started to thrust into her and a long low groan sounded out around Mel's gag. He felt her body starting to tense again. He pumped his cock repeatedly into Mel keeping a demanding pace. He felt her body buck and spasm, he felt that tell tale tightening of her whole body and he pulled his cock almost completely free before slamming it back inside her tight asshole, deep and hard. Mel screamed out around the gag, her body convulsing as the most intense orgasm of her life slammed through her. The entire world disappeared from around her and she was left to free fall through the sensations that were overwhelming her as Alex rode her ass hard and fast seeking out a climax of his own, prolonging the experience for her.

Just as Alex found his own climax he reached forward and tugged the rings from Mel's nipples, the extra throb through her now free nipples made her come again, the burn in her nipples matching the burn in her clit, and the delicious friction in her ass from Alex's cock. As she screamed out again around the gag Alex gripped her hips again harshly, his entire body tensing, and thrust hard, slamming his cock to the very depths of her, his balls slapping against her sopping pussy. He roared her name as he climaxed hard deep inside her, his entire body convulsing.

"Jesus..." he panted afterwards, letting go of her hips and running his hands through his hair. Mel was leaning fully against the back of the chair, her face against the backrest, her breathing staggered like she had just finished sprinting flat out. Alex's hands trailed along her back softly, from backside up to her shoulders, he undid the buckle on the gag, and carefully removed it from Mel's mouth.

She sighed when it came away from between her lips, "Mmmm" she mewled. Alex smiled at her lying against the chair with her eyes closed. He dropped the gag to the floor and moved himself ready to regretfully withdraw his cock from Mel's body. He held her hips and guided himself back, letting his still semi erect penis slip from her ass. Mel groaned against the chair. Alex reached down to the cuffs on her ankles and undid the buckles on them, letting them fall to the floor. He moved to behind the chair, and released the cuffs on her wrists allowing them to fall to the floor with the others. He moved through the room into the bathroom, and turned on the bath taps, letting the water fill the bath. He returned to the room, and lifted Mel's robe from her bag, and a wash bag of toiletries from his own. He moved around Mel to scoop up all the restraints, the gag, and other items, putting them all away.

Alex moved to beside Mel's curled form on the chair and stroked her cheek. She stirred and smiled at his touch. He let his hand drop and moved to the bed, turning down the covers. He then returned to the semi-conscious Melody, and scooped her up in his arms. She nuzzled against him her hand idling playing with his chest hair as he took her into the bathroom.

He set her on the closed toilet lid, and moved to the bath to turn off the taps. He poured in some essential oils and waved his hand through the water to swirl it around. He turned back to her, lifted her in his arms again, and lowered her into the water before slipping into the tub behind her. She gasped as her backside hit the water, but when Alex tucked himself in behind her, she adjusted herself and leaned back against him, snuggling up to him. He held her close against him, wrapping his arms around her and cherishing her. He nuzzled gently at her neck, silently adoring how she felt tucked in against him.

Eventually Mel let out a sigh and started to absently run her fingers along the arms that Alex had wrapped around her. She felt like she was in a safe and protected little cocoon when he held her like this and let her come out of the subspace that he seemed to always be able to send her into.

"Are you back with me now?" he asked her softly.

She smiled and tilted her head to look at him. "I think so, but only just." She reached out her hand to caress his cheek. He nuzzled against her touch and closed his eyes. *God I never want to be without her.* He thought to himself. Mel dropped her hand back into the water, Alex opened his eyes and reached for the sponge on the side of the bath tub. He dipped it into the water and gently let it soothe Mel's shoulders and neck. She hummed, and shifted in the water to allow him to give her back the same treatment.

"I love these baths." She hummed in contentment.

Alex paused his actions, catching his answer before it fell from his mouth. "I love looking after you." He replied instead, his hand moving against her skin again. *Don't say it!* His inner critic warned. Alex knew better than to tell Mel how he was feeling, but he was torn, she was the first person in a very long time that he actually wanted to take that chance with. He fought hard and pushed those thoughts down, willing himself to act as naturally as he could.

When he had finished rubbing Mel all over and encouraged her from the tub, he tenderly dried her off, and made her bend herself over the bathroom counter. He lifted a small jar from beside where she was leaning, opened it, and ran a dollop of the clear balm across her striped backside.

Mel jumped at his touch.

"Shit, is that sore?" he asked concerned.

Mel laughed a little. "God no, it's freezing!"

"You will be sore, just like you are after a good spanking, and it will probably last a few days longer, but that balm will help it." He said as he massaged the last of it into her skin. When he was done, Mel turned and looked at herself in the bathroom mirror. Admiring the red marks across her backside with a smirk. Alex turned after retrieving her robe and caught her look in the mirror.

"You're proud of those aren't you?" He asked with a grin.

Mel nodded her head. "Damn right!" She grinned back.

Alex held out the robe for Mel to slip her arms in, and as he slid it over her shoulders he pulled her back against his chest and wrapped his arms around her. "I'm proud of you," he breathed against her ear, "you were amazing, no one can take the crop like you can." He smiled.

Mel turned abruptly in his arms to face him, her expression suddenly serious. "None of your other submissives had the crop?" She asked with a furrowed brow.

"No one has ever made it past three with the crop. You took ten, and I get the impression in time you would be capable of more than that." He said solemnly.

A shit eating grin grew across Mel's face and she pressed her lips against his. "That, my darling, is because I fucking rock!" She grinned when she pulled her lips from his.

Alex laughed and kissed her back. "You certainly fucking do!" He scooped her up in his arms again, and carried her out to the bed. She slipped her robe off, and slipped under the covers, allowing Alex his ritual of tucking her in. He moved round the bed, dropped his towel to the floor, and slid between the covers with Mel. He pulled her against his chest, spooned in against her, holding her in his arms.

He kissed her shoulder and whispered in her ear. "Sweet dreams Jellybean." He reached back and turned off the lamp, his arm going back around Mel as he did. She took his hand in hers and kissed the back of it softly.

"Sweet dreams Alex." She smiled softly.

Within seconds both of them were fast asleep.

CHAPTER 20

Mel awoke the next morning to find she was still wrapped up tightly in Alex's arms. She lifted the arm that was over her body, and slid herself forward to the edge of the bed. She swung her legs out and sat upright, feeling for the first time that delicious throb and tenderness in her backside that the night before had left her with.

She got up slowly from the bed so as not to disturb Alex, and padded silently across the floor to the bathroom with her robe in her hand. Once she had used the bathroom, she stood in front of the mirror again, admiring her red lines. She ran her fingers across her skin gingerly, nervous that she would cause her skin to sting with her touch. Movement on the edges of her vision caught her eye and she looked up to find Alex standing behind her completely naked and grinning as he watched her inspecting her striped backside.

"Like what you see Miss Anderson?" He asked her with a wicked grin.

"Yes Master Lex. I trust that I have suitably compensated you for the issues that you felt the need to raise with the hotel?" She asked him with a cheeky smirk.

Alex moved in behind her, his hands firmly on her hips, and his heavy erection evident at the crack of her ass. "Perhaps Miss Anderson." He whispered against her ear before pressing his lips against her neck.

Her back arched against him, and she moaned from his attention on her most sensitive spot. She turned her head back, taking advantage of their height difference and captured his lips with her own. He moaned into her mouth and pulled her tight against him. His tongue slipping between her lips, finding her own, and playfully twisting around it. His hand caressed along her hip, over her side, and reached for her breast.

He released her lips from his, and growled in a low rumble. "Let's have a shower." Before pulling her towards the shower and turning on the water, seizing her mouth again with his own, pushing her backwards under the warm flow of water from the shower head.

~ ~ ~

Mel laughed as she walked out of the hotels door and went to Alex's Range Rover with a spring in her step.

"I can't believe you are making me go to the zoo." Alex pouted behind her as he carried their bags.

"Oh stop moaning like an old man!" She scolded with a grin.

Alex dropped the bags into the back of the car and grabbed Mel's wrist, yanking her hard against him, his hand reaching for her ass, turning her so that she was against the Range Rover. After a fast glance around he reached under her sundress and dipped a finger into her pussy, causing a gasp to escape from her lips, and her head to fall back with her eyes closed.

"Could an old man have you like this Jellybean?" Alex grinned, and pulled his finger from her wet folds. She looked at him with an intense gaze, and watched as he put his finger in his mouth and licked her juices from it. He smirked as her face blushed.

"Get in the car!" He grinned, and walked off to driver's side of the vehicle. She glared in his direction before moving to the passenger side of the car and slipping into the seat beside him.

~ ~ ~

Mel's eyes went wide with excitement when she looked at the Asian lions. "Look at them!" She cooed. Alex grinned at her as she took him by the hand and pulled him closer to the enclosure. "Aren't they beautiful! They are so noble!" She smiled at him and once again he felt the warmth of her spirit radiating out from her and blanketing him. *You're in love with her, you complete idiot.* The voice inside told him. It was completely right, but that just wasn't something that Alex wanted to admit just yet. Admitting that he was in love with her, would like poking a sleeping bear where his fears were concerned. He would freak out, he knew this, and he wanted to avoid that for as long as possible. He never wanted to be in a situation where he felt that compulsion to run from Mel.

He watched her grinning with a childlike glee as she moved around the zoo from enclosure to enclosing, stopping to read the information on each of the plaques, announcing random facts to Alex as she did. He found himself lost in her, and basking in the joy and excitement she had.

They spent several hours roaming the grounds of Dublin Zoo, and all too quickly was heading for the time when they would have to leave, and head back up to Belfast. Alex pulled her in against him.

"We need to make tracks soon. We've a good two hour drive ahead of us, and I would like to take you for dinner before we go!" He smiled at her.

"Oh okay... On one condition!" She said, bargaining like his nieces and nephew regularly did.

"Go on?" He grinned.

"I want to go to the gift shop and get a cuddly lion." She grinned.

Alex laughed at her. "You are such a brat!"

She grinned back at him even more. "And you know that is EXACTLY why you have me around." She said before raising her eyebrow suggestively, kissing him on the nose, and walking off in the direction of the gift shop.

~ ~ ~

Alex glanced over to where Mel was asleep beside him, clinging to a cuddly lion he had bought for her. As he drove along the road heading back to Belfast, his mind wandered over everything that was happening between him and Mel. He thought about Natalie, and everything that she had done to him, and he started to debate if that was something that Melody would ever do to him. He shook his head at the thought. *No, that wasn't remotely possible!* His critic told him. *You might be a feckless asshole, but there's no way that girl would ever do that to you.* It reminded him, and he thought about how the reality of the situation was more likely to be him hurting her and wrecking her trust forever rather than the other way around. He sighed at the thought, he couldn't do that to her, he didn't want to do that to her. He reached over and turned on the radio and turned it down low, the sound of Eminem filled his ears with Rihanna telling him that she loved the way he lied. Guilt nagged at him, and he pressed the button to change to the CD Changer.

~ ~ ~

She woke to find Alex rubbing her arm and calling her name softly. "You're home Jellybean." He told her. She stretched with a soft sigh and undid her seatbelt before stepping out of the car.

"Are you staying?" She asked as she walked towards her front door. Alex lifted her bag from the back of his Range Rover and walked towards her.

"I can't tonight Jellybean, I have to do some work tonight before an early meeting in the morning, and we both know that I get no work done when you're around." He grinned at her and kissed her on the nose.

Mel wrapped her arms around him on the doorstep. "This is very true Mr Matthews, I know that you have real problems resisting me." She grinned kissing his cheek. "But, since this weekend was your treat to me, you're going to keep next weekend free for me!" She winked and him and gave him a brief kiss.

"I think that sounds fair." He grinned back at her. He pulled her tighter against him and leaned in for a deeper kiss. His lips pressed against hers, his arms went round her waist and held her close. His tongue tangled with hers, and he moaned when her hands tangled in his hair and she tugged. He broke their kiss and growled.

"Stop tempting me woman." He breathed, holding her face in his hands, his forehead against hers.

"Then bugger off before I drag you inside and have my wicked way with you." She grinned at him.

"Yes Ma'am." He grinned and kissed her on the nose. He gave her another brief kiss before moving away from her, and heading back to his car. He got in and started the engine, Mel stayed on the doorstep watching as he left. She blew him a kiss as he drove out of site, and he gave her a wave.

Once he was out of sight Mel turned and went inside, locked the door and took her bag upstairs. Once she had cleaned her teeth and changed into her pyjamas she crawled into bed and fell asleep cuddling her lion, thoughts of Alex swimming in her mind.

CHAPTER 21

Mel smiled when Alex closed his front door and headed over to her car. "All set?" She asked him as he got in the passenger side.

"As ready as I'll ever be!" He smiled, leaning across the car and giving her a brief yet smouldering kiss. "Are you going to tell me where we're going?" He asked.

Mel laughed. "Did you tell me when we went to the aquarium?" She looked at him out of the corner of her eye as she backed out of his drive and onto the street.

Alex sighed dramatically and folded his arms over his chest. "No."

"Exactly." Mel grinned and drove out of the area that Alex lived in.

20 minutes later Mel parked her car on one of the Victorian streets behind the university, near the entrance to the Botanical Gardens. "We're here." She advised him. Alex looked around suspiciously.

"Botanic?" He asked, pointing in the direction of the park gates.

Mel smirked at him and raised an eyebrow. "You'll have to wait and see Mr Matthews." She took her seat belt off, grabbed her bag, and got out of the car. Alex watched her before doing the same himself. He stood on the pavement and waited as Mel locked her car, and walked around it and onto the pavement. "Come on." She beckoned over her shoulder as she walked off down the street. Alex jogged to catch up and soon fell into step beside her.

"Are you going to tell me yet?" He asked.

"Nope!" She smiled over at him.

They walked side by side down the street and round the corner, onto the university campus, and up along the side of the library that Mel was so familiar with. Mel led them into the Botanical Gardens. The gardens were gorgeous in September, the leaves on the trees were starting to change colour and the first few had already started to fall. They followed a path past the famous Palm House, and towards the entrance gate. At the gate, she turned left and headed up to a large building. "We're going to the Museum?" Alex asked with a smirk.

Mel smiled. "For starters, yes." She held out her hand for Alex to take it. He placed his hand in hers and they walked up the steps and into the Ulster Museum.

Once inside they were greeted by member of staff who presented them with a map of the exhibits. Mel pulled Alex towards the lifts. "Start at the top, and we'll work out way down." She informed him and she pressed the button to call the elevator. Alex smiled at her enthusiasm and let her drag him along.

When they got off the elevator in the top section of the Museum, Mel was instantly attracted to the displays of glassware and pottery. She looked at each of the items with enthusiasm, and it was an enthusiasm that was fast to rub off on Alex. She ran her fingers over a large piece of green glass called Cat and Dog, smiling. "Isn't it fantastic?" She asked.

Alex looked at her and the piece of art, admiring the curves in the glass, and trying to decide which piece was the cat, and which was the dog. "I'm an architect. Of course, I'm going to like all this kind of thing. Materials, and how they are used, and diffuse light, etc." He smirked, and she frowned at him.

"Okay, Mr Big shot!" She scolded, poking him in the arm and wandering off to some of the other exhibits in the large glass cabinets that covered this section of the floor.

When Alex finally caught up to her as she was browsing the pottery on display, she took his hand again and said, "Come this way." as she pulled him towards a large double door. He walked with her, pushing the door open ahead of her allowing her to walk in first. Alex glanced around realising that they were in one of the Galleries within the Museum. He watched Mel disappeared down some steps and through another door. He followed behind and found himself gazing at her as she gazed at postcards of fashion from the early twentieth century.

"Look at this." She grinned. "A 1920s flapper, all glitz and glamour without being too much." She said, pointing to the image in the frame. She walked slowly along, taking in every last image in the exhibit. Alex walked along behind her, taking in every expression that graced her face. He followed behind her as she walked into another gallery area, this time with more classical landscapes of the impressionist era. Her face lit up as she wandered around the room, and he enjoying taking in both the artwork, and his companion.

They toured around the art zone of the museum, Mel delighting in what was on display, Alex listening to her thoughts and opinions, and enjoying the opportunity to discuss art and materials and light, as they were used in each of the paintings they viewed.

Eventually, they arrived at the Ice Age exhibit. Mel went to look at the elephant skulls and the other items. Alex found himself at a quiz point, where he was asked what he thought each item was. He got the first two correct and then Mel joined him. They debated the answers with each other, and a few times, Alex refused Mel's answer for his own, when he got it wrong she laughed, and teased him for it.

They drifted through the other exhibits until they found themselves at Alex's favourite, he took Mel's hand

and led her into the exhibit. "Look at these." He said, looking over the glass case which held the 'Earth's Treasures' displays. He talked to Mel about the minerals and gemstones in the cases, and talked about the influence things like copper had on the colours that were produced. Mel smiled, watching Alex light up about something that clearly fascinated him.

"I had a collectible set as a child. You got a magazine and a sample of the mineral every fortnight. I loved to read about how they were formed, and found." He caught Mel's grin in the darkness that draped the exhibit. "I know!" He smirked back at her. "I'm a geek!"

She giggled and leaned in against him to kiss his cheek. "You're adorable!" She smiled. Alex grinned and pushed her back into a dark corner of the exhibit, pinning her against the wall, and crushing his lips against hers, demanding entry to her mouth with his tongue. Wanting her, needing to feel her against him. She kissed him back deeply, moulding her body into his.

There was a loud cough from behind them. They broke apart and Alex grinned his killer smile at the curator. "Sorry about that." He smiled, holding up both hands. "Won't happen again!" He promised, taking Mel by the hand and pulling her out of the dark and round the corner to the next exhibit. Mel's face was flushed, and she was biting her lip trying not too laugh.

"Oops!" Alex laughed once they were out of earshot of the staff member.

Mel slapped his arm. "Oh my God! I feel like a kid being told off by a teacher for snogging at the bike shed!" She sniggered. Alex just grinned at her and slid his arm around her waist, holding her against him, hip to hip.

"Come on." He laughed.

Two hours later they were walking around the gift shop of the museum, casually browsing all of the things on display there. Alex picked up a triceratops and made a face as he walked in through the air towards Mel.

"I think he needs to come home with you." He told her. "Tricky needs a home he says."

"Tricky?" She smirked.

He smiled. "Yes, Tricky the Triceratops. He says who's that gorgeous creature over there, can I go and meet her and go home with her?" he said a serious expression on his face.

Mel's shoulders started to move up and down with laughter and she shook her head, taking the stuffed toy from Alex's hands. "You're crazy!" She chuckled. They paid for 'Tricky' and he took her hand as they walked back down the steps into Botanic Gardens.

"Let's go for a walk around it all." Alex suggested, holding out his arm for Mel to grab his elbow. Mel smiled, hooked her arm around his and fell into step beside him.

As they walked, they talked. Mel asked Alex about his family, and he told her about his sister Emily, her husband Ben, and their three children, who were also his godchildren. He shared tales of the kind of things the kids would get up to and how much Ben loved his sister, and how they had become friends as he got to know Ben through his sister.

The more he shared with her, the more he found himself wanting to share even more. He wanted to open up to her like he hadn't been able to do with anyone since Natalie. *You trust her doofus!* His inner voice told him. For the first time, in a long time, he decided that he actually agreed with what his inner voice was telling him. He did trust Mel.

Knowing that he trusted her, he couldn't stop the words coming out of his mouth when he confided in her about his parents, and how they had been killed when he had been fourteen, and Emily had been twenty. He told her about the car accident that had taken both of them one May evening as they drove home from an evening at the theatre. Mel had stopped holding his arm at that point, choosing to wrap her arms around his waist, and pull him against her.

"I'm sorry to hear about your parents Alex." She murmured against his chest. He felt her comfort wash over him. He felt her warmth and light reach every last cold and dark corner in his soul. He sighed, relaxing something deep within him that he hadn't even realised had been tensed.

"It was seventeen years ago now." He said, wrapping his arms tight around her, and pulling her against his chest. "Its not as hard to bear as it used to be." He told her, kissing her forehead.

They stood there in a tight embrace as the world around them paused, leaving just them moving around in their own little bubble. Alex put a finger under her chin to tilt her head up to his, and leaned over to briefly brush against her lips with his own.

Mel moved back when he ended their kiss, keeping an arm around his back as they walked along, Alex mirroring the gesture his arm around her. "I know what you went through losing a parent." She shared with him. "My dad passed away when I was eleven." Alex squeezed her tight against him when he heard what she had to say. "He had a heart attack. He was only forty-five." Mel felt the familiar tightening in her chest when she talked about her dad. It had been fifteen years, but sometimes, the grief caught up to her when she least expected it.

"A right pair we are." Alex smiled as he hugged her against his side with the arm he had draped around her back. "What do you say we head back to the house, order a Chinese takeaway, and see what terrible film is on TV tonight?" He suggested.

She smiled at him. "Sounds like heaven!" She said enthusiastically. They turned down one of the paths that crisscrossed the park, and headed to the exit beside where Mel's car was parked.

When they arrived back in Alex's drive he paused before getting out of her car. "I just wanted to say thank you. I've had a lovely day, and it's been really nice to be able to share my sister and my parents with you." He smiled, leaning across the car to kiss Mel on the cheek.

She looked at him and felt her heart somersault. Words gathered at the back of her throat, but she couldn't form them into anything coherent. "Let's go order some food." She smiled, reaching for the car door. Alex did the same, and Mel locked her car while he opened his front door for them both.

CHAPTER 22

Alex shared the last of the wine between their glasses, before picking his up as he continued to talk. "So, what led to the Computer Science?" He asked, taking a sip from his glass.

Mel smiled and played with the stem of her glass while she pondered her answer. "I don't know... I've always liked computers, taught myself everything I knew before going to university, fixed a lot of computers for friends and family things like that. Played about with some web design, liked the logic that there was behind it all I guess. Everything is black and white. On or off." She smiled, and asked, "What about you? Why architecture?"

Alex put his elbow on the back of the sofa and rested his head in his hand. "Honestly?" He asked. She nodded. "Promise you won't laugh?" Mel laughed and instantly covered her mouth with her hand. "I'm sorry!" She giggled. "I promise I won't laugh at your reason!" She promised, forcing a serious face. Alex rolled his eyes shaking his head. "Okay." He sighed. "I loved coming up with building designs in Lego." Mel grinned and Alex frowned. "You promised!" He accused her. She grinned even more then. "That has to be the cutest reason in the world! There's a soft side to you Alex Matthews!" She beamed at him.

"Shhhhh! It's a secret." He blushed, taking another mouthful of his wine. He swallowed and looked at her. He felt like he was seeing her with new eyes over these last few weeks. He longed to touch her, caress her, and even make love with her, but he wanted it as Alex, not as Lex. He wanted it to be slow and tender, and not some lust fuelled unison. The only problem was, that wanting this made Alex feel like a nervous teenager trying to elicit that all important first kiss.

Mel let her head fall onto the back of the sofa, and she closed her eyes. "What were you like when you were younger, Alex?" She asked him.

"Tall, skinny, cocky as hell. You would have hated me." He laughed, and she smiled. "What were you like Mel? He asked in return.

"Ohhh I was chubby, loved books, wanted to be an English Lit teacher or a writer. And yet, even then, a geeky sci-fi fan who played about with computers." She explained, opening her eyes, tilting her head round to look at Alex without lifting it from the sofa. Alex set his glass on the coffee table in front of them and moved to take Mel's from her hand so it could join his on the table. He slowly moved towards her, shuffling along the sofa to be closer, before lifting a hand to cup her face and softly caressing her lips with his own. His kiss was tender, yet heated. It told her that he wanted her, yet needed to somehow savour her too. She ran her own hands through his hair lazily, enjoying the relaxed way he was kissing her. He pulled his lips from hers and let them gently kiss and nibble down her neck. A sighed moan escaped from Mel's throat as Alex nibbled on her neck close to her shoulder. "I love to hear you making that sound." He breathed against her ear, before returning his mouth to hers in another luxuriously slow kiss. Again, Alex lifted his lips away from hers, and he watched as her eyelids fluttered open, hooded with desire. She watched as he stood and offered his hand out to her. She offered her hand to him, and he took it, kissing her knuckles and pulling her off the sofa. She came up against him, chest to chest, and stood looking deep into Alex's now almost black eyes. He hooked an arm around her waist and kissed the tip of her nose, he captured her hand in his, let his other slip from her waist and moved towards the doorway, pulling her with him.

He led her to the stairs, walking up them, and towards his bedroom. He paused at the doorway and looked deep into her eyes. "I want to take you to bed Mel." He told her. "But I want it to be just you and me, I don't want to tie you up. I want... Just us... Is that okay?" He asked her. She gazed up at him and licked her lips. "Yeah." She nodded. Alex smiled at her. "You are beautiful." He told her and kissed her again while caressing her cheek.

Without breaking their kiss Alex turned Mel round and walked her into the bedroom, closing the door behind them. Slowly he pulled her t-shirt over her head, parting from her lips only long enough to move her top over her face and away from her body. His hands stroked over her skin, across her shoulders and down her back, cupping her backside through her jeans. Mel reached for the buttons of Alex's shirt, breaking their kiss so she could slowly undo the buttons, savouring each sneaky peak as more and more of his torso was exposed. With three buttons left to undo she leaned forward, nuzzling her nose against Alex's light sprinkling of chest hair, kissing his chest softly as she finished opening his shirt. She pushed it from his shoulders and slid it down his arms. She kissed across his chest to his nipple, flicking it with her tongue. Alex exhaled a groan, and Mel continued to kiss across his chest, her hand following behind at waist height caressing his bare skin. She circled him, planting a string of tender little kisses across his back from shoulder to shoulder, her hand dropping lower to skim across Alex's pert backside, before coming back round to his front, gracing his other nipple with attention. Alex's hand reached to cup her face and pull her in again for a more urgent kiss. His hands grabbed her hips, pulling her against him, skimming over her ass and up her back to unfasten her bra. He slid the straps off her shoulders and down her arms, letting it fall, exposing her breasts to his skin. Her already pebbled nipples pressed against his chest, and he moaned against

Melody's mouth. Mel's hands went to Alex's neck and snaked down over his chest squeezing his muscles, her fingertips grazing his nipples as her hands roamed over his stomach, and stopped at the button and zipper at the fly of his jeans. She undid his fly without breaking their long kiss, a kiss that increased in desire with every passing moment. She broke her lips away from his, leaving him breathing quickly, instead skimming her lips over his skin, down his neck, over his chest, stomach, before resting on her knees, she stopped at his waist. She reached up and inched Alex's jeans and boxers down his legs to his feet where he stepped out of them. She looked up at him, and while never taking his eyes from his, she slipped out her tongue and licked along the entire underside of his rock hard cock, from his balls to the tip which was already dripping with pre-cum. Alex shivered at the sight and sensation of what Melody was doing. She then worked her way back up his now naked form to his lips.

Alex wasted no time in removing the last of Melody's clothing. He popped the button at the top of her jeans, pulled down the zip, and slid them down her legs before she stepped out of them. He was at the perfect level with her pussy, and he couldn't resist nuzzling his face in against her sex, and taking a long lick to return the tease that Mel had previously tortured him with. She gasped, and her body shivered at the contact. He then kissed a trail from her hot, wet sex to her breasts. Alex took one of Mel's ample tits in each hand and kneaded them, his forefinger circling around her nipples at he did. Mel moaned, her eyes closing and her head falling back. His lips found her neck and he nuzzled in against her. Her hands grabbed his shoulders and squeezed. Her nails making little indents into his flesh. He dipped his head and ran his tongue over Mel's peaked nipple, feeling it harden even further when he latched his lips around it and sucked it into his mouth. One of Mel's hands instantly in his hair, gripping at it, holding him to her breast, needed the intense feeling he was building within her to be stoked to a blaze.

When Melody realised that Alex was trying to work her into frenzy in a very leisurely manner, she put her hands on his chest and pushed him back, breaking his contact with her. She prowled forward, pushing him back until Alex felt the edge of the bed at the back of his legs. Mel pushed him back further, and he fell back onto the waiting king size. She again ran her hands over his body, down over his strong thighs, and then stood over him, taking in all that lay before her. Alex could feel the heat of her gaze scorching every inch of his skin that her eyes roamed over. His cock bobbed, throbbing painfully against it lay ridged against his stomach. "Move up on the bed." She instructed, "Lie roughly in the middle." She told him. Alex shimmied himself into the position that

Mel wanted him in and gazed at her. She placed her knees on the bed and crawled up beside him, before she straddled his thighs, and spread her naked body over his. His hands instinctively went to her hips, holding her against him while he lifted his hips up against hers.

Melody kissed Alex's chest, she was relishing the chance to be able to touch him and kiss him, and roam her hands over him in a way that he previously would have restricted her from. Her tongue flicked over one of his nipples and a low growl sounded in Alex's throat. He wrapped his arm around her and flipped her underneath him. His fingertips stroked across her jaw, down her neck, across her collarbone and down her arm. His lips followed the path that his fingers took as far as her collar bone. From there his tongue licked across her chest, before circling a nipple, his lips clamping around it as he sucked it into his mouth. Mel arched her back against Alex's mouth, needing more contact. He untucked his hand from underneath her, and his thumb and forefinger teased her already pert nipple into a tighter peak. She groaned, starting to squirm with need beneath him. "Alex... please!" She begged with a sigh.

"Please what, Jellybean?" He asked her, lifting his mouth from her extended nipple, taking the opportunity to move to her other breast with his mouth.

"I need to feel you inside me." She whimpered.

Alex lifted his head and looked at Mel, his lips hovering over hers. "I know, trust me, I'm going to take care of you tonight. I promise." He explained, and he let his lips connect with hers briefly.

Alex shifted on the bed, and moved himself to between Mel's legs. He lifted her foot and started to kiss and nibble from her toes slowly across her foot, over her calf, he paused at the back of her knee and offered it a lick that made Mel gasp before he continued along her inner thigh. Once he reached the apex of her thigh, he lapped a long single lick through her wet folds, her entire body twitched at the contact, and a long hiss escaped from her mouth. Alex lifted his head and grinned at her, before lifting her other foot and repeating the process on her other leg. By the time he reached her pussy again, Mel was balling her fists in the bed covers and moaning, her back arching off the bed, desperate for the attention she needed to climax. He settled himself between her thighs and let his tongue dance through her wet labia once again. "I love how you taste." He breathed against her sex before nuzzling in against her, his tongue mixing between circling her clit, to long deep strokes into her. Mel's hips rose to meet his mouth and he suckled on her clit, nibbling and teasing as he listened to her pant and moan above him. He lifted his hand and pushed two fingers deep inside her. It was all she needed, he felt her clench around his fingers as he thrust them slowly in and out of her. Her juices flooding his mouth, his name on her lips as she called out in ecstasy. "Oh fuck! ALEX!" She cried as he continued to nurse every last shiver from her body.

Alex continued to greedily lap at her pussy until her body began to rise up against his mouth again. He covered her sensitive little nub with his mouth again and sucked on it, flicking over it with his tongue between sucks. Mel moaned out loudly and grabbed a handful of Alex's hair in her hand. "So good!" She sighed out in a moan. He wanted her to come for him again, craving her orgasm like it was his own. Again he slid two fingers inside her, pushing in deep and finding that little bunch of nerves on the front wall of her vagina. He took his other hand and pressed it on her stomach just a fraction. A second later Mel's pussy grabbed hold of his hand as it convulsed around him and she screamed out, her whole body tensing as her back arched off the bed. Alex used the flat of his tongue to tease more and more shivers from her body, coercing her with the flat of his tongue on her clit.

He eased his fingers from where her body was clenching around them, and looked her deep in the eyes as he licked her wetness from his fingers. "I could taste you all day long Jellybean." He smirked as desire and post orgasmic bliss merged together in her eyes, and she licked her lips. He kissed her mons and started a trail up along her body, over her stomach, towards her breasts.

His tongue circled a nipple, his hand reaching the other to tease and fondle her. His normally rough and greedy touch was sensual and tender, and Mel felt her heart explode with the feelings that she was having for him. The tenderness that he was expressing to her now via his touch was all she needed to know that she was completely in love with him, and that time had come when she wanted more. She wanted so much more now.

She held his head to her breast and he sucked her nipple into his mouth, applying a delicious amount of pressure, serving to tease her, to put her on edge with need. She moaned out his name.

"Mmm?" He moaned in question against her nipple.

"I need you Alex." She groaned, writhing against him.

He pried his lips from around her nipple and looked at her, his hand moving to beside her. "I'm always going to give you what you need Jellybean." He told her and shifting his position to directly between her thighs. As he stared deep into her eyes he pushed the head of his cock against her wet pussy, letting it dip in between her labia, and find its rightful place deep inside her in one long slow stroke.

Mel gasped as his invasion, a burn instantly starting deep within her as her body became accustomed to his entrance. She felt captivated by his eyes and couldn't remove hers from his. She moaned as Alex started a slow pace, grinding against her in circles, allowing his cock to pull out slightly, before teasingly sliding back in deeper.

"Oh Alex." She sighed. "Fuck me harder!" She encouraged.

Alex kissed the tip of her nose. "No Jellybean." He panted on as he ground his hips against her, and moved deep inside her. "This isn't fucking." He said, and brushed his lips against hers in a brief kiss. "Mmmm, God Mel." He groaned. "This is just you and me. Let me worship you." He appealed, and leaned in to kiss her again.

He let his tongue roll over hers at the same pace that he rolled his hips against hers. Goosebumps rose over Mel's skin, every last nerve in her body was tingling. His words and tenderness started a warm feeling that ran over every last inch of her, and his sensuous rhythm inside her, created a burn that smouldered inside her groin, and radiated heat out to the tips of her fingers and toes, and the top of her head.

She wrapped her arms around him, holding him tight against her, her hips falling into a rhythm with his. Sweat glistened on the skin of them both, as both moved against each other keeping a slow and sensual tempo. Mel stroked her hands over Alex's back, caressing his taut muscles. He dipped his head to her lips, her neck, and her shoulders. His hands ran over her, her hips, her breasts, and cupping her face.

Alex could feel Mel's pussy start to pulse, he knew that she was going to come soon. He wanted to drive himself into her hard, but he held back on that urge, instead keeping up his leisurely pace. Mel wrapped her legs around the back of Alex's thighs, holding him against her, helping to increase the amount of friction he was creating on her clit with his pelvis. Her body started to tense, she felt the explosion of pleasure growing, and she held on tight to Alex, her fingertips digging into his back.

A low growl vibrated through Alex's chest, and Mel knew that his climax was as close as hers. She stared deep into his eyes, needing that intimacy, wanting to be completely engulfed by what was happening between them. "Alex..." She started unable to finish the sentence.

"I know..." He panted, his eyes piercing through to her soul. As she looked into his eyes she felt her orgasm rip through her. She arched her back against him and cried out his name over and over, her eyes never leaving his. Alex felt her body tensing, and clamping down on his cock as her climax erupted. The intensity of her orgasm and the connection between them as they looked into each other's eyes was enough to start his climax too. He thrust deep and hard inside her, erupting into her, calling out her name.

"Mel, oh Jesus Mel!" He called before crushing his lips against hers, lavishing attention on her mouth with his tongue. Every fear he had previously had melted away, and he wanted to be hers, completely, for as long as humanly possible.

There were things that Alex wanted to tell Mel, and even though the words still wouldn't form in his mouth, he knew that it was going to happen, and he no longer wanted to fight it. He sighed as he withdrew his cock from her body, before falling onto the bed beside her. Mel shivered when he moved away from her. He pulled her in tight against his body and wrapped his arms around her, pulling the sheets and duvet up over them. She snuggled in against him, needing to keep the contact and intimacy they had just experienced.

She looked at him and smiled. "Thank you." She said, cupping his face tenderly.

"Anytime Jellybean." He smiled and kissed the tip of her nose. "You've changed me these last few months, you deserve my appreciation for that." He murmured sleepily. "Now go to sleep." He grinned.

She smiled broadly back at him. "I'm glad I've been around for the journey." She leaned forward and kissed him gently. "Night Alex." She whispered against his lips.

"Night Mel." He replied, snuggled into her before they both drifted off to sleep in each other's arms.

CHAPTER 23

Mel woke the next morning to find she was in a tangle of limbs with Alex. She sighed in contentment, enjoying the feeling of being wrapped up with him, and enjoying the memories she had of the night before. Things had definitely changed between them. Mel knew now without a shadow of a doubt that she was in love with Alex, a realisation that filled her with warmth.

Alex stirred, the smell of sex and Melody flooding his nose. He felt her against him and couldn't help but pull her close against him. She wiggled her butt against his hard cock that was now pressing against her backside, tempting her.

He kissed her bare shoulder. "Stop wriggling Jellybean." He growled playfully. Mel shifted her ass back against him and glanced over her shoulder, her look playful and mischievous. Alex grabbed her backside parting her ass cheeks and sliding his throbbing erection between her cheeks, grinding it against her.

"Stop pushing your luck." He smirked at her, nipping her shoulder with his teeth. His nip made her tense her ass against him, and he rolled back away from her, reaching for the drawer in his bedside table. In a few second, he was back against her. She heard the click as he flipped the lid on a small bottle of lubricant.

Alex squirted some lubricant from the bottle into his hand and moved his hand to his stiff cock, covering it in the slippery lotion. Once his dick was well covered he slipped his hand against Mel's asshole, slipping the last of the lubricant over her tight hole. He pushed the tip of his prick against her and reached around to let his finger find her clit. As his fingertip grazed that sensitive little nub, she moaned and pushed back against him. His lips nibbled on her shoulder as his hand worked her wet pussy.

"Alex!" She pleaded.

"Shhhhh." He whispered, and rocked his hips, pressing his cock into her, begging entry. He felt Mel relax against his insistent pressure, and his cock slipped past the ring of muscle in her ass.

Mel groaned loudly as Alex tilted his hips and slid his cock deep into her most intimate place.

"Are you okay?" He asked.

"God yes!" She moaned pushing her backside against him, willing him to start thrusting into her.

Alex kissed her shoulder softly. "No Jellybean, slow is so much better, remember?" He said, starting to work himself deeper and deeper into her ass in a deliberate and sensual grinding of his hips. He removed his hand from her clit, and brushed it on her lips allowing her to taste herself. Mel licked his fingers, savouring the taste of her own pussy. She moaned as the tang of her juices touched her tongue. As she did, she felt Alex's cock throb deep in her ass.

His hand went from her lips to her nipple. He circled around it with his moist fingertips before teasing it between his thumb and forefinger, pulling it out from her breast a little, mischievously encouraging her body to respond to him more. She grabbed his hand and held it against her breast, encouraging him to knead into her flesh instead of torturing her stiff little peak. He ground his hips against her, his cock pushing deep into her ass, and she let a moan escape. She shifted against him, hooking her legs over the side of his legs as he pulled back a little before driving his hard dick into her again, sliding all the way in.

He wrapped his arms around her and pulled her tight against him, grinding his hips against her backside, his cock moving in and out, filling her completely. His fingers went back to between her legs and he ran them through her wetness. He grazed her clit, and he felt her ass clench around him. He knew that she was already close.

His fingers slipped inside her pussy, first one, then two, and he thrust his hand against her in perfect time with his dick deep in her ass. She was panting and writhing against him, needing more, wanting to come.

"Oh Alex! PLEASE!" She begged him.

Alex rubbed his thumb over her clit as he fucked her with his fingers. "Come for me, Mel!" He encouraged, feeling her tighten around him. As soon as Mel heard his words, her orgasm ripped through her. She arched her back and panted as the world fragmented around her in a blinding flash of pleasure. Alex jerked his hips against her, thrusting hard into her ass before he came deep inside her. "Fuck Mel!" He growled as he climaxed.

He kissed her shoulder as they shivered together in post orgasmic bliss. "You look and sound so beautiful when you fall apart with my cock inside you." He murmured against her bare skin. She grinned at his compliment, and leaned against him, soaking in his warmth, and the skin-to-skin contact with him.

Alex nuzzled into her neck as she leaned against him, holding her, not wanting to burst their bubble. For the first time, in a long time, Alex felt complete, and that was all because of Melody.

"Are you busy at the start of October?" He asked, nipping at her shoulder.

Mel's eyes opened and she looked at him. "Why?" She asked with a smile.

"I have a gala to go to, and I wondered if you would join me?" He murmured nervously.

"Not sure I could cope with a vibrator in my knickers at an event like that." She answered him with a grin.

Alex frowned. "No Jellybean, as my official guest, it's in the Hilton hotel with a lot of bigwigs." He gazed into her eyes. "What do you say? You'd have to get a gown and all that kind of thing." He asked.

Mel thought about it for a moment before grinning back at Alex. "I would love to go with you." Then realisation about something else that Alex had said hit her and she groaned. "Oh shit... I'm going to have to wear a dress..." She mumbled. Alex let out a deep laugh. "I don't *do* dresses!" She complained.

"You will look amazing in a gown Jellybean!" He smiled. "Let's go and get a shower." He said, and pulled his semi-erect penis from her ass.

"Mmmm..." She murmured at his withdrawal. He moved back and rolled her towards him, face to face. He brushed his lips over hers.

"Shower, breakfast, and then perhaps we should just come back to bed." He whispered as he kept his forehead against hers.

She smiled at his plan. "Sounds like a great plan to me." She breathed against his mouth before crushing her lips against his, grabbing his hair in her hands, running it through her fingers. He moaned against her mouth, his now completely erect cock rubbing at her hip. She pulled her mouth from his and pushed away from him, jumping up out of the bed, and heading for the door of his ensuite bathroom.

"Let's get that shower then." She grinned over her shoulder. Alex growled and bounced up out of the bed, striding towards her.

"You're in big trouble now Jellybean!" He warned her as he closed the space between them. Mel squealed and ran for the bathroom laughing.

CHAPTER 24

"I'm so excited!" Jacob exclaimed as they walked towards the shopping mall.

Mel laughed. "I'm glad one of us enjoys shopping sweetie." Mel sighed. She hated shopping, especially for something as fancy as a gala. She had never been as grateful for her gay best friend as she was at this moment in time.

"What's our budget?" He asked, practically jumping up and down and clapping like an excited child.

She shrugged. "I don't know yet Jake, it depends on how much I like what I see, but I have my credit card with me if that helps?" She smirked when she saw Jacob's eyes light up. She had never seen anyone love shopping for clothes the way this man did.

"House of Fraser first, and if that doesn't work, Debenhams!" Jacob planned.

"Yes boss!" She grinned, earning her a frown from her friend. "Come on Ms Westwood." She laughed linking her arm around his and pulling him towards the doors of the House of Fraser store.

They found their way to the formal wear section and Jacob started moving around all the rails ready to pick as many dresses as he thought would suit Mel. Mel stopped him before he did. "I know what I have in mind Jay.

Floor length, floaty, nothing covered in glitter. Classic, elegant, refined. Understand?" She asked, holding on to her friend's arm. Jacob nodded and gave her a quick salute.

The first thing that Jacob reached for was a silver chiffon gown, covered in beadwork. Mel shook her head. "Jacob!" She scolded. "Nothing too glittery!"

Jacob grinned. "But sweetie, this would look fabulous on your figure."

Mel raised an eyebrow, and Jacob put the dress back on the rail in a huff. "Fine!" He sulked and went off looking again. A few minutes later he was back at her side again with a floor length fitted cream gown with black lace over the top.

"Oh!" Mel murmured as she ran her fingers over the dress. "Okay, this one is one worth trying on!" She said taking the dress off Jacob and hanging it over her arm to keep for trying on after more browsing.

Feeling victorious Jacob disappeared off between the rails again. About five minutes later he returned again, this time with a one-shouldered rich dark purple ruched gown with a little glitter on the shoulder. "Oh Jake!" She said in awe when she saw the dress. "It's gorgeous! Definitely one for trying on!" She said, taking the dress off him and draping it over her arm. "What do you think of this one?" Mel asked showing him a royal blue taffeta creation.

"Oh sweetie! That colour is amazing, you have to try it on!" Jacob cooed. She smiled and tucked the next dress over her arm. Both friends went back to looking, and by the time Mel was ready to head to the changing rooms she had seven dresses draped over her arm.

Jacob knew the woman working on the fitting rooms, and she allowed him to go in with Mel to one of the larger cubicles. He sat on the stool of the corner of the fitting room and waiting while Mel put on each dress in turn. They both agreed that no matter how gorgeous it was, the cream and black lace dress was not for her. They narrowed it down to three dresses, and when she tried the last dress on Jacob's mouth fell open.

"Oh my God sweetie! That is the dress! I mean it is *THE* dress! It's amazing!" Jacob grinned, pleased with the success of an afternoon of shopping.

"You really think so?" Mel said, twirling around in the outfit.

"Melody Anderson, if you do not buy that gown, I am never speaking to you ever again!" Jacob warned her.

Mel laughed. "Okay! Okay! I'll get it!" She smiled shaking her head. "So we're done?" She asked.

"Oh hell no darling, you need accessories!" Jacob frowned.

One look at her friend's face and she was laughing again. She couldn't help it, the man really did love to shop. "Accessories?" She sighed. "You mean we're not done yet?"

"Do you want to look fabulous or not?" Jacob asked, putting his hand on his hip like he was about to scold her just as a mother scolds her child. Mel held her hands up in defeat.

"Okay boss! Don't kill me, I haven't paid for anything yet." She laughed, and even Jacob had a hint of a smile on his face. "Come on." She said, linking her arm with his, and draping her gown over her other arm. "Let's shop some more then." She laughed, as Jacob rushed them off in the direction of the shoe department.

~ ~ ~

Several hours, and several hundreds of pounds later Mel had been completely kitted out for the Gala. Jacob had made sure that not only had she a dress and heels to die for, but that she also had the jewellery, the makeup, and a potential hairstyle to go with it all. She smirked when she thought of all the fun that her friend had had just shopping with her.

"Penny for your thoughts, sweetie?" Jacob grinned from across the dining table in the Japanese restaurant they were eating at.

"I'm just thinking about how much you enjoying spending my money!" She grinned.

"Oh shut up! You'll be the belle of the ball! It was worth every penny!" He said screwing up his face at her.

As the waitress set her bowl of rice and chicken in front of her she couldn't help but grin and agree with her friend. "You did me proud today Jacob Oakley!" She grinned, lifting a mouthful of food with her chopsticks and savouring the delicious flavours.

The pair chatted about their shopping, Mel's gala with Alex, and Jacob's boyfriend Marc. Mel listened as Jake told her about Marc's course in college, and what they had been up to recently. She had never been sure about Marc and his intentions towards Jacob, but he seemed to make him genuinely happy, and that was all she really wanted for her friend.

"So when are you seeing him again?" Jacob asked her.

"Tonight, and then we have an evening out planned the night before the gala." She grinned, delighted at the thought of seeing Alex again.

"Make sure you don't tell him about that dress!" Jacob warned her.

Mel laughed. "Oh I won't don't worry! I want to wow him with my entrance!" She grinned.

She lifted her phone from her pocket and tapped out a message to Alex.

Hey handsome. Just found the perfect dress for the event in the Hilton! Still up to see me later? Xo

No sooner had she hit send than Alex's reply came through.

Of course I will be seeing you later! You are something I am always 'up' for ;-) A xo

Came the reply. Mel smirked and nibbled on her bottom lip as she looked at her phone.

"Someone got a reply she likes!" Jacob teased her.

She stuck her tongue out at him and grinned and Jacob couldn't help but grin back at her.

"He really seems to make you happy." He remarked. Mel thought about it for a second.

"He does Jake, he really does!"

They finished their food with general chit chat and Jacob settled the bill. Mel linked her arm with Jake's as they walked back to her car.

"Are you sure you don't mind dropping me off at Aiden's house sweetie?" He asked her as they stood at the machine paying for their parking.

"Not at all, his house isn't that far from here, it's all good." She smiled. She pulled the ticket from the machine and they walked over to where her car was parked.

Mel drove to the area of town where Aiden lived with his parents, and pulled up outside his house.

"You're going to look fabulous in that dress sweetie!" He told her as he took off his seatbelt and turned towards her.

She ignored his compliment. "Thank you so much for helping me today!" She smiled as Jacob leaned across the car to give her a hug, which she gratefully accepted.

"I'll talk to you tomorrow sweetie." He said as he opened the car door.

"You will, we're meant to be heading to the library again!" She reminded him.

"Oh hell!" He grumbled. "Text me and let me know what's happening?" He asked.

Mel laughed. "Will do sweetie, see you later, and thanks for today!" She waved as Jacob closed the car door behind him. He waved as she drove away

~ ~ ~

Mel picked her phone up off her kitchen counter when it alerted her to an incoming text message. She found a message from Alex in her notifications.

Hey Jellybean x today's been awful, how does a movie marathon and a Chinese takeaway sound? A xo

Mel smiled after a day out shopping with Jacob, a night on the sofa curled up with Alex sounded like bliss.

Sounds like a perfect plan to me! Xo

She replied. Mel dragged herself upstairs for a bath before Alex arrived.

~ ~ ~

Alex pulled into Mel's drive just after seven. He had suffered a long and challenging day, and he wanted nothing more than to snuggle up with Mel and let her usual warmth radiate through him. He grabbed the bag of food from the passenger seat and strode up to the front door. He tried the handle and called out to Mel as he walked in.

"Kitchen!" Came the muffled reply.

Alex locked the front door and pulled the curtain before heading down the hall to the kitchen. Mel was bent over loading the dishwasher when he walked in. He dumped the bag on the counter and grabbed Mel by the hips and ground his pelvis against her. She laughed and slapped at his hands.

"Oi you!" She giggled. "You'll knock me head first into the dishwasher!"

Alex wrapped his arms around her waist and pulled her up against him. She turned in his arms and wrapped hers around his neck.

"Hello handsome!" She grinned.

"Hello gorgeous!" He smiled back.

Mel leaned in and pressed her lips to his. Alex held her close and let his tongue dip into her mouth. She moaned and knotted her fingers in his hair. He pulled his mouth from hers.

"Jellybean..." He growled. "Dinner's getting cold."

She kissed his nose. "Hmmm, can't have that now can we?" She smirked. Alex swatted her on the backside.

"No we bloody can't!" He scolded.

She grinned. "Well, it's not like you haven't been in my kitchen before! You know where everything is, don't let me stop you!"

Alex glared at her, and Mel burst into laughter. She grabbed the bag of food and started to lift the variety of packages out of the bag. Alex opened the cupboard and lifted out the plates, setting them out in front of Mel before reaching into the drawer beside him for knives, forks and spoons. He and Mel worked together effortless, two cogs in the perfect machine, each moving around the other seamlessly dishing out their food. Once everything was served they grabbed a plate each, and went into the living room to the sofa.

Alex lifted the remote before Mel got to it. "Oi!" She laughed elbowing him in the ribs.

"OW!" He laughed in fake pain. "Watch it you!" He pouted.

Mel set her plate on the floor and reached for the remote again. "You don't get to pick what we watch!" She grinned at him. He held the remote out of her reach.

"I'm your guest!" He smirked. "Is this how you treat all your guests?" He asked.

"Only the ones who steal the bloody remote – hand it back!" She scolded.

Alex grinned at her even more and set his plate on the floor with hers. "Have lots of gentleman callers, do we?" He grinned.

She stuck her tongue out at him. "Only when my boyfriend isn't around." Alex's eyes went wide for a split second and Mel caught it. "Well, not my boyfriend..." Alex didn't let her finish her sentence, or take the words back; he pulled her against him and pressed his mouth to hers. She moaned against his mouth, and their kiss naturally broke apart.

"Must be a damn lucky man to have you as his girlfriend." He said softly.

Mel seized the opportunity and grabbed the remote. "He is, especially when he lets me have the remote control!" She smirked.

Alex laughed, shook his head and lifted his plate and Mel's from the floor, placing hers in her lap. She pressed the HOME button on the remote, and called up the onscreen menu.

"What are we watching? It better not be a chick flick!" Alex smirked, putting a forkful of food into his mouth.

Mel rolled her eyes. "Oh yeah, I'm really a chick flick kind of girl!" She snorted, and continued to navigate through the menus. She went into the on demand section, and found the movie that she was looking for. "Ha! There it is!" She said in glee.

Alex glanced at the screen. "You like that movie?" He asked her in surprise.

"No, I *love* that film! Why?" She looked him with confusion.

Alex grinned. "Because that my dear Melody, is one of my favourite films!"

"You're an Arnie fan?" She chuckled.

"Who isn't?" He beamed, and she pressed play to start their viewing of 'Terminator'.

When the film was over, Mel was snuggled against Alex's arm. "That is a brilliant movie. It never gets old. Shame there's only one thing that spoiled it." She said softly.

"Spoiled?" Alex questioned. Mel looked up at him.

"The love story! John Connor basically sets up his mum and dad, because he gives his dad a picture of his mum, and his dad falls in love with her picture? Oh come on!" Mel scoffed.

"Not into the mushy stuff?" Alex smirked.

"Time and a place dear boy, and in the middle of being chased by psychotic metal men from the future is definitely not it!" She explained, and he laughed. "Don't you laugh at me!" She warned, which only served to make him laugh more. Mel glared at him, put her hand on his thigh and rubbed down to his knee. She wrapped her fingers around his leg and tickled the back of his knee.

"Can you ride the donkey?" She asked him with a giggle.

"Ahhh!" Alex shrieked and grabbed Mel's hand. "Stop that!" He laughed.

"Stop laughing at me!" She demanded with a smirk.

"Okay! Okay! I give in!" Alex howled with laughter.

Mel took her hand away from his leg, and smirked. "Ticklish Mr Matthews, I'll have to remember that one."

Alex grinned back and pulled her across his lap, smacking her backside. "And you need to remember that I won't think twice about giving you a good spanking!" He laughed. She wriggled on his lap and fell to the floor with a bump, laughing as she did.

"Never mind the spanking," she smirked up at him, "let's go to bed." She moved from the floor, and stood in front of him, holding her hand out to him. Alex turned off the TV, dumped the remote on the sofa beside him and took Mel's hand to follow her upstairs to bed.

She smirked at the doorway of the bedroom. "I'll be back." She grinned before disappearing into the bathroom.

"That was terrible!" Alex called after her. He stripped down to his boxers, and pulled back the covers, while he waited for his turn in the bathroom. When Mel came in he grinned at her, and in his best Arnold Schwarzenegger voice said, "I need your clothes..." and paused.

"You don't need my boots and my motorcycle?" she asked with a grin.

"Hell no! Just your clothes off would be perfect!" Alex said with a wink, and walked off to the bathroom.

When he returned, Mel was already in bed and starting to doze off. "Still awake?" he asked, and she murmured something unintelligible in reply. Alex sniggered to himself and stripped off his boxers before getting into bed beside her, and turning off the lamp. He pulled her in against him, and wrapped his arms around her.

"Goodnight Jellybean." He whispered to her in the darkness.

"I love you Alex." She sighed softly.

Alex froze unsure what to do. He listened in the darkness and somewhere in his mind he registered that Mel's breathing was slow and deep. *She's asleep!* His inner critic explained. Alex let go of the breath that he had been holding and fell asleep.

CHAPTER 25

Alex heard the scream from the bathroom and rushed to the door bursting in. Natalie looked up at him with a bloody piece of toilet paper in her hands. "Alex!" She cried out staring at him.

"Shhhh!" He said, moving towards her and stroking her face. "It's going to be okay, come on, get up and straighten yourself up and we'll go straight to the hospital. It'll be fine." He rushed off to grab the keys to his beat up old Honda; Natalie emerged from the bathroom and headed to the front door of their apartment. Alex was hot on her heels, he wrapped an arm around her in comfort and ushered her to his car.

~ ~ ~

They looked at each other as they sat in the room waiting for the doctor to come in and perform an ultrasound scan on her to check on the baby. Alex clung to Natalie's hand. He kissed her knuckles, "It's going to be okay." He soothed.

Tears fell down Natalie's face. "You don't know that! Oh God, I'm losing our baby... I know I'm losing our baby!" She wailed.

A doctor walked into the room and Natalie wiped the tears from her face quickly. The doctor, a tall black man smiled at her grimly, and touched her arm. "It's okay, *don't panic, we're just going to do a scan and check that everything is okay with the baby. Sometimes bleeding can be a symptom of something else." He told her. He pulled the blanket back to expose Natalie's stomach and squirted some of the special gel onto her skin. He lifted the probe from the holder on the side of the machine, and started to press it against her stomach, attempting to get a good look at her unborn baby. He was silent as he worked, and Natalie and Alex both held their breath waiting for the doctor's verdict.*

He stopped pressing against her stomach and replaced the scanner back on the holder. He took a piece of tissue paper and wiped the excess gel from Natalie's stomach and he pulled the blanket back over her exposed skin. "Okay," he said, "I'm really very sorry to tell you, but I can't find your baby's heartbeat, I'm afraid you are having a miscarriage."

A sob erupted from Natalie. "No!" She cried. "Please no!"

The doctor nodded to Alex. "I'll give you a few minutes to take this all in." He said, and left the room quietly, as Natalie clung to Alex's shirt.

"This cannot be happening Alex!" She sobbed. "Our baby can't be dead." She said shaking.

A tear ran down Alex's cheek as he held her close to him. "I'm so sorry baby." He said trying to soothe her.

~ ~ ~

"We need to go and collect his ashes today Nat, you have to get up baby, please." Alex said to the form lying in the bed. Natalie had been lying there since she had been released from hospital after the birth of their dead son. She only left the bed long enough to visit the bathroom, the rest of the time she was in bed either asleep or non-responsive.

"Natalie!" He shouted. "NOW!"

Natalie threw back the covers like a petulant child being raised from their bed to get ready for school. "Fine!" She hissed at him through gritted teeth. She stomped into the bathroom, and slammed the door. Alex heard the water running and sighed. He couldn't believe this had happened. His son was gone, and the woman that he had created that life with was withdrawing from him. Things were really starting to fall apart.

~ ~ ~

"I can't believe you haven't fucking told him yet!" Malcolm shouted.

"Keep your damn voice down." She hissed. "You don't think that I might have been a bit more concerned about the fact that I was losing our baby Malc?"

Alex stood at the door and listened, something was wrong. He recognised that voice, something wasn't right. They seemed to be completely unaware that he had been slamming the front door shut just moments before. "I lost our son." She told Malcolm.

"I know you did." His voice barely audible through the partially open door. Alex could hear the sounds of sobbing, and the soothing sounds that his friend was making.

"I promise I'll tell him soon, I just can't face it so soon after this." She cried.

"Shhhh!" Malcolm soothed.

Alex pushed the door gently, letting it open wide enough to get a clearer view of the pair. His stomach turned to lead and sank to his feet in an instant that he saw her Melody was holding on to his best friend.

It didn't happen like this, he thought.

"Mel?" He asked in confusion.

"Shit! Oh my God, Alex! It's not what it looks like. I can explain..."

~ ~ ~

Alex sat bolt upright in bed. A cold sweat covered his entire body and he was shaking like a leaf. He looked at the alarm clock on the bedside table. 6:39 a.m. it blinked. His stomach was churning, and he bolted for the bathroom. He heaved, and the emptied his stomach's contents into the toilet bowl. *How? How could you think such a thing of her?* His inner critic asked, and he could practically imagine it standing shaking its head at him. He ran his fingers through his hair and tears prickled in his eyes. Guilt at thinking the worst of Mel twisted in his guts and he heaved again over the toilet again.

A knock on the bathroom door made him jump. "Alex, you okay?" Mel's voice sounded concerned. *Shit!* He thought. *She's heard me in here throwing up!*

"Yeah, just an upset stomach I think." He called out to her. "Must have been the takeaway."

Alex sighed and tried to calm himself down. He would never be able to explain to Mel the real reason for him being sick. "I'm just going to jump in the shower." He called out.

Mel moved away from the bathroom door and went downstairs while Alex got into the shower. She made herself a cup of tea, lifted the Pepto-Bismol out of her cupboard, and went back upstairs.

Alex was just drying himself off when she walked into the bedroom. He glanced quickly in her direction when she came in. "You okay?" She asked him.

Alex shook his head. "Not really. I think I'll just go home, sod work." He sat on the edge of the bed and started to pull on his boxers.

"You can stay here you know. I don't mind." She said, and handed him the bottle of medicine. Alex stared at the little bottle of pink liquid and felt his stomach churn again. He needed to go home, he needed to escape and think about what he was doing, how to get a grip of the situation before it spiralled out of control. He set the bottle on the bedside table and continued to get dressed.

"Thanks Jellybean, but I think I want the comfort of my own bed, know what I mean?" He didn't look in her direction; he just slipped his feet into his shoes and stood. Mel took a sip of her tea and looked at him. She felt so sorry for him, she didn't like to see him ill, she wanted to help, but she also knew that when she was sick, all she wanted was her own bed, and to be able to 'die' in peace.

"Call me if you need anything?" She asked as he slipped his t-shirt over his head.

He looked over his shoulder at her and gave a grim smile. "You'd be the first person I'd call." He grabbed his bag and headed for the door. "I'll not kiss you." He nodded. "Just in case it wasn't the food, you know, in case it's contagious." He told her. She nodded and eyed him up suspiciously.

"Okay." She agreed. He walked out of the bedroom and down the stairs in silence. Mel followed him to the door and watched him leave. She hoped that he would be okay, and resolved to text him later to find out how he was doing.

~ ~ ~

Whatever it was that Alex was suffering from had stopped Mel from seeing him for five days now, but he was back in work, and he was texting her more often, and had reassured her that their evening out was still going to happen.

Mel was standing in front of her full-length mirror, with a selection of possible outfits laid out on the bed. She was lifting each one in turn, holding them up against herself, and giving them careful consideration. She was nervous. There had been a hint of something going on with Alex all week, she understood that he had been under the weather, but there was something else, something just persistently nagging at the back of her mind.

When she finally decided on the perfect outfit, she spent time arranging her hair and putting on her make-up. Tomorrow was the night of the gala, so she didn't want to be out too late, and had decided that she was going to drive into Belfast instead of calling a cab. They were meeting in The Apartment bar just round the corner from Mel's place of work. So she knew of a few places in the area to park in.

She checked herself one last time in the mirror before grabbing her jacket and bag, and heading downstairs and out to the car. She drove the twenty-minute journey singing along to her rock playlist on Spotify, parked on the street outside her job, and walked the few hundred yards to the bar. When she got in, she looked around for Alex, and when she didn't see him, she looked at her watch. *7:50 p.m. Just a little early.* She thought to herself, and walked up to the bar and ordered herself a drink while she waited.

When she looked at her watch again it was ten past eight, and there was still no sign of Alex. She went to the bathroom, checked her makeup, and walked back to the bar, looking around for him. He was still nowhere to be seen. She lifted her phone out of her bag and dialled his number. The phone rang and rang without reply. *Probably just parking.* She thought, and ordered herself another soft drink.

It was half eight when she looked around again, expecting him to appear in the crowd and apologise profusely for keeping her waiting for so long, she gave his phone another try, this time it went straight to answer phone. She sighed, and sent him text.

Hey you, I'm standing in the Apartment Bar. I'm leaving in 20 minutes if you haven't arrived. Hope you're okay xo

Mel waited, the twenty minutes passed, and still there was no sign of Alex. She downed the last of her drink, checked her phone to see if there were any missed calls or messages, and when she saw that there was no response from him she got up and left.

CHAPTER 26

She couldn't believe that he'd stood her up last night. She had stood at the bar for over an hour nursing a Coca-Cola with ice. She had tried to call him, but his phone rang without answer and then switched over to answer phone. She was worried about him, what if he had been in an accident. He hadn't called her back or text her, which wasn't like him. She had made up her mind to call him in the office and see what happened to him. Tentatively she dialled the number and waited to hear it start to ring.

Alex looked at his phone and sighed. It hadn't stopped ringing since he walked into the office this morning, one of the contractors on the building he was working on had gone into administration, and he was tied up in mopping up the mess that had been generated because of it. "Matthews." He barked into the receiver when he picked it up. "Hi, Alex." Mel's voice spoke in his ear. "Jellybean." He sighed.

"Are you okay? I was worried about you when you didn't show last night." She said with concern.

"I'm sorry, it's just the shit has hit the fan here and I have had a lot of stuff I needed to fix. I can't talk Mel, I've got 6 people waiting for me in the conference room." He sighed.

"I get it, I'll see you tonight?" She asked him, looking for reassurance.

"Sure." He replied.

"See you then handsome." She said, her smile apparent even over the phone.

Alex put his head in his hand, "I'm sorry Jellybean. I'll talk to you later." He said, and hung up before waiting for her reply.

You can't even tell her you giant prick! His inner critic said. "FUCK!" he shouted, slamming his fist onto his desk. His phone started to ring again, and this time he picked up the whole thing, tugged the cable and launched the phone against the wall, watching it splinter into pieces.

Mel primped and preened the entire afternoon, having her hair done in a swept up messy up-do, with tendrils left loose and curled. She had her make-up perfected, smoky eyes, long thick eyelashes, and a dark red stain on her lips. Her dress was made from chiffon in a long floating maxi-dress style, trimmed with rhinestones around the neckline and shoulder straps. She was due to be at the Hilton in the Lagan Suite by 8. The taxi dropped her off outside, and she made her way through the revolving doors, and walked up the stairs, crossed the mezzanine and through the doors of the Lagan suite. Half of it was set up for the banquet dinner, and the other half was set up for mingling, drinking and dancing. People were milling around the room, champagne flutes in hand, chatting among themselves. She walked in and scanned the room, seeking out Alex.

Her eyes finally feasted on him in his tuxedo on the far side of the room. Talking to a group of middle aged businessmen. She lifted a flute from a tray as a waiter walked passed, and proceeded to make her way across to where he stood. She was behind him, almost close enough to touch him when a tall blonde caught her eye. She was gliding across the room towards Alex, and Mel noticed his whole body tense and his jaw twitch when he noticed her approaching. She sidled up to him, pulled him to her, kissed his cheek, and put her mouth to his ear not making any attempt to hide what she was actually saying. "My God, I've missed you." Suddenly Alex's hands were on the woman's shoulders, pushing her away. "Alex, how long has it been?" She purred at him.

"Not long enough, clearly." She smiled at him as if the acidic tone he had spoken to her in had been nothing other than a little harmless surprise. Mel watched as another woman quickly arrived by Alex's side, draping her arm across his shoulders as Alex hissed at the woman again. "What do you want Natalie?" He asked her. The second woman put her other hand on Alex's chest, and Melody felt hers tighten. "Should I be worried that you're manhandling my fiancé?" The second woman asked the blonde. *Natalie, wasn't that what Alex called her?* Mel thought. "Jules, this is Natalie Carter, you remember? The bitch I made the mistake of dating in college?" He spat.

Juliet extended her hand to Natalie. "I've heard so much about you Natalie, I'm sure you'll appreciate why I don't say it's a pleasure meeting you." Juliet said her eyes burning into Natalie. "Alex darling, Mr Goodridge was looking for you at the bar, why don't you go speak to him, while I have a little chat with Natalie here?" Juliet smiled sincerely, looking up at him, pushing him back away from Natalie, and unknowingly back towards Melody. Juliet took a firm hold of Natalie's arm and started to escort her back the way that she came.

Alex turned to see Mel looking at him, she was frozen to the spot, her face had drained of all colour, and her eyes were wide in shock. "Melody." He breathed, and he stopped dead in front of her, unable to move. She swallowed hard. "You're here with someone else?" She asked with a croak.

Alex nodded.

"And she's your fiancée?" She asked, the tears welled up in her eyes and she prayed they wouldn't spill while he was looking at her.

"Does it matter who she is, Mel?" He replied avoiding the question.

"How long?" She snapped her hurt brewing into anger.

"How long what?" He asked not understanding.

"How long has she been with you?" She bit at him.

"Three years this October." He sighed. Technically he was being honest. Juliet would be working for him for three years by the time October arrived. He sighed, looked at his feet and spoke again. "It wouldn't have worked, Jellybean. I'm sorry."

"Don't dare call me that!" She spat out at him, her tears finally winning the battle as they spilled down her cheeks. "You are a complete fucking asshole Alex Matthews. Don't ever contact me again!" She said, wiping her eyes and taking off across the room. Pushing her way through the crowd, picking up speed the closer to the exit she got.

Juliet put her hand on Alex's shoulder. "Was that...?" Her voice trailed off, and Alex finished the sentence for her, "...Melody." Juliet's hand covered her mouth in shock. "Oh Alex... You didn't?" Juliet asked rhetorically. She knew exactly what he had done and why. She sighed. "You're such a prick." She scolded. Alex glared at her and raised an eyebrow. She took in his expression and cut him off before he had a chance to reply. "Don't you dare pull that boss, employee bullshit with me! We are friends, and friends are meant to tell each other when they are being stupid. And you are being a complete fucking idiot.

You love her! And you just let her walk away, thinking Christ only knows what!" She ranted in a tirade. Alex just shrugged and shook his head, his eyes back on his feet. "I know Jules. Believe me I know." He turned and walked towards the bar as Juliet watched. Alex was the best boss she had ever had, and they were good friends, and she knew that she would end up watching him drink himself to oblivion this evening. She also knew that all she could do was damage control, she would make sure he wasn't abusive to anyone, and that he made it home in one piece.

~ ~ ~

Mel pulled the quilt over her head trying to ignore her phone's ringtone, it had been ringing almost back to back now for 20 minutes. She snatched the phone from its charger and answered it. "What do you want Jonny?" She snapped.

"Melody Kate Anderson!" He scolded. "What kind of friend would I be if I left you to stay in bed FOUR days later?" He asked her.

"A decent one! Now please Jonny, just leave me the fuck alone." She retorted.

"I'm at your door. If you do not get down the stairs and let me in right now, I'm using the key you gave me, and I'll be straight up to bounce on your bed!" He told her, sounding smug.

"Why the fuck did I ever give you that key!" She sighed. "Hold on, I'll be down in a minute!" She told him and hung up.

She gave some serious thought to just leaving Jonny outside, and remaining in bed, but the thought didn't last long. She knew Jonny well enough to know that he would do exactly what he said, and use the emergency key that she had once given him. She pulled herself from her bed, wrapped her dressing gown around her, and went to open the door for Jonny. Once he was inside, she padded back up to her bedroom and lay back down pulling the quilt over her. Jonny followed her and sat on the edge of her bed.

"So is this all you're going to do now?" He asked her quilt covered form. "The Melody Anderson I know doesn't let a man get to her like this. Not ever!" He told her, an anguished groan rising out from under the covers as he did. She flipped the quilt away from her face and turned to look at Jonny.

"ENGAGED! The bastard is engaged, Jonny!! How? Huh? How am I meant to just get over that? There is no way to describe how I feel right now. You wouldn't understand!" She stated angrily.

Jonny stared at her intently. "I wouldn't understand?" He repeated in disbelief. "Clare... Remember her Mel? Don't fucking tell me I wouldn't understand!" Mel winced and kicked herself inwardly. Of course, she remembered

Clare, the gorgeous young student that Jonny had dated, fallen in love with, and then found out she was married to one of the younger professors. She had been there for him as he was now here for her. She sighed. "I'm sorry." She said softly, her words full of remorse. Jonny leaned over her and kissed her forehead. "Forgiven." He told her. "But for fuck's sake Mel, go and get in the damn shower, four days of lying in your own self-pity has left you ripe!" He grinned at her and she opened her mouth in mock shock and offence. "And brush your damn teeth!" He added. "I'm going to go and make you breakfast. If you're not down in 20 minutes, I'm coming up to shower you myself!" He smiled, almost daring her to challenge him.

"You wouldn't dare!" She challenged back.

"Try me." He almost growled in a low seductive voice.

Mel shuffled in the bed and held her hands in the air. "I'm going! I'm going!" She lifted herself off the bed and Jonny slapped her backside as she did. "20 minutes, Miss Anderson!" He warned as she disappeared into the bathroom, and he went downstairs to start preparing her tea and some breakfast.

20 minutes later Mel lumbered down the stairs to the smell of eggs bacon and coffee drifting from the kitchen. She walked in behind Jonny stirring eggs around the pan and couldn't resist wrapping her arms around him for a tight hug. He moved the pan off the heat and turned

round to meet her, wrapping his arms tightly around her as she snuggled into his chest. "I got you baby, you're going to be okay." He sighed softly, kissing the top of her head. Mel relaxed into his arms and found the tears starting to erupt from her eyes again. "You better not be crying Anderson!" Jonny joked softly, holding her tighter still.

"N-no." She stammered, trying to prevent a full on sobbing session from starting.

"Good. Go set the table, I'll bring out breakfast, and we'll talk about it." He told her, kissing her head again before giving her a tight squeeze and pushing her out of the way of the cooker.

~ ~ ~

For the rest of the morning, Mel sat and talked to Jonny about what happened. She poured out everything. How she and Alex had been together, how Alex had acted, everything, all her thoughts, her feelings, her anger, her pain, her tears. Jonny sat and listened to everything she had to say. When she was done he took her hand. "Sounds like he loved you very much Mel. No matter what other lies he told you. I don't think that was one of them." He smiled at her sympathetically.

"That doesn't stop how it hurts Jon." She sighed. She let her head fall against her hands, waiting for another wave of tears to claim her.

"I know, baby." He said. "You need to get out of the house for a while Mel, it's not healthy staying in here all day." She lifted her head, about to protest when he interrupted. "Please? The cinema or pool in the Student's Union?" He asked.

"Fine." She sighed, giving in already. "Let's go to the cinema first, then I might feel like going to the SU after. We'll see." Jonny grinned at her, and she trudged off upstairs to get ready.

~ ~ ~

Mel laughed as she left the college film theatre. "How did you know that was on?" She asked Jonny grinning.

"Oh, come on, you know it's the 30th anniversary of 'Back to the Future'! How could they NOT show it?" He grinned back at her. She sighed contentedly at him. "Thanks, Jonny. I needed this." He took her hand and pulled her in against him giving her a squeeze.

"Pool? I think it's time I kicked your ass again!" He laughed. She gasped at the suggestion that he would kick her ass with a smile, and elbowed him in the ribs. "Oh, you think so hot shot?" She asked laughing.

"Ohhh hell yeah!" He grinned back at her.

"Come on then!" She smiled, pulling him by the hand the quarter of a mile from the film theatre to the Student's Union building. They stopped at the crosswalk just in front and waited for the lights to allow them across the road. "Just so you know, if I find even a hint that you've gone easy on me because of the circumstances, I'm never giving you a lift anywhere, ever again!" Mel joked looking at Jonny. The lights changed and she started to walk across the road. She registered briefly a look of horror cross Jonny's face. She didn't get the time to turn and see what was causing the look, a split second later she felt a crippling pain in her leg as something large and heavy slammed into her. She felt a slightly weightless feeling in her guts, and suddenly she was falling. She heard a scream and wondered briefly if it had been her own voice she heard. A moment later and she felt an enormous flash of pain vibrate through her head. She looked up to see Jonny looking down at her, his face pale, his voice frantic. He was holding her hand, every last inch of her cried out in agony. "You're okay baby, you're going to be okay." He told her. "Someone call a fucking ambulance!" He shouted out. Just then Melody's eyelids became too heavy to keep open, and the blackness that had been lurking on the edges of her vision swallowed her. Jonny looked at her lifeless form in front of him and a tidal wave of grief slammed into him. *No!* He thought. *Jesus no, please don't let her leave me!* He pleaded with the universe. But it was too late. She was gone.

CHAPTER 27

Jonny looked at his college friends approaching as he stood at the bar. Dylan held out his arms, and Jonny stood, accepting the hug and the manly pats on the back that his friend offered. "You okay, bro?" Dylan asked. Jonny nodded, unable to say anything else, the sting of tears threatening.

"I still can't believe what happened to Mel." Nate announced over Dylan's shoulder, pulling Jonny into a hug of his own. Jacob looked at the other three men and shook his head. "She wouldn't like this. She wouldn't want us all here moping." He said to the group.

"If I hadn't forced her to leave the house." Jonny sniffed. "It's my fault this happened." He said shaking his head. He had replayed the events of that night over and over and over in his head, torturing himself, guilt seizing him in a vice-like grip. Dylan put his hand on Jonny's shoulder. "You weren't driving the car that hit her Jonny. You weren't the one drunk and behind the wheel!" He squeezed his friend's shoulder, reinforcing his support and trying to shake some sense into him.

Jacob and Nate went to the bar to order a round of drinks for them. Dylan stayed with Jonny. "Mate," he started, "it could just have easily had been you, and I would tell her the same thing. This was NOT your fault!"

Jonny just shook his head. "Have the police said anymore?" He asked.

"No, they found the car abandoned, and aside from the few leads from the CCTV in the area, they have nothing." Jonny sighed.

"Have you called him?" Dylan asked.

"Not yet. How the hell do I tell him?" He asked. After Melody's accident Jonny had confided in Dylan a lot of what she had told him about Alex, their relationship, and their breakup.

"The guy's a prick, but I think he'd want to know." Dylan shrugged, just as Jacob and Nate arrived at the table with four pints of pear cider.

Jacob held up his glass in a toast, "To Mel!" He said. The other friends all held their drinks up, clinked their glasses together, and called out the same toast, "To Mel!"

~ ~ ~

Jonny sighed, his finger hovering over the call button on his phone. He had meant to make this call for days. Every time he put it off. How did he break the news to Alex about Mel? The man was engaged, but when Mel had told him about how he was with her, it struck a chord within him, he knew that no matter what happened, he had clearly cared deeply about her. He took a deep breath and pressed the button. He let it ring, hoping that Alex wouldn't answer, just as he was about to hang up, a voice barked down the line.

"Matthews."

"Alex?" He asked.

"Yes." Alex replied. "Who am I speaking to?" He asked.

Jonny let out a breath, "Alex, you don't know me, my name's Jonny, I'm a computer science student with..."

"...Melody?" Alex finished.

"Yeah." Jonny paused, not really knowing what to say. "Alex, I don't know how to tell you this, but, Melody was involved in an accident on Wednesday night. She was hit by a drunk driver. Listen, can I meet you somewhere?"

Jonny heard Alex gasp.

"Is she okay?" He asked.

Jonny took another deep breath. "No Alex, no, she's not."

~ ~ ~

Within an hour Alex was sitting at a table in the Clement's Coffee shop in the centre of town, waiting for Jonny to arrive. Every time someone came in Alex's eyes leapt to the door, waiting to see who it was. *You pushed her away, and now you're never going to see her again.* His inner voice started on him. *Well played douchebag, well played!* Alex sighed. He knew that the critic was right. He might have already lost the only woman he ever completely belonged to. He couldn't think that like. He wouldn't let himself think like that. *Serves you right if she is gone!* His inner voice chided. He sank his head into his hands as a feeling of grief threatened to take over him.

At the sound of a throat clearing beside him, he looked up to find a blue-eyed man with light brown hair looking at him. "Alex?" the man asked. Jonny put his hand out to Alex for him to shake. Alex took his hand, shook it and pointed to the seat opposite. "What happened?" He couldn't wait any longer to hear Jonny's story about the night of the accident.

"I was about to ask you the same thing." Jonny replied.

Alex sighed. "Please, I can't take it, what happened to her?" he pleaded. Jonny sighed too.

"We were out on Wednesday night, I took her out to cheer her up. She was heart-broken Alex." He said glaring at the forlorn face across the table. "We were just about to cross the road in front of the Student's Union. The light went green for us to cross, she stepped out onto the road; she didn't see him coming. Next thing I knew she was lying on the road bleeding from her head." Jonny closed his eyes and shook his head. The memory of seeing Melody hit by a car had haunted him every second since the accident happened.

A waitress came over and offered to take their order. They both asked for a large regular coffee.

"I'm glad she was with you when it happened. I wouldn't have wanted her to be alone when..." Alex's voice trailed off, he tried to swallow the lump that had formed in his throat, but it wouldn't go away, he couldn't breathe around it. His chest constricted tightly, and he actually felt his heart crumble into dust, a hollow, vacant cavity left in its place.

"I can take you to see her if you want to." Jonny offered. "The ICU doesn't really allow non-family members but I'm sure they would understand if I explained."

Alex stared at Jonny, unable to take in his words. "What?" he asked not really sure of the meaning behind what Jonny had said. The waitress returned and set down their cups. Jonny smiled to her, and she went back to her other customers.

"She's in intensive care Alex, I'll take you to see her if you want." Jonny offered again.

Alex's head sank into his hand again. "Jesus Christ." He breathed. He looked up at Jonny. "I thought she was dead." He said, matter of fact.

"I know." Jonny replied. "I'm sorry I let you think that. I didn't realise that's what you probably thought until I had hung up. It's been a tough few days." He sighed. "She's got a fractured tibia, she'll be in plaster for a while. She's got bruised ribs, and she gave them a challenge with some internal bleeding. But when she fell she hit the traffic island in the middle of the road with the back of her head. She had bleeding on the brain, and she's in a medically induced coma to let her brain recover. It's just a waiting game now to see if she wakes up." Jonny told him. Explaining what happened to her never got any easier.

Alex glared at him. "I love her. I should never have hurt her." He told Jonny.

Jonny glared back at him. "No, you fucking shouldn't have." He sneered angrily. "Care to explain why you did?" He queried.

"Do you really want to know?" Alex asked him.

Jonny stared at him. "If I'm going to let you back near my girl for more than a look, then you are damn right I want to know what the fuck happened with you." He snapped.

Alex took a deep breath. "When I was in college I dated a girl called Natalie Carter. She was a year younger than me and she was my universe. I fell for her and I fell hard. We dated, we fell in love, and she got pregnant in my final year." Alex told him.

Jonny took a sip of his coffee, taking in what Alex was telling him. "What happened?" He asked.

'She lost the baby." Alex continued. "Turned out it didn't really matter anyway because she'd been fucking my best mate the entire time. The baby was his, not mine."

"Oh." Jonny said, taking another sip of his coffee.

"Yeah…. It destroyed me. One minute I'm in love, the next minute I'm mourning the death of my first child, then I find out she was not only a cheating bitch, but that I'm breaking my heart for a child that isn't even mine." Alex took a drink from his own cup and continued. "For a while after that I drank… A lot…Once I picked myself up, I started to dabble in dominance. It allowed me control. It allowed me to break up with them when they got too close. And it became empty and not enough the second I met Melody." He exhaled. It felt good to finally tell someone what had happened to him.

Jonny stared at him across the table. "What about your fiancée? Jules?" Jonny asked him.

"I'm not engaged." Alex replied.

"You broke off your engagement?" questioned Jonny.

"I was never engaged to begin with." Responded Alex. "Juliet, my personal assistant was with me that night. Natalie had cornered me, and Jules came over to save me. She draped herself over me and asked Natalie to back the fuck off. She's a close friend, and she was looking out for me." He explained. "I was already running scared with Mel, I didn't deserve her, and I still don't. She misunderstood the situation, and I used it as an out. It was a shitty thing for me to do. I never wanted anyone to get to me the way that Natalie had, and I knew that I was completely under Mel's spell. Now I realise the only thing I fear more is never getting a chance to see her again."

Alex blew out a long breath. One thought rattling repeatedly in his head. Never again would he ever let Mel go. She had to be okay. She had to know how much he loved her, valued her, how much he was hers.

Jonny snapped Alex out of his thoughts with a clearing of his throat. "I get it. I don't like it. You cut her so deep Alex, she was really hurt by what you did. But I do understand. If she wakes up, then you should definitely tell her, and let her decide for herself if she should forgive you." Jonny held out his hand for Alex to shake. "I'm not saying we can be mates, but I'll not try to persuade her to not listen."

Alex shook Jonny's hand again. "That's fair." He nodded.

Jonny looked at this watch. "It's visiting time. Do you want to go to the hospital?" he enquired. Alex nodded. "You drive don't you?"

"Yeah, my car is in the car park of my office building a few streets over." Alex said. They both got up and walked to Alex's car to drive to the hospital.

~ ~ ~

Alex stared at Melody lying in a hospital bed, tubes everywhere, a machine to the right constantly beeping in time with Melody's heartbeat, and a respirator on the other side doing her breathing for her. A nurse appeared over his shoulder. "Go on in, love. Talk to her, hold her hand. It's okay." Alex smiled grimly at her. He slowly walked over beside Mel's bed, sat on a chair and touched her hand. Relief and grief swept over him in equal measure. He would forever be indebted to Jonny for telling him what happened, for allowing him the opportunity to be there with her, and for having the grace to hear him out. He wrapped his fingers around hers and kissed her knuckles. "Hey Jellybean." He whispered against the back of her hand. "You scared the shit out of Jonny! He thinks it's his fault, silly man, I know that it's mine...." His voice faltered as his emotions overwhelmed him, he rubbed his eyes with the back of his hand. "I'm so sorry my sweet Melody. If I hadn't been such a coward you wouldn't be lying here." His head dropped to her hand, and his shoulders shook in silent sobs.

When Alex woke another nurse was in the room changing her IV bag to a new one, checking her blood pressure, and her blood oxygen levels. "How's she doing?" He asked him. "She's doing well." The nurse told him. "She's stable, the swelling on her brain seems to be going down. Her coma is medically induced so the consultant will make the decision to let her come round on her own soon I'm sure." He continued, trying to reassure Alex that Melody was making good progress.

"Thank you." Alex said humbly.

The nurse shrugged with a smile. "It's my job mate, it's what I do." He stated.

Alex didn't move from beside Melody's bed for three days. Eventually, Jonny and one of the regular nurses convinced him to go home, sleep in his own bed, and maybe even check in on work. "I promise I'll be staying right here." Jonny said reassuring him.

"You'll call me if she wakes up?"

"You'll be the first person I contact. I promise!" Jonny said, holding up 3 fingers like a boy scout. Warily Alex got up and left the hospital. He wanted to sleep for a while, get a decent shower and a shave. He'd need to call in with Juliet and see how everything was going. But then, he would be back at Mel's side, and he'd stay there until she woke up. *If she wants to even see you when she does wake up!* His critic reminded him. *Maybe she won't*. He thought. *But I'm damn well going to find out.*

CHAPTER 28

Jonny held Mel's hand with both of his, his forehead resting on their joined fingers. "You can't leave me Mel, I love you. I can't deal with shit without you here." He told her sleeping form, tears spilling from his eyes. Mel squeezed Jonny's hand. "Dumb ass." She croaked at him. "Like you could be trusted to be without me." She mumbled her voice broken from tubes that had been in her throat.

"Do you promise?" Jonny asked her, squeezing her hand tight and holding it against his cheek.

Mel started to laugh. "Ow!" She whispered and abruptly stopped laughing. "Shit that hurts, stop making me laugh!" Her free hand moving to rub over her tender ribs.

Jonny kissed her hand. "Sorry baby. I'll go get a nurse to get you checked out okay?"

"Yeah." Mel whispered weakly.

Nurses and doctors had rushed to her side, and dozens of questions and checks were made. "You're a very lucky woman, Miss Anderson. It doesn't look like you will have any brain damage or any long term injuries." The doctor informed her.

Jonny grinned at the news, "Thank God!" Melody thanked the doctor, and they all departed, leaving her alone with Jonny again. He took up a seat right beside her, holding her hand as he had before. "I'm so relieved Mel. I've been so worried. I never want to lose you."

Mel gifted him with a warm and genuine smile. "Do you seriously think that you could get rid of me that easily?" She touched his cheek. "I love you too, you know." Jonny leaned over and kissed Mel softly. They both closed their eyes and leaned their foreheads against each other.

Alex listened from the doorway. Fists balling at his sides, his jaw twitching and his lips pulled in a hard line. *What are you going to do genius, fight him over her bed?* The inner critic nagged. He cleared his throat, Mel's eyes shot over to the doorway, and Jonny sighed and moved back into his seat again. "You're awake!" He said moving towards the opposite side of the bed to Jonny.

"What are you doing here?" She asked, glaring at him.

"Jonny told me what happened."

"He's been here every day Mel." Jonny informed her.

"I don't want you here!" She groaned at him.

"Mel..." Alex pleaded.

"Jonny get him out of here... Please." She asked, turning back to her friend, squeezing his hand, and refusing to look in Alex's direction.

Jonny sighed. "Alex you should go." Alex went to respond, but the look on Mel's face defeated him. He hung his head and turned to leave.

"I'll be back in a minute." Jonny said as he followed Alex from the room.

As they arrived in the stairwell Alex turned. "So you love her, huh?" Alex asked as he gripped the railing of the stairs.

"This is the conversation you want to have now?" Jonny replied. The look on Alex's face made him answer. "Of course I fucking love her. You've met her, you know how amazing she is." Jonny sighed.

"How long have you been in love with her?" Alex snarled.

Jonny laughed at him. "Are you kidding me?"

"No, I'm not fucking kidding you. How long?" He said angrily, raising his voice.

"Keep your fucking voice down mate! They'll throw us both out!" Jonny pleaded.

Alex ran his hands through his hair, gritted his teeth and asked again, he needed to know how long Jonny had been in love with Mel, he needed to know if he had a rival for her affection. And Jonny would be a major rival, he hadn't let her down, rejected her, broken her heart. No, that had been all Alex. "I don't understand why it's such a difficult question to answer." He spat out.

"And I don't see why it's any of your business!" Jonny replied.

"It's my business because I'm in love with her!" Alex exclaimed back.

Jonny smirked smugly. "Well for someone who's in love with her you have a funny way of showing it."

Alex glared at Jonny. "I know this. Do you think you're telling me anything I don't fucking know?! For fuck's sake Jonny, just answer the question, how long have you been in love with her?"

Jonny sighed. "I'm not *in* love with her you dumb shit. But of course I love her, she's my best friend, the other half of me. Men and women can be just friends for fuck sake!" He said, throwing his arms in the air.

Alex's face turned crimson. "You're not *in* love with her?" He asked again sheepishly.

"No! But you really must think a hell of a lot of her to be getting so damn jealous." Jonny reasoned.

Alex put his hands on the railing and bent over, letting out an enormous sigh. "She's it for me Jonny." He said softly and lifted his head to meet Jonny's gaze. "I fucked up big time, and I need her know just how wrong I was."

Jonny sighed and leant against the wall in the empty stairwell. "Then fight for her. She'll not give in easily, and knowing her she'll give you a rough ride along the way, but if you truly feel that way about her. You got to fight for her Alex."

Alex sighed. "I know." He straightened, and put out his hand for Jonny to shake it. Jonny shook Alex's hand. "Thanks for listening to me, and letting me be here with her."

"You got it bro." Jonny smiled.

Alex smiled back grimly and walked off down the stairs.

~ ~ ~

"You told him?" Mel asked when Jonny walked back into the room and sat beside her.

"You don't think the fact that he hasn't been home in three days kind of proves he wanted to be here?" Jonny replied glumly.

Mel sighed. "You know what he did Jonny."

"Mel, I'm not fighting with you about this. I talked to him, I heard what he has to say, and because of that I brought him here to see you. You can talk to him yourself when you're good and ready." He explained.

"And if I'm never ready Jonny?" She asked almost in accusation.

Jonny shrugged. "Then you're never ready. I'm not taking sides here baby." He reached forward and took her hand in his. "Get out of this place first. Then you can decide about it all." He smiled at her and stroked her hand.

Mel squeezed his hand back. "Three days straight huh?"

Jonny smirked. "Yeah baby."

Nothing else was said between them until the nurses came in to check on Mel a few hours later.

~ ~ ~

That evening Mel was moved to a more general ward. Jonny had called all their friends to let them know that she had woken from her coma. Dylan was the first to pop his head around the door of her new room.

"Look who's finally awake!" He grinned at her. "Jesus Christ woman, you'll try anything to get out of your part of our Master's project!" He teased her, grinning at seeing Mel awake again finally.

"Good job I can't get up yet mate, or you'd be getting a slap you cheeky bugger!" She grinned back at Dylan when he leaned over and kissed her forehead.

"Don't scare us like that again missus!" He warned her.

"Oh I don't think she's any plans for that!" Jonny laughed from the doorway. "Not if she knows what's good for her!"

Mel stuck her tongue out at him as Dylan settled himself in a chair by her hospital bed. Jonny grabbed himself a chair and was just settling down when an enormous bouquet of flowers came through the door, followed by Jacob. Jake handed the flowers to Dylan and leaned over Mel in a hug. "Oh sweetie!" Jacob said, soundly clearly chocked up. Mel winced.

"Jakey! My ribs!" She groaned.

Jacob jumped back off her. "Shit! Sorry! Are you okay?" He panicked. Jonny nudged him on the arm and nodded his head towards the chair that Dylan had put out for him. Mel laughed and shook her head as her friend settled himself guiltily into his seat.

"Feeling better to be down here?" Jonny asked.

She sighed. "God yes! They don't poke and prod you as much on this ward!" Just then there was a small knock on the door and Nate walked in with his band mate Cassidy.

"Hi guys!" Mel smiled. Cassidy grinned and walked up to Mel, giving her a kiss on the cheek.

"Nice to see you awake woman!" She told her and then perched herself on the bottom of the bed. Nate moved past Cassidy and draped his tall form over Mel gingerly.

"You scared us." He whispered in her ear. "We don't want to lose you!" He mumbled, kissed her cheek and stood, taking hold of her hand to give it a squeeze.

The group settled themselves around the bed, and the chatter started about what Mel had missed. Eventually a nurse came in and told Cassidy off for sitting on the bed. She took Mel's blood pressure and generally checked her over.

"Visiting time if over in ten minutes!" She scolded as she headed back out the door. Cassidy stood against the wall, frowning. Nate glanced at Cassidy and smirked.

"We better head off if we want to catch the train." He said nodding in her direction. She sighed and pushed off the wall with her foot, moving to give Mel a gentle hug goodbye.

"Get your ass out of here soon!" Cass told her.

"Damn right I will!" Mel grinned.

"You better Mel!" Nate continued after Cassidy paused. "There's a lot of project work waiting for you!" He winked, leaning over to kiss her forehead. Mel groaned.

"God, you can't even manage for a week or so while I get hit by a car?"

Nate grinned. "Nope!" Mel laughed and rolled her eyes, she smiled and waved as Nate and Cassidy left. Dylan shifted in his seat.

"I'm going to disappear off too missus." He smiled at her and she smiled back warmly.

"I'm going to walk out with Dylan." Jacob announced, getting himself up out of his chair before Dylan could even move towards Mel. Jonny smirked and cast a glance in Mel's direction. She caught Jonny's look and started to smirk herself. Dylan looked at Jacob "Pervert lips, I've told you before, I'm not turning for you." He smirked wryly.

"Dammit a boy can dream!" Jacob pouted with a smirk.

Mel and Jonny both erupted with laughter, and Dylan gave Mel another careful hug. "We'll be back to see you soon missus, until then try and be fit enough to get your ass out of here!" He joked.

Jacob leaned over and gave her a kiss on the cheek, taking care not to touch her ribs this time. "Hope you're feeling better soon sweetie." He smiled warmly. Mel smiled at them both.

"Thanks for coming guys." She smiled back affectionately. Both men walked out of the room with a smile and a wave, and she was left with just Jonny.

There was a moment of comfortable silence. Jonny had missed his friend's sassy mouth and support while she had been in her coma and the opportunity to share in her conscious company was all he needed. "You okay?" Mel asked after a while, reading the expression on Jonny's face and guessing he had something on his mind.

"Yeah baby, I'm good. Just thinking that's all."

She smirked. "Yeah, I thought I could smell burning."

Jonny grinned. "Cheeky bitch! I've missed that smart mouth." Mel grinned back at him, and took his hand in hers and gave it a squeeze. "I was just thinking about the accident."

Mel's smile faded. "Jonny..." She warned.

Jonny gave her hand a little squeeze back. "Look I'm just going to say it because I think it needs said. I blame myself. If I hadn't taken you out, you wouldn't have been knocked down that night. I'm so sorry Mel." He said, his head hanging in guilt and shame.

Mel shifted in the bed to put her other hand on Jonny's shoulder. "No! Jonny, it wasn't your fault sweetie! You have nothing to be sorry for!"

"I could have lost you... We all could have lost you, and all because I wanted to make sure that smile stayed on your face that night." Jonny moved closer to Mel, and rested his forehead against her hip. "I'm sorry. I'm so, so sorry." He murmured against her.

Mel's heart broke to think that her friend would blame himself for what happened. This wasn't his fault, she didn't blame him, and she told him so in her own way. She lifted her hand and stroked the back of his head, before lifting her hand and slapping him firmly on the back of the head. "You're such a dipshit. This isn't all about you, you know. I was the one hit by the bloody car." Jonny lifted his head and rubbed where Mel had clipped him. "The only person I hold to blame for all of this is the selfish son of a bitch who was driving that car while drunk, and the last time that I checked, that wasn't you!" she scolded him, her expression stern.

Jonny looked up at her with wet eyes, tears threatening.

"If you even dare say the 's' word one more time, I will get out of this bed and kick your ass." She glared.

Jonny's solemn look evaporated, replaced instead with a smirk. "Baby, if you think you are fit enough to get up and kick my ass I would welcome that in a heartbeat!"

Mel smiled, and touched her hand to Jonny's cheek. "It was never your fault, and I won't have you saying anything else. Understand?" She smiled.

Jonny leaned his head against her hand and closed his eyes. "I'll do my best to keep that in mind." He said grimly as she continued to stroke his cheek.

The nurse from earlier in the evening arrived at the door of Mel's room. "Visiting time is over now." She announced, before turning on her heel and disappearing off back down the corridor. Jonny smiled, and took Mel's hand from his cheek into his hands.

"Apparently I need to leave." He smiled at her, squeezing her hand between his own. Mel smiled back, and Jonny felt the warmth and affection radiating from her. He leaned over to kiss her head, and she caught his head in her hands, and kissed him softly on the lips instead. "You were never to blame for any of this Jonathan Tyler, and you better not forget that!"

He kissed her cheek and leaned against her softly in a hug. "I'll try." He murmured in her ear.

"You better buster, or I will be kicking ass, and you know it!" She warned with a grin.

Jonny grinned back and kissed her forehead. "I better go before that nurse comes back and drags me out by the balls." He smirked.

Mel laughed, and Jonny moved towards the door. Just before he left he looked over this shoulder. "I'll see you tomorrow." He smiled and walked out the door.

Mel settled down in the bed, and fixed the covers round her. As she drifted off to sleep her mind wandered to what had been said earlier in the day about Alex. She thought about what happened to them the night of the Gala, and she thought about what Jonny had told her about him not leaving her side for three days straight. She thought about the last time she had slept beside him, warm strong arms wrapping around her and she drifted off to sleep.

~ ~ ~

Mel had been out of hospital now for two weeks. Her mother had been driving her crazy, she had been there at her house staying with her to help out with the things that she couldn't manage by herself. Jonny had been there every day, and the others in their group had taken it in turns to call by and see how she was doing.

"Mum, really, I'm fine. You need to get back to your own house. I can manage, I promise. Jonny said he'd call round later, and you know that I will be on the phone to you the second I need you." Mel smiled to her mum.

"Do you promise? I know what you're like Melody Anderson, you're a stubborn bitch, you take after your dad." Mel's mum scolded.

She rolled her eyes. "Yes Mum! I'm sure. Go!" She smiled, practically pushing her mum out through the front door.

Her mum kissed her on the cheek and gave her a hug before hunting through her handbag for her car keys. "As long as you're sure love." She smiled.

"I am, and I'll phone if I'm not. I promise." Mel replied.

Mel stood in the doorway and watched as her mum left. She waved, and when her mum's car had disappeared from sight, she closed the front door and let out a huge sigh. *Halle-fucking-lujah!* She thought to herself, relieved that she was back to the peace and quiet that her house usually offered her. She loved her mother dearly, but she loved her own space, and privacy more. As grateful as she would always be to her mum for the support she had given her over the last few weeks. She needed the time to collect her thoughts, and decide what she was going to do about Alex.

Her phone chirped in her pocket as she limped down the hallway to the kitchen to make herself a cup of tea.

How's my girl today?

Jonny had texted her. She smiled. He was someone else that she would be forever grateful to. Jonny was the only reason that she was still sane after her mother had lived with her for the last two weeks. She typed out her reply and hit send.

She's enjoying the peace and quiet! The mothership has headed home at last! :D

She set her crutch to the side and hobbled around the kitchen. Her phone chirped again and she looked at Jonny's reply.

So a day in relaxing by yourself then? Or can I harass you later? ;-)

She smirked when she read his reply.

You can harass me later Sir. But you better bring supplies! I want chocolates and films! LOL x

The kettle finished boiling and she poured out the water for her cup of tea. Her phone chirped one more time.

On one condition... Text Alex. You said you wanted to hear the truth from him. So arrange it.

Mel sighed. She knew that Jonny would eventually push her to act on her decision sooner or later. They had talked about Alex and the truth that he claimed he needed to share with her. She had agreed that she needed to hear what he had to say, even if it was only for closure and to give her peace of mind. She had been delaying contacting him to make arrangements to see him though.

Okay boss! I'll text him today I promise!

She replied to Jonny. Within seconds her phone chirped again.

You better! I'll check!

She rolled her eyes at the message on her phone, lifted her cup of tea, and once her phone was back in her pocket, lifted her crutch and limped her way into the living room. Once sitting on the sofa and reasonably comfortable she pulled her phone out of her pocket again, and began to tap out a new message.

Hi x Sorry it's taken me a few weeks to get in touch. I'd like to hear your explanation for what happened now, if you're still willing to tell me. Are you free on Saturday?

She pressed send before tucking her phone back into her pocket, and turning on the TV.

CHAPTER 29

Mel pulled into the driveway at Alex's house and turned off her car's engine. She was glad she had an automatic, and didn't need both legs to be able to drive. *Just find out why and leave.* She thought to herself over and over. She wanted to know what had happened that night. But she was worried about what Alex would say; she worried about seeing him again, and how she would react in his presence. She finally got out of the car, locked it and went to door on one crutch, and rang his doorbell.

"Hi." Alex said meekly when he answered the door.

"Hi." She murmured back, walking in past him and heading straight for the lounge. She turned to watch him walking in behind her. "So I'm here, what do you want Alex?" She asked him, coming across as harsher than she had really intended.

Alex gestured towards the sofa as he walked towards it. "Sit, please?" Mel glanced at him, and then looked behind her, moving to the chair that was the furthest from him. She looked at him, waiting for him to start his explanation, to say something that would make the tiniest bit of sense to her. She set her crutch beside her as he stared.

"Can I get you a drink or anything?" He offered.

Mel looked at him. "No thank you."

"Cup of tea?" He asked again. He looked at the expression on her face and he sat down, knowing that she wasn't going to let him take a minute longer than he needed to.

"Can you explain it, please? I don't want to be here any longer than I have to." She said confirming what he had thought.

Alex bowed his head, his heart ached seeing her. He wanted to make it up to her. He wanted to tell her now all of the things that he was scared of before. "Okay... But before I tell you what happened, I just want to explain to you that I never meant to hurt you. At this point, I'm just grateful you are here, and willing to hear me out, I won't hold you to anything else, I don't deserve anything else."

Mel sighed. "Stop." She said, raising her hand. She didn't need this, she couldn't hear this, she wasn't sure how long her resolve to listen to him was going to last. "Alex, please don't. Just say whatever it is you wanted to say."

Alex sighed and started to explain. "Okay. I'm not engaged Mel. I was once a long time ago, and I'll explain that later. But the only person I've been seeing is you."

A laugh erupted from her and he looked up at her. "Alex I saw the two of you together. I heard her call herself your fiancée, you even told me she was yourself."

He held her gaze, willing her to believe him. "Jules isn't my fiancée. She's my assistant."

Mel thought for a moment, thinking about that time that she surprised Alex at his office for lunch. "I've been to your office. That woman wasn't the one sitting outside."

Alex remembered it too. "The day you were in my office," he told her, "my assistant went home sick, and Kate was standing in for her."

She thought about what he was telling her. Trying to make sense of it in her head. Wondering if there was any truth to what he was telling her. Somewhere in her, she wanted to believe him. He was getting to her, and she wanted to get away from him. She needed to get the upper hand with him again, she couldn't weaken. "Why would your assistant drape herself over you and claim to be your fiancée Alex, what kind of idiot do you think I am?" She asked.

He sighed, running his hands through his hair. "I don't take you for an idiot Jellybean I really don't."

The second that his pet name for her registered in her brain she melted. She sprang up from the seat looking like a deer caught in the headlights of a car. "Don't call me that name, I can't deal with that." She said shaking her head, grabbing her crutch, about to move for the door.

Alex stood and went to reach out to stop her. She stopped in her tracks and pulled herself back from him like he carried the plague. He pulled his hands back and offered them up in the air like a sign of surrender. He didn't want to make her run, he would have walked over hot coals at that moment just to have a few more seconds of her company. "Please, sit back down?" He said apologetically.

Mel looked at him, and thought about what she really wanted to do. To sit, or to run. This time, she picked sit. "Just..... Don't, okay?" She said, perching herself back on the edge of the chair.

Alex sat too, rubbing his jaw in his hand. "Sorry, just habit I guess. I won't say it again, I promise."

She nodded, and Alex started to explain. "Do you remember the other woman who was there? Blonde, tall, complete fucking asshole?"

Mel stared at him with distrust. "Can't tell if she was an asshole or not, but yes, I remember her." She snapped.

Alex bit his bottom lip as he looked for the right words to explain this whole mess to Mel. "Juliet is my assistant and my friend. The blonde piece of work was my ex. Natalie Carter." Mel looked at him. She wanted to hear more, but she wasn't sure how this would relate to her, and what Alex had done. She was torn.

"Can I have a glass of water, please?" She asked.

Alex bounced up from his seat and into the kitchen. He returned a few minutes later and handed the glass to Mel. His finger skimmed against hers as she took the glass from him, and she held her breath. Alex looked away and sat back down.

"I'd like to tell you about Natalie, but you have to let me get it all out, because it's hard for me to talk about, and to be honest, aside from my sister, Juliet and well, Jonny, no one else has been told what happened. Not by me anyway." Alex explained. Mel nodded, took a sip of her water, and waited. Alex thought back to the day that he had first encountered Natalie Carter. Telling Mel everything as he went.

He told Mel how he had seen Natalie from across the grassy courtyard in the middle of the Lanyon building, the oldest part of their university campus. He described her as tall, with green eyes and long straight blonde hair. She had caught him looking at her and grinned. They quickly found out that they were on the same course, and spent the rest of the induction week hanging out together, and getting to know the campus and their classmates together.

He told her how they had become fast friends, and eventually he had plucked up the courage to ask her out.

He explained that he and Natalie had become a couple, and he started to think that she was the love of his life. In the second year, he told her that Natalie had changed her degree subject, and while they remained in the same faculty they were no longer in the same classes. He said that outside of classes the pair were generally inseparable, that was until Alex's final year. He said he had become incredibly busy with his final project and exams, but he spent every spare second with Natalie.

"She was my world. I'll never forget that night after my final exams when she told me that she was pregnant. I've never been so delighted and yet so fucking terrified in my whole life up to that point. We set a date for our wedding, and we planned for a life with us and our baby. About two months later, she began to bleed. I rushed her to the maternity hospital, and we found out that she was miscarrying. I sat in that hospital with her 17 hours while she went through labour, and essentially gave birth." He sighed, the weight was lifting off his shoulders. It felt good to finally be letting go of the hurt that he had held in his heart for so long. To be free of the fear that it had bred with it. He chanced a look at Mel, who was sitting with a shocked yet remorseful expression on her face.

"How far along was she?" She asked with genuine sorrow.

Alex puffed out his cheeks and let out a long breath. This was the hard part. This was the part that would explain to Mel why he was such a cold hearted ass who didn't really deserve her. "17 weeks," he explained, "so while it was officially a miscarriage, in reality she delivered a tiny little baby boy. She named him, she got a photo of him. I took her home the next day, and she and I cried, the plans we had made suddenly up in the air. I'd had a son, and he was gone."

Alex saw the look of pity cross Mel's face. It made him sad, and yet hopeful. He knew that she cared about him still, but at the same time, she hadn't heard the worst of the story of what Natalie had put him through. He needed to see it through and finish his story. His face grew grim and he continued. "But that wasn't the worst of it. A couple of days after she got out of hospital, when she was due to go and collect the baby's ashes, I find her and my best friend having an argument in our bedroom. They didn't hear me come in, I stood in the hall outside the room and heard their conversation. Why hadn't she told me that the baby was his? Why hadn't she called him so that he could have been there for her in the hospital? How my best friend had been with screwing my fiancée for a year and a half, right under my nose!" He finished angrily.

Mel looked into his eyes. "What did you do?" She asked softly.

Alex looked at her expression of concern and laughed "I punched the living fuck out of him and walked out that night. I did go back about a week later after I had calmed down. She tried to convince me that she and I would be okay and that we could work it out, that she was sorry." His head fell into his hands and he rubbed them over his face, he sighed. "I just couldn't look at her." He explained. "I've never trusted anyone since. Not until I met you."

Mel sighed and tried not to think of the underlying meaning of what Alex was saying. He had bombarded her with information and she needed to try and take it all in. "And this is the tall blonde there that night?" She asked to clarify. Alex nodded, the other woman there that evening had indeed been the woman who had broken his heart, and ripped apart all of his dreams. "But what has this to do with Juliet?" She asked.

Alex licked his lips, he needed a stiff drink. He was telling Mel more than he had ever told anyone. "Jules knows about Natalie. Every once in a while Natalie appears at one of these functions. When I used to go to these things alone, she showed up I ended up drinking half the bar and pissing off some clients." He laughed and continued. "The last time it happened, Juliet said she was sick of my shit and that she was going with me instead. Figured that was easier than kissing client ass for months afterwards." He sighed. "The night you saw her, was the first time Natalie had showed up while Jules was there. She just did what she thought she needed to in order to stop Natalie making a scene or pissing me off."

Mel thought about what Alex was saying. She felt overwhelmed with information. She needed time to process, and get things straight in her head. She looked at him. "But that doesn't explain why you said she was your fiancée when I asked you." She pointed out.

Alex had known this moment would happen from the second that Mel had asked for the truth, and to explain himself. He took a deep breath and let it out in a puff. He swallowed and started to answer her. "That happened because I'm a fucking coward. I've been falling deeper and deeper in love with you for months now." He told her. "Normally that scares the shit out of me, I never let it get that far with a submissive." He said wringing his hands nervously. "But with you, I always want more, and wanted to take a bigger risk, but that scared the ever living fuck out of me, and when you asked me if I was with Jules, I saw an out and I took it. Falling for you, and then Natalie turning up, just pushed me too far, and I needed to bolt. I'm a pathetic bastard Mel, I can't dress it up as anything other than that." Alex leaned back on the sofa and cast his eyes to the ceiling. He had told her; admitted his crutch was domination, he admitted that he was damaged goods, that he had been a complete idiot for pushing her away.

"Has there been anyone since Natalie pulled her mind-fuck?" She asked softly.

He turned his head to look at her, she needed to know that this was the truth. She had to see it on his face t' he was being honest. "No. Never. I used domina· maintain distance and keep control. If they got t or expected more than what I was comfortable giving, I just went out and found myself a new submissive." He admitted. Mel raised her eyebrows at his brash honesty. "I know, it makes me seem like a cold hearted fuck, and I have to be honest, until I met you I probably was."

Mel shook her head. She wanted to believe him, but he was right he sounded like he was too cold-hearted for it to be true. "But you love me?" She asked scornfully.

Again Alex caught her gaze. "With all my heart."

Mel found herself laughing at his sentiment. "So much you walked away and left me?" She scoffed laughing.

Alex closed his eyes and swallowed, her comment stung, he knew she was right. "Mel... I... I'm sorry, I have no excuses, just fear." He tried to apologise. He knew that it wasn't enough, but those words were all he had, and he didn't know what else to say. He could have shown her just how much she meant to him, but he knew that she wouldn't let him touch her.

"I almost died Alex." She said softly.

Alex could feel the tears forming in his eyes. He couldn't bear to think about the fact that he had almost lost her forever when she was hit by a car. He sighed. "I know, and it woke me up, I could have lost you Mel, and I have never been more terrified in my life than at that moment. That you could have been gone, and I wouldn't be able to hold you, or tell you I was sorry, or how I really feel about you."

Mel sighed. She had to explain to him, for him to understand that he wasn't the only one who had been hurt. That he wasn't the only one who had been scared because of the possible outcome of her accident. "It's made me reflect too, Alex." She told him. "Life is too short to waste it on someone who just isn't worth it." She said.

Alex closed his eyes. *She thinks you're not worth it asshole, and you know deep down that she's right. You let the best thing in your life walk away because you were a scared little pussy!* His inner critic told him. He winced at the harshness of the notion. He covered his face with his hands, trying to push those thoughts out of his head. "Do you think I'm not worth it?" He asked.

She wanted to tell him that he was worth it. He had been through a lot and she could understand part of what was going on in his head. But she wasn't ready to let go of the hurt that he had caused her first. "Jesus Alex, I can't decide that after all I've just heard. Let's just say I haven't made up my mind yet." She told him. It was all she could give him at that moment.

He nodded. "Okay."

"Is there anything else to your confession?" She asked.

Alex thought about it for a moment. "Just that I love you." He said with a shrug. "I hope that you can understand why I am how I am, even if you can't forgiv it."

Mel thought about the information overload; she thought about what she wanted to do next. The first thing that she wanted to do was talk to Jonny. She could talk to him and he'd help her figure this out. "You have given me a lot to think about. I need time to digest it all." She said at last.

Alex cleared his throat, fighting back emotions. "I understand."

"I'll let you know what I decide, okay?"

Alex nodded. "Take as long as you want."

Mel stood and shifted about nervously. "I should go."

Alex stood, gazing at her. "Okay." He swallowed. There was a pregnant pause. Neither of them willing to part from each other's company, but neither of them really knowing what else to say or do. "Can I hug you? Would that be okay?" Alex asked anxiously, hoping he wasn't pushing her for too much.

Mel looked at him cautiously. "Okay."

She stepped forward and moved into his arms as he put his around her and pulled her in against him. She put her head on his chest and for a moment was lost in the warmth of his body and his smell. He wrapped his arms around her and held her tight against him. His nose filled with the flowery smell of her shampoo. They both stood wrapped in their embrace, trying to make the moment last that little bit longer. Mel sighed and braced her resolve for being able to leave. "I'll talk to you soon." She said, and moved herself back away from his chest. Her entire body feeling the loss of contact from him. Alex swallowed hard, he felt like she was taking a part of his soul out of his body at that moment. The feeling that he was going to never see her again washed over him and he fought the urge to pull her back against him and never let her go.

"Okay... And thank you for hearing me out." He said the raw emotion spilling into his voice.

Mel fought the tears in her eyes that just wanted to spill down her face. "It's okay." She sighed and walked towards the door.

Alex followed her in silence to the front door, his shoulders slumped, his head hanging low. Mel walked out the door and got into her car. She couldn't bear the thought of looking back and seeing any shred of hurt on his face. She started the car and drove out of the driveway and down the street. Alex closed the door and sank the floor behind it. Tears flooded his eyes and streamed down his cheeks. A sense of dread filled the pit of his stomach. *She's not coming back you know. You well and truly fucked this one up!* His inner critic gloated.

When she was finally around the corner and out of view from Alex's house. Mel parked the car at the kerb and crumpled. Her face was instantly awash with tears, and her shoulders shook as she sobbed. She cried for the hurt Alex had caused her, she cried for the hurt that s¹ knew that she had just inflicted on him, and she cried for the past that had damaged him so much.

CHAPTER 30

Once she was ready to continue driving, Mel called Jonny. "Are you okay?" He greeted her as he answered the phone.

"No." She replied.

"Come and get me. We're going to yours for a movie night and a good long hug!" He told her, once she had agreed he hung up the phone and got ready for her arrival.

~ ~ ~

Jonny walked into Mel's lounge with a large bowl of popcorn and dropped himself onto the sofa beside her. "So he told you everything?" He asked, and scooped a handful of popcorn into his mouth.

"Yes..." Mel sighed, "But Jesus, Jonny what the hell am I meant to do with that?" She asked him, lifting popcorn and stuffing it into her own mouth in exasperation.

Jonny tried to chew some of his popcorn before he replied. "I don't know baby." He said, and rubbed his hand on her leg in an attempt to comfort her. "I guess, whatever you feel you should be doing with it."

Mel looked at him clearly not amused with his suggestions. "And what if I don't know what the fuck I'm meant to do with it!" She sighed.

Jonny smirked, "Remember when you had been fooling around with Aidan, and then, he left for University, and you kind of kept hooking up for a while, and eventually he got a girlfriend." He asked.

Mel raised an eyebrow at him. "You better have a point here buster..."

Jonny just gave her a cheesy grin, "I always have a point baby. You remember him, right?"

Mel shook her head and decided to play along. "Of course I remember him." She said and lifted more popcorn into her mouth.

"You asked me what I thought, when you had a chance to see him when he was home, but was very much in a relationship." Jonny reminded her.

Mel rolled her eyes at him. "I'm still waiting for a point..." She warned. Jonny held his finger up. "Wait." He advised. "What did I tell you to do? What pearls of wisdom did I supply on you, what diamond advice did I give at that point?"

Mel laughed at him. "Nothing, as I remember you flat out refused to reply to my messages about it."

Jonny grinned at her and held out his hands like he was supplying her the answer. "I know I did... Because you are a beautiful and smart woman, and you don't need to be told what to do! You already know. You don't need my validation to make it anymore right for you." He smiled, waiting for her reaction. Mel put her arms around Jonny and squeezed him tight. "Thank you."

He grinned and winked at her. "See, I told you there was a point."

She laughed at him and fake punched him. "Yeah, took you long enough to get there though."

Jonny groaned as Mel's fake punch made contact, laughing; then he smiled and looks at her sweetly. "Seriously... I love ya, and you're too smart to get it wrong."

Mel's heart melted. This was why she loved Jonny; why they were the closest of friends and always would be. He always had the right thing to say to make her feel better. She snuggled in against him, and he smiled put his arm around her and kissed her on the forehead, resting his head on the top of hers. "Film night now?" He asked.

"Yeah." She smiled.

Jonny pressed play on the remote and the pair settled down with their popcorn and watched 'Fight Club'.

~ ~ ~

Two weeks passed after Mel had called into Alex's house to hear him out and find out exactly what had happened on the night of the Gala. She had thought long and hard about what Alex had told her. She had talked things over with Jonny and he had been his usual helpful self, offering her very little in the way of advice while showering her in support. She had part of a plan coming together in her head about what she wanted to do. She just needed to start to put it all into action.

Mel took a deep breath and dialled the number to Alex's office.

"Matthew's Architecture, Mr Matthew's office?" Came the voice down the line.

"Juliet?" Mel asked.

"Yes, who am I speaking to?" Came the reply.

Mel sighed. "It's Melody Anderson." She said hoping that she wouldn't have to explain anything.

"Oh, hi... Do you want to talk to Alex?" Juliet asked.

"Actually, I was hoping to speak to you. Can I meet you for lunch today?" Mel enquired.

There was a moment of silence. "I can probably get some time at 12:30 if that suits you?" Juliet said down the phone.

"Perfect." Mel agreed. "Do you know the coffee shop just down the street?" She added, and paused to hear Juliet's response. Juliet agreed that she knew where the place was and that she would be able to meet Mel there.

"I know I shouldn't really ask this." Mel started. "Can we keep this between us?" She requested.

Juliet sighed. "I don't think it would help him if he knew that you were going to be there to be honest." She admitted. Mel thought about asking more than that. But she resisted. Instead she thanked Juliet, said that she would see her at 12:30 and hung up the phone.

~ ~ ~

Juliet knocked on the door to Alex's office and entered. She stood watching him as he frowned at the paperwork in front of him, and looked back to the computer screen.

She cleared her throat to get his attention. "Boss?" She called, waiting for him to look up.

"Oh hey Jules." He said, glancing in her direction and sighing. Since Mel had kicked him out of her hospital room he had been a mess. Juliet could tell from the look on his unshaven face that he clearly wasn't sleeping. Her heart ached for her friend, she knew that aside from losing Mel, he was struggling with guilt. When she had called to his house to check on him the night after he had shared the truth of his past with Mel, she had found him drunk in his study. He had rambled on about his part in Mel's accident. When she asked him to explain, he had apparently decided that if he had "had any balls" and not "ruined everything" with how he handled Mel's questions at the Gala, she wouldn't have needed to be out with Jonny that night, and wouldn't have been there to be knocked down. While Juliet couldn't fault his logic, she didn't see what good would come from him putting himself through that kind of self loathing. She had taken his scotch, gave him some paracetamol and a pint of water, and tucked him into bed. She saw the same look in his eyes now.

"I'm just going to take an hour out and grab some lunch and run a few errands. Do you want me to bring you anything?" She asked.

"Bottle of Black Bush would go down a treat." He laughed.

"Whiskey will not help you right now, and I'll be damned if I'm letting you waste a good bottle of Black to wash away your guilt." She scolded.

Alex smirked. "True, a situation like this calls for some Jack Daniels." He laughed a little when he caught her glaring at him. "I'll be fine Jules. But I could murder a coffee before you go, if that's okay?" He asked. Juliet nodded, and turned to make Alex a coffee.

When she came back with his mug of hot Americano, she set it on his desk. "I'll be back in about an hour." She advised. Alex didn't even lift his head from his work this time. He just held up his hand in a wave.

"No worries, see you when you get back." He murmured, deep in concentration. Juliet shook her head, left his office and grabbed her handbag before heading for the elevators.

~ ~ ~

Mel sat at the table, nervously tapping her good foot on the floor as she hugged her cup of tea, the other was still wrapped in plaster and proving increasingly itchy.

374

She sat thinking over the situation as it lay in front of her. She needed to figure out what to do about Alex. She needed to know if she should go and see him, and hear him out after all. He had offered to tell her "the truth" and she was so unsure of what to do next. Jonny had been his usual self, not advising her of what she should do, knowing that she would eventually figure it all out for herself. She rubbed her temples, feeling the start of a headache forming, her accident had left her with regular headaches, thinking about Alex seemed to bring them on even more.

"Mel?" A voice said, snapping her out of her meandering thoughts. She looked up at the petite blonde standing in front of her.

"Juliet?" Mel asked.

Juliet nodded and held out her hand for Mel to shake. Mel took her hand and looked into the green eyes that were currently regarding her with compassion.

"Have a seat, I haven't ordered yet. Just needed a tea while I contemplated the universe." She smiled as Juliet sat down opposite her.

Juliet smiled back. She was already understanding why Alex liked Mel, there was just something about her that made you warm to her instantly. A waitress came over to their table and they both ordered some food.

"How is he?" Mel asked softly.

Juliet sighed. "He's not too good if I'm honest. He's drinking a lot of scotch, he's not sleeping all that well, and he blames himself." She explained, watching Mel's reaction. Mel's heart sank. She couldn't stand the thought of Alex miserable, let alone blaming himself.

She sighed. "Why is he blaming himself?" She asked.

Their waiter appeared with their food, and Juliet paused before answering. "He thinks it's his fault." She explained as the waiter walked away. "He believes that if he had handled the situation better at the Gala, and been honest and told you what was really going on, you wouldn't have been out with Jonny that night, and been hit by the car." She finished, and took a sip of her coffee.

"Oh for fuck's sake." Mel sighed. "I've had the same shit from Jonny! If he hadn't taken me out I wouldn't have been there, and wouldn't have ended up in hospital." Her shoulders sagged and she sat back in her chair, and began looking in her bag for some painkillers. "The only person to blame for me being knocked down is the wanker who was driving in the car drunk." She said weakly before putting two tablets into her mouth and swallowing them with some mouthfuls of tea. "Juliet, I don't know if Alex mentioned it, but he explained everything to me two weeks ago." Mel paused to see what Juliet would say.

"He had mentioned it. But I didn't want to push anything with him, so I haven't asked all the details." Juliet offered.

Mel turned her cup on its saucer. "I have come to a decision about what I want to do next. But I need a little help with it." She said, absently staring at the cup as it revolved. She looked up at Juliet. "I understand why he did the things he has. But..." As she spoke Juliet's face fell a little expecting the next part to be bad news for her friend. "... I'm not ready to let Alex find out that I want to fix things just yet." Juliet stared at Mel, and she laughed. "You thought that I was going to give him some bad news didn't you?" She smiled.

Juliet smiled too. "I did. But I'm very glad to hear that you're not!" she explained.

Mel grinned. "Me too."

"So what are you going to do?" Juliet asked.

Mel's face lit up and she raised an eyebrow. "Well..." She started, before explaining to Juliet her plan.

~ ~ ~

At the end of an hour, the pair had become firm friends, and Juliet was feeling delighted to hear how things would be panning out for Alex. She was also a little surprised to hear how wonderfully devious Melody could be. Her plan was very sneaky, and brilliantly thought out. Jonny would be the go between from Juliet to Mel since Mel didn't want Alex to see her before she was ready.

On her way back to the office, Juliet stopped to get a sweet chilli chicken salad for Alex, knowing that he now needed to get himself sorted out.

~ ~ ~

Two days later, Jonny took a visit to Alex's office. He was there to introduce himself to Juliet, and to see Alex, and let him know how Melody was getting on. A decoy visit, made to make Alex think that Mel still wasn't willing to see him.

The lift door opened and Jonny walked out and around the corner towards Alex's office. Juliet was sitting with her head down working on some paperwork. Jonny stood in front of her and coughed a little to get her attention.

"Can I help you?" She said as she lifted her head. Jonny getting a first look at her face, and into her emerald green eyes. He suddenly lost the power of speech, he couldn't take his eyes off her, or make any of his words pass his lips.

"Sir?" She asked smiling, "Can I help you?"

Jonny came back to earth with a bump and coughed a little again, feeling suddenly self conscious.

"Sorry, are you Juliet?" He asked.

"You're Jonny." She told him, and he nodded licking his lips. "Mel said you would be over today."

Jonny took a deep breath and willed his body to start behaving and listening to his internal commands. "Yeah, sorry. I'm Jonny Tyler." He smiled and stuck his hand out for her to shake.

Juliet stood and put her hand in Jonny's to shake it. Instantly a tingling sensation swept up her arm from where he touched her and she felt her heart start to speed up. Jonny grinned at her and she wondered if he could read the sensation that he was generating within her. His cheeks had a hint of colour and she looked deeply into his bright blue eyes. She swallowed and took her hand from his. "I'll let Alex know that you're here." She said as she licked her lips.

Jonny's eyes swept down over her lips as the tip of her tongue slipped over them, and he felt his cock stir in his jeans. *Well, fuck.* He thought as Juliet left from where she was standing in front of him, and went to the door of Alex's office to knock and introduce Jonny.

Juliet gave Jonny a quick glance and a smile as he walked past her and into Alex's office. He looked over his shoulder at her and smirked as she closed the door behind him.

Alex strode across the office to shake hands with Jonny. "Has something happened to Mel?" He asked, anxiety clearly showing in his voice. Jonny put a hand on his shoulder.

"She's fine." He told him. "She's doing okay actually. I just thought that I would come in and let you know. I know she's not been in touch." Jonny said, his voice trailing off in regret. He was starting to like Alex. He seemed to genuinely feel for his best friend, and anyone who seemed to love Mel as much as he did was okay in his book.

"Has she said anything about that?" Alex asked.

Jonny sighed and shook his head. "Sorry mate, she hasn't. But I thought that you might like to now that her cast is coming off in a week, her ribs are healing nicely, and most of her bruising is gone."

Alex smiled a genuine smile and looked relieved. "How's her head?" He asked.

Jonny smiled. "Still on her shoulders for now. She's still giving me shit, so she seems fine to me." He laughed. "She gets headaches, but the doctor has said that they are nothing to be worried about, it's just her brain complaining about the accident. They might fade in time, but he has warned her they might just be a new 'feature' of her life."

Alex moved to the sofa part of his office, and dropped himself into the chair. "I can't help but blame myself for all of this." He said as he ran his fingers through his hair. Jonny looked at Alex, and couldn't help but share his thoughts and feelings on the whole situation.

"I know how you feel mate. I keep going over the fact that if I hadn't took her out that night, or if I hadn't suggested going to the SU after the cinema, that things might have been a hell of a lot differently. I get that you feel guilty mate, really I do, I have that feeling every damn day when I see her on her crutches, or wince in anyway, or taking her painkillers. It's fucking gut wrenching." Jonny said, sighing and dropping himself into the chair at the opposite end from Alex.

"But that's not your fault Jonny, it's mine. If I hadn't been a gutless cunt, she wouldn't have needed you to cheer her up at all." He said, holding his face in his hands.

Jonny put his hand on Alex's shoulder again. "I get it. I really do. But I'll tell you what Mel told me when I was telling her the same thing you're telling me." He sighed. "She told me, and a quote 'Thanks dipshit, stop making it all about you, I was the one hit by the bloody car.' And she followed it up with, 'The only person I hold to blame is the selfish son of a bitch who was driving that car while drunk.' If she can let me off with an ear bashing, I'm pretty sure she'd be doing the same thing for you. Don't you think?" Jonny let his hand fall from Alex's shoulder, and slouched back in the chair sighing.

"She wanted me to come here and tell you how she was." He explained.

"But she doesn't want to see me." Alex said, stating rather than asking.

Jonny shook his head. "I'm sorry mate, I don't know. I just do what I'm told."

Alex looked at him, his face looking pained. "I've got to head to Aberdeen for a conference in two weeks time. Would you tell her that if I haven't heard from her by then, that I'll understand that she doesn't want to talk to me anymore, and I'll leave it at that?" Alex asked.

Jonny nodded.

Juliet knocked on the door and walked in. "Alex, your next appointment will be here soon." She informed him, while casting a long glance in Jonny's direction. Jonny's eyes met hers and she caught a trace of something in his glance.

"I better head off then." Jonny said, clearing his throat and looking away from Juliet's gaze.

Both men stood, and Alex held his hand out to Jonny. "Thanks for letting me know how she's doing." Alex said his expression grim.

"No worries man. I'm sure she'll be in touch at some point mate, you just need to give her time." Jonny reassured him while shaking his hand.

Alex sighed moved back behind his desk and Juliet held the door open for Jonny to leave. Once the door was closed Juliet turned back to Jonny.

"Has he been like that the whole time?" Jonny asked her.

Juliet nodded. "Pretty much." She held out an envelope to Jonny. "Mel asked for this. Give it to her, and tell her everything is arranged."

Jonny gazed down at the envelope. His friend hadn't told him her plan, but he understood that she knew what she was doing. He reached for the envelope and his fingers skimmed over Juliet's hand. He felt the sparks buzzing in his hands where their skin had made contact. His eyes shot to hers, only to find hers already staring at him. *She feels it too.* He thought to himself. Juliet's face flushed with colour, and she coughed a little, breaking the moment and looking away from Jonny's eyes.

Jonny swallowed and pulled his hand from hers. "Thanks Juliet, I'll make sure she gets this." His eyes dropped to the envelope in his hand. "I really hope she knows what she's doing." He mumbled.

Juliet smiled. "I think she does, yes."

Jonny smiled back. "Thanks, I'll take this over to her now... It was nice meeting you."

"You too." Juliet replied with a grin.

Jonny walked away not turning back until he was safely in the elevator. He glanced at Juliet one last time as the doors closed, and sighed when the car finally started to move. *What the fuck was that?* He thought to himself. He'd never reacted to a woman like that in his life before.

Once he was out on the street he pulled his phone from his pocket and called Mel.

"Hey, listen I have an envelope for you from Juliet. Are you ready to tell me what the fuck you're planning

383

now?" He asked when she answered the phone and then listened to her reply. "I'm on my way over now then. I'll be about 25 minutes." He replied, and hung up the call, putting his phone back in his pocket.

CHAPTER 31

Juliet drove Alex's Range Rover into the drop off point outside George Best Airport and turned to look at her friend. One look at his face and she could tell where his mind was but she wouldn't be able to say anything that was going to make him feel any better.

"Ready to rock and roll?" She asked smiling at him.

Alex sighed. "I guess." He glanced at the phone in his hand, and checked for what felt like the millionth time that he hadn't missed a message coming in from Mel. When he saw that the screen was blank he sighed again and looked at Juliet.

"I just thought that... Well, I *hoped* that she would have been in touch." He said, staring at the rain falling on the windscreen.

Now it was Juliet's turn to sigh. "Just because you haven't heard from her, doesn't mean you won't. It just means she's not ready yet." She said, and reached out to squeeze Alex's shoulder in support.

"I told Jonny to tell her that if I hadn't heard from her by my trip to Aberdeen, that I would take it that she didn't want to hear from me anymore, and leave it at that." He reminded her.

"I know you did boss." Juliet replied glumly and let an uneasy silence fill the car for a moment before she interrupted it. "You better get a move on, you don't want to miss the check in."

Alex wiped his hand over his face and puffed out his cheeks with a long exhale. "Yeah. You put all the details in my briefcase didn't you?" He asked Juliet, checking he had everything that he needed.

"Yes I did. Almost everywhere was booked up, so you're in a spa hotel called Ardoe House, it's on the other side of Aberdeen from the airport, so there should be a car at the airport to collect you. Just look for the sign with your name on it." She informed him.

Alex lifted his briefcase and his holdall from the back seat, and leaned over to give Juliet a kiss on the cheek. "Thanks for all this Jules. I'd be lost without you." She smiled at him, and he reached for the door handle. He opened the door and jumped out, striding for the covered area of the drop off point. He waved as Juliet pulled away, and he made his way across the road, and along the path to the front of the terminal. Once he had himself checked in, he sat and waited for his flight to be called. He checked his phone one last time for a message from Mel, when there wasn't on he turned his phone off and tucked it into his briefcase ready for the flight.

~ ~ ~

Mel stood in the main area of the airport wearing a navy trouser suit and white blouse, her long hair up in a neat bun and she waited. From the information Juliet gave her, Alex's plane had just arrived and he would soon be coming through security. She couldn't stand still. She was moving from foot to foot, nervous in case she missed him. She knew that he was coming to Aberdeen for the International Conference on Architectural Technology, and was expecting a car to pick him up. He just wasn't expecting it to be her that was collecting him.

She stood with a sign, just like they do in the movies, making sure it was high enough to conceal her face, and waited. The seconds slowed, and what seemed like hours passed before the other passengers started to appear. Mel bit her bottom lip anxiously. Eventually, feet appeared in her line of sight under the sign. "I'm Mr Matthews." Alex said, and she could hear how tired he was. She moved the sign from in front of her face, but he wasn't looking at her. "Certainly Sir." She said, and his eyes were on her in an instant, a shocked look on his face.

"Mel?" He asked, not believing his own eyes. *You've lost it now buddy, you're seeing her everywhere!* He thought.

"Yes Alex, it's really me." She smiled tenderly.

"What are you doing here?" He stared in disbelief.

"You were expecting a car to collect you, weren't you?" Alex nodded.

"Well, I'm your driver." He tried to move, but his limbs wouldn't do what he told them to. Mel watched his expression closely and moved closer, her hand going to

387

his cheek. He gasped at her touch. She leaned in and put her lips against his. His body awoke at her kiss, he dropped the bag he was carrying and his arms circled her, pulling her tight against him. Her tongue licked along his lips, begging him for entrance; he parted his lips and her tongue slid between them. She kissed him to tell him everything that she couldn't find the words for. That she had missed him; that she forgave him; that she wanted to be with him, and he listened to what her body told him. He finally pulled his mouth from hers, panting. "God I've missed you Jellybean."

She smiled. "I've missed you too Alex, so damn much."

"I'm sorry Mel, I'm so so sorr-" Mel put a finger over his lips, stopping him mid apology.

"Shhhhh." She whispered softly.

Alex held her hand away from his mouth. "Let me say this... Please?" He felt the tension leave her arm, and she let him move it away from his lips. "I was wrong Mel. I thought that being hurt was the biggest risk out there. But when I thought that I had lost you, I knew I was wrong. To lose you, without giving us a chance, and without you knowing how completely I love you, that would have been the biggest mistake of my life."

Tears glimmered in Mel's eyes, threatening to spill out. "Say that last bit again?"

"I love you Melody Anderson."

Mel smiled, "I love you too Alex. But, please don't run on me again."

"Jellybean, the only place I'll ever run, is after you."

Mel's tears escaped, and he pulled her against him. His mouth on hers, his tongue invading her mouth, his need for her obvious. After a few heated moments he tore his mouth from her and quickly bent to pick up his discarded bag. "Let's get the fuck out of here." He demanded pulling her hand. "We have a lot of time to make up for, and a hotel room waiting for us!" He grinned. Mel smiled and picked up the pace beside him. Hand in hand they walked out of the airport, ready for whatever the future gave them, ready to face it... Together.

The End.

Acknowledgements:

This is going to be a LONG list lmao, you might want to hold on to your hats!

Nancy Henderson – you were the first author to share the love. You had patience, you answered my insipid questions, and most of all you introduced me to the groups where I met everyone else. Thank you so much for that.

Addison Kline – There will never ever be enough words on this planet to explain the gratitude I have for you. You have been my constant champion! You have put up with my sulks, my tears, you have kicked my arse on every occasion necessary (and some that weren't lol). You have answered every question I have, you lent me your street team members, you lent me your beta readers, and generally you kept me on track to make Lex's Melody what it is today; finished, complete, and ready to make its mark in the world. You have taught me how to do so, so many things, the most important thing being to pay it forward. You my friend are one of the most amazing people I will ever have the privilege of knowing. From the bottom of my heart I thank you, and hope that I can at least attempt to repay the amazing kindness you have shown me.

Christy Carter – Yes, you wench! I am humbled by your faith in me, and the amount of time and effort (like Addison) you have been willing to show me. Our friendship was forced through a mutual adoration for a certain local lad (to me at least) called Jamie Dornan, you have been my beta reader and have at times held up my street team in the most amazing streams of pimping posts (even braving temporary bans! Lol) But most of all you have become a true friend, allowing me to return the favour by being your beta reader (to a fucking awesome tale that I can't wait for more of!), and even claim that I inspired you to do something about it. I am honoured to call you my friend. <3

Kim Brown - <3 what can I say! You are an amazing friend, and I wouldn't swop the friendship that we have for anything. You are so supportive and caring and lovely. I can't wait to meet up with you at future UK book signing events! I also can't wait to show your Mr Riley the same love you have shown Mr Matthews!

Rebecca Moree – Another sweetheart that I completely adore! You are a lovely friend, and I love the long chats we have about our books, and characters, and a poor girl being left on her knees for a few days in a seemingly endless blow job lmao ;)

Deb Olliff (a.k.a. Olivia Quillbender) – Another Jamie Dornan admirer in our midst ;) You have been my beta reader, my sometimes editor, and my always friend. I have loved our long chats about Alex and his behaviour!

To my Beta Readers – I love you all, you have read about Mel and Alex with such enthusiasm. (and put up with my radio silence for a while!) Thank you so much <3 your support has been amazing, and I appreciate it so so much.

<3 Wendy, Aimee, Jen, Kelly, Lisa, Deb, Clare, Sandra, Jackie, Rannie, Nik, Carrie, Linda, May, Christy, Kristi, Kellie, Addison, Kristy, Rachel and Danielle <3

To my Street Team – You guys are just fantastic! I could not have managed this without you amazing people spreading the love (and my book teasers) with everyone you could! I love you guys!

<3 JustJenn, Rachel, Jan, Christy, Leanne, Maria, Amy, Kristy, Wendy, Kellie, Deb, Annette, Carrie, Danielle, Jackie, Clare, May, Kristina, Addison, Kim, Nik, Nadia, Nicole, Kelly, James and Jen! <3

To the Irish Eejits (Mandy, Sam, Krissy) – talking to my local lovelies helped to keep me sane! The craic is always 90, and the general cock talk is always a giggle!

James Pyper – You made the off-the-cuff remark "God you've read so many of those you could probably write your own." I took that idea to heart, and Lex's Melody was born. <3 you sweetie! :D

To the real Jonny, Jacob, Nate, and Dylan – You know who you are (and you'll be getting a proper mention in each of your own books lol) my two years in Belfast Met wouldn't have been anywhere near as enjoyable or funny without some of the crazy things that we talked about, or did (and therefore passed on to Mel and her gang!) <3 you guys!

To my daughter – You are the most amazing child a parent could ever dream of having. You are a constant support; you have (despite being a teenager) been a loving, caring and incredibly mature person. I love you with all my heart, and I am so grateful and blessed to be able to say that I had even some small part in the fantastic person you are already turning out to be.

To my family – I know that I have hidden most of the notion of this book from you, and generally try to keep the real me and the author me separate. But you all shaped me into the person that I am today, and without you, none of that personality would be woven through all my characters. I love you all with all my heart.

To all the blogs who allowed an unknown/new author to come in and take over your blog – THANK YOU! To Kelly's Kindle Konfessions for popping my takeover cherry! To Literary Lust, Breathless Ink, and Bad Boys and Bedtime Stories who along with Kelly allowed me to reveal my cover in a four blog simultaneous takeover frenzy! And to name some of the blogs who invited me to party on their pages for a while: Hot Books and Hotter Book Boyfriends, Hooked on Books, Obsessed by Books, Just One More Page, the list is a long one, but I value all the amazing bloggers out there, and the friendships that they have extended to me. You all do an amazing (and sometimes thankless) job. We indie authors would be lost without you, and I hope you all know just how appreciated you all are (including any blog not mentioned in my little shout out). You all provide an amazing gift to us as readers and authors alike.

To EL James for writing the first book to start me down the path to erotica, and where I am today. While 50 Shades wasn't the first "naughty" book that I read, it was certainly the most influential and without it, I might not have ever made it to where I am now.

To all the other authors that I have come to love as a reader, and in some cases, now own every book they have ever written, including (again, this isn't a complete list, just the ones that come to mind as worth a mention) Beth Kery, Julie Kenner, JS Scott, Sylvia Day, Jodi Ellen Malpas, Harper Sloan, Victoria Ashley, Whitney Gracia Williams, Brooke Cumberland, Mia Sheridan, Scarlett Metal, Laurelin Paige, Alice Clayton, Emma Chase, SL Jennings, Christina Lauren, Charlotte Stein, Raine Miller, RK Lilley, and many many more... Without your temptingly hot reads, my friend would never have suggested that I try writing my own book.

36800802R00238

Made in the USA
Charleston, SC
15 December 2014